C000174283

THIN-ICE SKATER

by the same author

novels
THIS SPORTING LIFE
FLIGHT INTO CAMDEN
RADCLIFFE
PASMORE
A TEMPORARY LIFE
SAVILLE
A PRODIGAL CHILD
PRESENT TIMES
A SERIOUS MAN
as it happened

plays
THE RESTORATION OF ARNOLD MIDDLETON
IN CELEBRATION
THE CONTRACTOR
HOME
THE CHANGING ROOM
THE FARM
CROMWELL
LIFE CLASS
MOTHER'S DAY
SISTERS
PHOENIX
EARLY DAYS
THE MARCH ON RUSSIA
STAGES
CARING

poetry
STOREY'S LIVES

general
EDWARD
(with drawings by Donald Parker)

DAVID STOREY

Thin-Ice Skater

JONATHAN CAPE
LONDON

Published by Jonathan Cape 2004

2 4 6 8 10 9 7 5 3 1

First published in Great Britain in 2004 by
Jonathan Cape
Random House, 20 Vauxhall Bridge Road,
London SW1V 2SA

Random House Australia (Pty) Limited
20 Alfred Street, Milsons Point, Sydney,
New South Wales 2061, Australia

Random House New Zealand Limited
18 Poland Road, Glenfield,
Auckland 10, New Zealand

Random House South Africa (Pty) Limited
Endulini, 5A Jubilee Road, Parktown 2193, South Africa

The Random House Group Limited Reg. No. 954009
www.randomhouse.co.uk

A CIP catalogue record for this book
is available from the British Library

ISBN 0-224-06449-5

Papers used by Random House are natural,
recyclable products made from wood grown in sustainable forests;
the manufacturing processes conform to the environmental
regulations of the country of origin

Typeset by Palimpsest Book Production Limited,
Polmont, Stirlingshire

Printed and bound in Great Britain by
Mackays of Chatham PLC

MEMO ONE (1)

6.1.71, 7:32 a.m.

1. My brother won't mind my mentioning this, for he's of the same opinion himself. So's his second wife, Martha, even tho' at the moment she's confined in a private lunatic asylum.
2. My brother is good-looking.
3. He has a six-foot-one-inch figure, grey hair, verging to whiteness on either side, dark eyes, each shaded by a canopy of thick, black lashes, a nose broken in a boxing tournament in the Royal Navy during or after the Second World War, a mouth which is thin and broad and clearly defined, cheekbones which are sharply pronounced, and a jaw which is firm and outward-projecting.
4. I, too, have acquired the same dark eyes and, altho' my nose has not been broken, my mouth, like his, is thin and broad. I have, in addition, the same caesarian fringe of curls and my cheekbones, like his, are sharply pronounced.
5. There are thirty-five (35) years between my brother and I. We share the same father but not the same mother. My own mother died within weeks of my being born, our father's second wife, who had her first and only child when she was forty-four (44) and our father was seventy-five (75). He died the following year and I have lived the whole of my life with my brother and his demented second wife. A third brother, two years older than the one I live with, resides somewhere in the north of England, but neither I nor his younger brother have seen him for as long as I recall.

8:00 a.m.

6. The area we live in is characterised by, amongst other things, an extensive area of open ground which sweeps down in a series of wooded undulations, interspersed with ponds and streams, to the congested hollow of the River Thames.
7. The house we inhabit stands adjacent to this area of open ground and, altho' the view over London is not available to us from any of our windows – merely the fronts of the houses opposite and the backs of the houses behind – a walk to the end of our tree-lined road will reveal, from the summit of a nearby hill, the whole of the city spread below.
8. In the evening, gilded by the sun, the basin glows, like the remnants of a fire, and in the morning, rising from a mist, it has the appearance of an inlet of the sea, a configuration of rocks and stones which, as the sun ascends, resolves itself into a bay, not of brine, but concrete, brick and steel.
9. All around us live intellectuals: doctors, teachers, politicians, lawyers; authors, artists, composers, poets. Marx and Freud lived here in exile; Keats, Coleridge, Constable and Shelley; Wordsworth, Dickens, Hunt and Southey; Lawrence (D.H. & T.E.), Wells, Galsworthy, Mansfield and Bennett (A) (1867–1931) have dined or wined or lived or walked or worked here in the past.
10. My brother has cultural aspirations. Not only is he keen on making money – lots, at which, tho' not to the extent he would have wished for, he has been successful – but, commensurate with this ambition, he is anxious to the point of dementia to be recognised for what he is.
11. Not one of the Florentine Medici (circa 1389–1492) exactly but someone who might, after a protracted inhalation of the crap he takes from time to time ('for recreation'), be mentioned in an adjacent breath.
12. He is a producer of motion pictures and even married a motion picture star, Miss Geraldine O'Neill, née Martha Sheringham,

and altho' he mentions the possibility of our feeling 'at home' in this haven of intellectuals, what he mentions more often as a virtue is not so much the high-class status of our neighbours, past and present, as the 'fact' that a place like this generates what he calls 'a feeling of community'.

13. He is very concerned about 'community'.
14. Not to the extent that he is about making money, but it runs his primary obsessions fairly close. Money and being recognised as a patron of 'the greatest art of the Twentieth Century'. 'Community,' my brother tells me, 'is what we're all about.'

MEMO TWO (2)

17.1.71, 9:17 a.m. (twenty (20) seconds).

1. Altho' we live in a house an apartment would do us just as well. Before we moved to these heights above the city we inhabited a flat in Curzon Street, one in Mount Street and, for a couple of days, an apartment in Berkeley Square.
2. Up here, however, according to my brother, we can enjoy the benefits of living 'in a village', where 'everyone knows everyone else' and where I might be found a decent school.
3. A day school is what we came here for. 'No boarding school for you, Rick,' my brother said, 'where they separate you from the community for three (3) parts of the year and no one ever sees you. I want you,' he says, 'to be part of the family.'
4. Even tho' the family is comprised only of my brother and myself.
5. 'We'll find a school where we can see one another, morning, noon and evening, and you can tell me what's going on in your life. None of this paying you off to live with a bunch of moneyed freaks. That would be too easy,' a homily he's not averse to repeating to anyone who happens to be around.

MEMO THREE (3)

19.1.71, 8:13 p.m.

1. My brother's one dread, I might as well admit it, is that I'll end up like his second wife. 'Promise me you'll *talk*,' he has said on more than one occasion and, whenever I assure him I feel all right, he will clasp his arm around my shoulder and, providing someone else is present, say, 'Richard has the makings of a director himself, in addition to which his teachers tell me he has, if and when he applies himself, a capacity to write. There's nothing a guy like this can't do. *Won't* do, once he gets his fucking finger out. Shall I tell you what? Everything with him has got to *count*. He's obsessed with fucking *numbers*.'

MEMO FOUR (4)

23.1.71, 3:19 a.m.

1. Our house is a Victorian structure (one of sixteen (16) in the street).
2. It has a bay-protruding ground-floor window which overlooks the road and, beside it, a porch with a flight of steps (8) below which is the basement flat in which live the two domestics of our establishment, Mr & Mrs Hodges (Jack and Edith). Above the ground floor, which comprises a sitting room, a dining room and a kitchen, are two further floors, the first of which is occupied by my brother's study, his bedroom, a bathroom and a guest room, and the top floor which is given over to myself, to a second bathroom, to a lumber room and to a room which my brother keeps in readiness in case his second wife comes back.
3. The building is not attractive: its windows are small, its proportions mean, its garden non-existent: a yard.

4. My brother is here to lick his wounds.
5. His second wife's name is Miss Geraldine O'Neill. She is fifty-seven (57) years old – five (5) years older than my brother. She was born Martha Sheringham (a Philadelphia banking family) and adopted her screen name when she signed a studio contract in 1938. She made a success of her first three films but only finally made her name in the 40s and 50s: twenty-nine (29) films of which I have seen twenty-seven (27) and, tho' I loathe the movies, loved or loved almost every one.
6. It was in the third from last of these she met my brother, when he played his only role beside her: a stagehand in a theatre where she is an actress making a comeback after the breakup of her marriage: a theme which projected itself into their subsequent life, for my sister-in-law had been married twice, once to a movie star who was killed in a car crash, and once to a business tycoon whom she divorced to marry my brother – the first man, she said, she had ever loved.
7. She was forty (40) at the time.

MEMO FIVE (5)

13.2.71, 11:57 p.m.

1. My brother's name is Gerry Audlin.
2. People used to think it fictitious (since his second wife was also known publicly as 'Gerry', he always referring to her in private, however, as 'Martha', sometimes 'Matty') only I can show them a photostat of his birth certificate which I carry around and which, as well as indicating his true age, confirms both Gerald and Audlin are authentic (born 3 October 1919). He served in the British Navy during the Second World War, part of that time as a liaison officer with the US Second Fleet,

where he broke his nose in a boxing match and was mentioned in despatches.

3. After the war he went to Hollywood under the aegis of an actor who he knew in the Navy and who gave my brother an introduction to the Studios where he met his second wife. He got into producing, having started as an actor, because Martha, as a condition of her contract for what turned out to be her penultimate picture, had my brother incorporated as a technical assistant.
4. My brother has produced more pictures than Martha has appeared in.
5. Altho' he lays great stress on our 'home', and has had my notepaper printed with 'Richard Audlin, 32 Leighcroft Gardens, London NW3 1LH' across the top, he has an apartment in town which I can only assume from counting his suits. In Mount Street he had thirty-two (32) and there are only sixteen (16) in his wardrobe at present. Similarly, his overcoats, of which there were twelve (12), only five (5) of which I can find in his built-in cupboards. Likewise his shoes, of which he has so many pairs I've never troubled to count, his shirts, his jackets, his jeans, his flannels which, together with his ties, hats, caps, scarves, underwear (incredible) and socks, indicate that he is not committed to where we live at present.
6. His office is in Grosvenor Street.
7. A rented Rolls collects him most mornings and returns him in the evenings. His apartment – wherever that is – is the place he goes to screw his girls.

MEMO SIX (6)

14.2.71, 2:37 a.m.

1. My brother has a great appetite for women.

2. He can't keep off them.
3. Whenever he tries, a melancholy descends upon him which is more frightening than the one which presently absorbs his second wife. Beneath the caesarian fringe of curls his brow is furrowed by a frown so deep it unites the shadows beneath his eyes. Not only his features but his face contracts. Likewise his six-foot-one-inch (73 inches) figure. Womanless, fuck-less, he looks something like a crab.
4. His hands are neither delicate nor strong.
5. None of these women has he ever loved.
6. I have noticed my brother's effect upon women so often that it might be assumed I'd be averse to seeing it paraded before me yet again. However, it never ceases to intrigue me. 'None of these women have I ever loved,' he often tells me, 'not as I love Martha. But I can't live like a hermit,' he will add, with a grin which, for me, is the most infectious thing about him. 'Martha understands, and, in any case,' he concludes, 'she'll often ask me how I'm "making out", which, as you know, is her way of enquiring how I'm getting on at present.'
7. There are always people in our house. My brother has not the capacity to sit alone for five (5) consecutive seconds. He is always on the telephone, whether he is in bed, sitting at a table or even on the john. He seldom supervises a picture now, deputising each one to an associate producer who, over the years, he has come to trust. 'Gavin's all right,' he will say about his principal assistant. 'He's scratched my back for so long it's right I give him a chance. The second he reckons I'm past it he's confident he'll take over.'
8. My brother's attractiveness to women is something of a gift. 'I made your brother,' my sister-in-law often said before she lost her head. 'He didn't know what he had until I showed him, and I'm not just talking about his fucking prick.'
9. My sister-in-law, whom I dearly love, brought gifts – if not

the gift – to my brother's life in showing him his true vocation; to her own life my brother has brought, as far as I am aware, precisely nothing. Her illness has been classified as paranoid schizophrenia and altho' early on she clung to my brother like he, for different reasons, must have clung to her, it must be with the realisation he could do little if anything to help her.

10. Her father was a banker. He died when Martha was eight years old but left Martha and her younger sister and their mother so well provided for that when my sister-in-law finally went to Hollywood it was never with the feeling she had very much to lose. There is a vulnerability about her acting – the pale blue eyes, the blonde hair, the high-raised cheekbones – which, whenever I see her films, reduces me to tears – something of a child, yet not a child, 'a sensitised, ironic, usurping creature . . .' (from one of her reviews).

MEMO SEVEN (7)

14.2.71, 3:27 a.m.

1. Ever since I can remember we've been on the move. My first few years were spent in Beverly Hills, then, at Martha's insistence, we came to England, living first in Beaconsfield (where she made her last film, *Farewell Tomorrow*), then in Putney, then in Curzon Street, then Mount Street, finally in Berkeley Square. 32 Leighcroft Gardens is the first vestige of a *home* I've ever had.
2. If, for no other reason, we shan't stay here for long.

MEMO EIGHT (8)

14.2.71, 4:17 a.m.

1. My room at the top of the house is bare.
2. You might have assumed I would have accumulated any no. of possessions, considering the no. of places in which I've lived. All I have accumulated is a record player, a pile of paperbacks, a fountain pen, a tape recorder, an electric toothbrush and a watch which tells the date as well as the time.
3. My bed stands in the corner of the room, unlike my brother's which occupies the centre of the room below.
4. Sometimes I lean back and contemplate the bleakness of the walls and wonder what it is that's missing.
5. There's nothing here I recognise.
6. My brother came back to England because my sister-in-law insisted.
7. Her knowledge of the country was derived exclusively from reading books.
8. The only books my sister-in-law read were the detective novels of Agatha Christie.
9. She left the only land (the only people) she knew and set up home in a rented house in Beaconsfield on the basis of having read the fictional accounts of the exploits of a female detective.
10. Peculiar to that stage of my life when I indulged in her delusions, I accompanied my sister-in-law everywhere, hiding in bushes, behind trees, in ditches, even peering in people's windows before being driven off by the occupants, my (then innocent) belief that this character of an amateur sleuth which she insisted on playing, and to which she appended the name Miss Sheringham, had been invented exclusively for my amusement. A belief which was only quashed when the 'murderer' we were evidently looking for was identified as none other than my brother – whom, confusingly, she referred

to by her father's name, Alfred Sheringham.

11. I was introduced early to the notion that my brother's wife was nuts. Her bathing, for instance, in her swimming pool in Beverly Hills, without any clothes on, when people she hardly knew were walking around, was merely the prelude to setting her hair on fire, to her cutting up her scrapbook with a knife – an introduction to the fits where, rigid, she would lie back in her chair, her cheeks swollen, her eyes distended, her skin green, her teeth bared, her tongue curled back in her throat (my brother trying to pull it back by inserting a pencil).
12. Her flight to England was Martha's attempt to hide her anguish from her friends, 'Where am I?' her most frequent question.

MEMO NINE (9)

14.2.71, 4:51 a.m.

1. Previously a writer lived in this house. I imagine I must inhabit one of his children's rooms. In one of the built-in cupboards I have found a number of rolled-up posters of pop stars and movie stars and one, curiously, featuring a montage of Hollywood Greats which includes the head and shoulders of Miss Geraldine O'Neill.
2. My brother acquired this house cheaply: the writer was wanting to divorce his wife, split the proceeds, and quickly re-marry.
3. Some house.
4. Some home.
5. Its modesty betrays an absurd desire on my brother's part to live down his income (in case its extent de-motivates me). 'You, too, can be a director,' he often tells me. 'You have an eye for detail.' Going on to add, 'The director of a film today

is the equivalent in the time of the Italian Renaissance of Michelangelo, Leonardo da Vinci, Raphael, Bernini, or any of those other all-time greats. In those days artists were looked down upon as workmen, just as directors are today. As for producers . . .'

6. The cinema is bullshit.
7. It only shows two things: charm (portrayed as sentiment) and melodrama (expressed as action). The area between the cinema never touches. The camera kills experience. Just like it killed Miss Geraldine O'Neill (or, in my eyes, Martha Audlin, née Sheringham, a rich Philadelphian waif).
8. Like an Italian immigrant family on the Lower East Side might persuade their eldest son to make it as Middleweight Champion ('Rocky Asshole'), so my brother encourages me. 'It would make up for all we have lost. Not only with Martha,' he says, 'but Ian too.'

MEMO TEN (10)

14.2.71, 5:14 a.m.

1. Ian is his son, by his first wife, who died at the age of seven (7).

MEMO ELEVEN (11)

27.2.71, Noon

1. One of the signs of the Medici complex is the atmosphere of a court that exists inside this house.
2. There is scarcely a writer whose name has been mentioned in the papers who doesn't, within a matter of days, find

himself at our front door and who is then commissioned to write, if not a script, a treatment.

3. The subservience of certain types is what my brother is noted for.
4. He is a 'Prince'. 'EXECUTIVE PRODUCER: GERRY AUDLIN' sits at the foot of every list of credits and, in the last few years, the legend has been prefixed to every title: 'A GERRY AUDLIN FILM'.
5. It's not only writers but celebrities from every walk of life who come to the door at my brother's invitation: academics who have made a splash, psychologists with social theories, politicians, actors, actresses, musicians, artists, poets.
6. In the basement are the professional couple who specialise in looking after my brother's needs yet whom my brother dislikes to see inside the house whenever the two of us are together: 'I have never enjoyed the privilege of using servants, even when Martha was around.' It must be something basic: the Hodges (meanwhile) rarely, in my experience, if ever, take offence.
7. Paranoia.
8. *My brother can't be certain that schizophrenia is not infectious.*

MEMO TWELVE (12)

1.3.71, 8:19 p.m.

1. The school is the only reason for our living in this neighbourhood.
2. Dover's Academy was founded by a gentleman of that name after the Second World War (when my brother was on his way to Hollywood). It occupies a large Edwardian house not fifteen minutes' walk from here.

3. Its fees are astronomical, being, as it is, the alternative to a state school where the fees are non-existent: what can they teach at Dover's that they can't teach anywhere else?
4. The absence of material ambition, the taking of drugs, the promulgation of ideas which would only be licensed by the most extreme political party, the high incidence of neurosis, psychosis, halitosis, erythema, intertrigo and seborrhoea are some of the more prevalent features of the place.
5. Mrs Dover, the founder's widow – altogether more formidable than the deceased himself – has bright pink cheeks, light blue eyes, a triple chin, blonde hair and weighs, by my estimation, well in excess of two hundred and twenty (220) pounds.
6. I like her.
7. In some respects I love her.
8. 'Do not take my kindliness for granted,' her look suggests.
9. She is the only woman I know who is not in any way attracted to my brother.
10. At the back of the school, overlooking the garden which has been turned into a tarmac yard, is Mrs Dover's office. It is cluttered with books and smells of dust and of the cumulative scents of the secretary and the typist who – the latter – comes in from time to time.
11. It's here that Mrs Dover has, on occasion, upbraided me for 'not smiling when I know you can', and, on one occasion, for 'not being as happy as only you know how'.
12. I have not smiled for as long as I remember.
13. 'You Americans,' she says, 'are all the same.'

MEMO THIRTEEN (13)

1.3.71, 9:10 a.m.

1. I must be mad.

MEMO FOURTEEN (14)

13.3.71, 1:13 a.m.

1. My brother is worried. He is busy with a film and is constantly in and out of the house, coming back, if I am there, to stand at the door and ask, 'Are you okay, Richard?'
2. If I say, from my bed, 'I'm fine,' he comes in another step and asks, 'How are you making out at Dover's?'
3. He uses three epithets to refer to me directly. The formal 'Richard' is used to indicate that we are two entities apart, like an artist – wondering whether his picture requires another dab – might, palette in one hand, brush in the other, step back for a broader look. 'Rickie' he uses as a sign of our confederacy, our capacity to be joined in a common venture, a call he might make (less and less often now) from the foot of the stairs when he is going out and thinks it might be a good idea for me to go with him. 'Rick' is intimate, a call from over his shoulder, his mind invariably on other things – like someone calling from a dream, the sound instinctive, if not unconscious.
4. I often wonder why he has me with him.

MEMO FIFTEEN (15)

17.3.71, 2:10 a.m.

1. My brother is an empiricist.
2. He picks up these phrases from other people.
3. He seldom reads a book: thirteen (13) of his films have been made from 'bestsellers' he's never read.
4. All he reads are synopses. It involves him reading the first few pages and the last of any project, asking, 'Anything go on in the middle?' and giving it the thumbs up or down. How he acquired this skill I've no idea.

5. He never goes to the movies. Some of the films he's made I'm convinced he's never seen. He is superficial.
6. He is superficial like the whole of his generation are superficial. Maybe the war killed something off. Maybe the war was the killing off and, for their parents, the war before that (1914–1918) the killing off of something else. Maybe all this shooting at things with cameras is the killing off in progress. How can I explain that to a man (or Mrs Dover) who talks of 'creativity' and 'genius' and, God help us, 'art'?
7. He is always buying pictures. He is eclectic. He knows where to look. Or, rather, who to have look for him. This is the principle of his working life. Some people have it. Most don't. Me not at all. Everything he receives is secondhand. One painter with an international reputation remarked to me on one occasion how my brother bought a picture of his for three hundred pounds, when the painter was a student ('a lot of money: one year's income, so to speak'), and sold it six years later when the painter, a prodigal talent, had become established, for fifty-two thousand dollars. 'I got nothing out of that transaction,' he said. 'Someone not a thousand miles from here is making a hell of a lot of money *off my back*.'
8. My brother will sit at a restaurant table and lay out half a million bucks while he asks the waiter for another drink.
9. How can he not be superficial when he has all that shit inside?

MEMO SIXTEEN (16)

1.4.71, Midnight

1. My brother is a skater.
2. He cuts fine figures.
3. I stand on the bank and admire his skill. 'A man who doesn't

initiate is no man at all,' he often tells me. 'That's what life,' he says, 'is all about.'

'Maybe I'm initiating by standing still,' I tell him.

'Standing still is passivity,' he says. 'It takes nothing to stand still. We stand still when we're born and we stand still when we die.'

'Maybe it takes more courage to stand still when everyone's on the move,' I tell him.

MEMO SEVENTEEN (17)

2.4.71, 1:13 a.m.

'I don't think I've ever told you about Ian,' my brother says.

'You mean how he died at the age of seven, the product of your marriage to your first wife who subsequently married a doctor who was hauled up in court for indecent behaviour with one of his patients and who later emigrated to Canada and from whom you've never heard again, your marriage having broken up as a result of Ian's death?'

He allows the facetiousness to drain away as he might something unpleasant in the john.

'Ian was a gifted child,' he finally declares. 'I'd do anything to have that boy back. Anything,' he tells me.

I am lying on my bed (I don't sleep well at night). My brother, having just come in the house, is standing in the doorway of my room. Moments before, not for the first time, he has informed me, 'This is a phase you're going through. You'll have to choose. From now on we're looking for commitment, Rickie.'

'By "we", you mean,' I ask him, 'you and Martha?'

'I don't think I've mentioned how Ian died.'

'You sat up two whole nights,' I tell him.

'It was meningitis. His mother went to pieces. I resisted. I guess the effect is still with me. It affects the way I respond to you. Whenever you feel I'm being rough and the sort of brother you wouldn't like, maybe you'll remember.'

'Sure.'

'Look around you.'

'Right.'

Maybe he means I shouldn't look too far. Maybe he means I shouldn't look at all.

'This is a society we live in of people who are lying down. We live in a lying-down situation, Rick. The people in this country no longer resist.'

'I thought you donated funds to the Labour Party,' I tell him.

'The Labour Party in this country is symptomatic of the lack of backbone. It's a panacea put on a gaping wound. A wound of indifference.'

'Why do you give them money?' I ask.

'Our father was a socialist.'

'I thought he was a bankrupt.'

'He was in textiles. He went bankrupt after the war. What has that got to do with it?' he says.

'Maybe he went bankrupt because of his ideals,' I tell him.

'He went bankrupt because he stayed in this fucking country, Rick,' he says.

'You've come back to it,' I tell him.

'Sure I've come back. Do you think I was glad to come back? I came back because of Martha. As soon as she is better I aim to leave. This country is a mausoleum.'

'You give money in memory of our father?' I ask, intrigued by this idea.

'I give money because you do what the natives do. It pays to donate to the Labour Party. Not for what it gives me but because without that I'd have no hope at all. I couldn't otherwise bear to stay in this place another fucking minute.'

He adds, 'When Ian died I thought for a time I wouldn't recover.

Not from his death – he was a beautiful child and so gifted it makes me weep to think of it – but that I wouldn't regain my faith.'

'In what?'

'In fucking life!' he tells me. 'I sometimes wonder how you see me, Rick.'

'I love you.'

'I know you love me. We love one another.' (Mention 'love' and the bullshit never stops.) 'In many senses, we're all each other has got.'

'And Martha.'

'And Martha.'

Of Martha, however, he's not too sure (those telephone calls from Hertfordshire when she comes on the line, invariably enquiring about the latest 'clue').

'I wonder if you recognise what I've been through,' he says.

'Sure.'

'There is a purpose to what I do.'

'Right.'

'Ian was the trigger. I wanted to prove there is another dimension to suffering. That the destruction of something that was wholesome and good wasn't the whole of what life's about.'

So he went to Hollywood, became an actor, met Miss Geraldine O'Neill and ruined her life.

'What I do is an act of faith.'

'It is.'

'I don't go in for this secularised theology which says it's circumstances alone that count.'

'That's right.'

'Free will is still an ingredient in my book, Rick. A painful ingredient. But also a beautiful ingredient of what experience is all about.'

'Sure.'

'Don't allow yourself to think that what you see around you is everything that's happening. That's arrogance. That's blindness.

Not to put too fine a point on it, I'd describe that as stupidity, Richard.'

'Right.'

He gestures round: bare walls (where's my personality, my persona, my *imprint* on the place in which I live, not least that part of it exclusively my own?): a bookcase, table, bed: fuck all.

'Maybe you preferred it in Curzon Street?'

'In a service flat?'

'How about Mount Street?'

'I hated it. Particularly all that panelling. It reminded me of a mortician's.'

He is about to ask about Berkeley Square, where we scarcely stayed a minute (Martha, on a 'home' inspection visit, screaming in every room) or the house in Beaconsfield ('All those trees,' I'd told him, 'are going to drive me fucking mad,' invoking Martha's detectival preoccupations), or maybe about the episode in Dumfries in Scotland, staying at the castle of a friend – a former friend – of Martha's. Or about the house in Putney, not to mention those we looked at and never went back to: a couple of thousand of those at least.

'That man telling us, the day we first visited it, how his wife went crazy in the kitchen.'

'It was in the bathroom.'

'I thought it was the kitchen.' (I hate to get things wrong.)

'The bathroom.'

He waits.

'Maybe it's the school,' he says.

'I like the school.'

'How about the teachers?'

'They're fine.'

'Mrs Dover?'

'Perfect.'

'Perfect?'

'Fine.'

'Some notable people have lived here in the past.'

'Here?'

'The *district*.'

'Right.'

'Freud. Marx. Keats.' He gestures beyond the confines of the room. 'Coleridge.'

He's been reading the plaques on the buildings – or has had Gavin do it for him.

'Where did you hear all that?'

'I read it in a guide.'

'A guide?'

'Sure.'

He looks at me with a smile.

'You read a guide?' The first book he concedes he's read.

'I read a guide to the neighbourhood. I wanted to be sure, when we moved here, it would be the sort of place you'd like.'

'You went to a lot of trouble,' I tell him.

'Why not? I get worried about you. I wake at night and think, "What am I doing for my youngest brother?"'

He is thinking, 'I come up to his room and find him in bed at four (4) p.m., and he has nothing to contribute to anything. Least of all a conversation.'

'I'm fine.'

'Maybe it's the gap.'

'Gap?'

'Between the generations.'

'It could be.'

'We have more in common than you realise.'

'What?'

'A similarity of feeling.' He gestures round – exclusive of everything, the gesture, but the building. 'The same sort of humour.'

'Sure.'

'We don't take any bullshit.'

'You work in it all the time.'

'Sure I work in it.' He laughs.

He waits for me to laugh. (Catch him laughing on his own!)

'A good job one of us works in something, Rick.'

'Right.'

'I was a pain in the ass when I was young.'

'You were?'

'Boy! Was I a pain in the ass!' He is about to add, 'To our father,' but since being a pain in the arse (as it then would be) to our father who went bankrupt in the textile trade and donated funds to the Labour Party is no great shakes in anybody's book, he adds, 'I don't think you see me as a brother.'

'I do.'

His look is peculiarly (uncharacteristically) intense.

'Somebody who cares about you, Rick.'

He adds, 'Martha cares about you, only she is in no position to show it at present.'

He thinks about all the other people who care about me and says, 'I, too, would like some help.'

'I do help, Gerry.'

'Sure.'

He waits for instances of the help I've given him to materialise but after an interval of several seconds that feel like hours declares, 'If I could see something positive that you were working towards, *that* would reassure me.'

'Right.'

'Even your friends are ass bound. I've never seen so many bums glued to so many fucking floors.'

'Right.'

'Maybe you feel science and technology have reached as far as these things can. That even fantasy has reached its limits.'

'I don't.'

'You don't?'

I move over on the bed.

'The only thoughts that come to an *ass*-bound thinker are thoughts that keep his *ass* to the ground. Maybe when you can enlighten me about all these remarkable thoughts you have maybe you'll come downstairs and tell me.'

'Sure.'

'How would I have been,' he says, 'if I'd given in to our father's failure and decided our future was bound up with our past? Like Jimmy, who's done nothing to redeem himself.'

'Who's Jimmy?'

'Jimmy is our fucking brother. The one,' he goes on, 'we never mention.'

'Is it,' I ask, curious about Jimmy, 'a matter of redemption?'

'It's a matter of justification,' he says. 'You have the means to take a step forward that I never had. I would have given my right arm to be an artist. I started off with nothing. Now look where I am.'

He doesn't wait for me to look too long: he closes the door and is gone.

A door is shut in the room below.

Moments later – a prevalent sound – the jocular tone of his voice on the phone.

MEMO EIGHTEEN (18)

'I hope you don't mind me calling?' I ask her.

Mrs Dover stands up behind her desk.

'Not at all,' she says.

'My brother suggested I might see you.'

'Glad you followed his advice,' she says.

She eases her bulk to the centre of the floor.

'What can I do for you?' she asks.

She indicates a chair in front of her desk.

'How is your brother?' she adds.

'He's fine.'

'How is his lovely wife?'

'She's making progress.'

'I'm glad to hear it.'

Behind her a window looks out to the back of the school.

'This,' she says, 'is a distinguished neighbourhood. Freud lived here in exile. Marx, and many more.'

A photograph of Mr Dover stands on the mantelpiece above what would have been a fireplace when the house was someone's home: adjacent to it is one of Mrs Dover – I wouldn't have recognised the sylph-like figure were it not that, on a previous occasion, she has pointed it out – in a mortarboard and academic gown.

'Keats lived here,' she adds, 'and not far from this building he wrote his famous ode. But this, of course, I don't have to tell you.'

'Which one?' I ask.

'To a nightingale.' She raises her hand. 'Shelley, Byron, Wordsworth . . .'

Invention, at least of dialogue, falters: all this she must have sold to Gerry when he first approached the school.

'My brother admires it, too,' I tell her.

'I'm sure he does.'

'He has referred specifically to its open spaces.'

'I'm sure his appreciation is as warm as mine.' Mrs Dover resumes her seat behind her desk. Her surprise at my appearance fades. 'Why,' she adds. 'I have your essay on the subject here. "Home Background".' She places a pair of spectacles on her nose. '"The wooded undulations interspersed with streams and ponds sweep down to the congested hollow of the River Thames". I've given it Alpha Plus. A somewhat bucolic appreciation.'

'Thank you.'

Removing her glasses she adjusts her dress, a voluminous garment buttoned at the neck.

'I was very much taken by your analysis of your family life. I so much admire your sister-in-law. She was and always has been my favourite. I saw *Taken to Paradise* five times, and I'd see it again, if I could, tomorrow.' She replaces the essay on the desk. 'Your brother tells me she stays in the country.'

'In Hertfordshire.'

'Such lovely places there as well. So close,' she adds, 'to Hampstead.'

'Yes.'

'How often do you see her?'

'Every month, if I go with my brother, though sometimes,' I add, 'I go alone. Particularly if he's busy. In which case,' I conclude, 'every two or three weeks. Over the summer holidays I go most Sundays.'

'What form does her indisposition take?'

'She thinks she's a female detective.'

'What crime is she seeking to solve?'

She blinks her pale blue eyes.

'She's looking for a murderer.'

'I see.'

Perhaps she does.

I wait.

'Who has been murdered?' she asks.

'Someone by the name of Martha Sheringham. Though the corpse, she tells us, is hard to find.'

'Does she know anyone of that name?' she asks.

'She used to.'

She nods: a double chin recesses into triple.

I am, it's true, enamoured – not of Mrs Dover in her entirety but of certain aspects of her which over the past two years I have, I suspect – self-analysis not my forte – idealised.

I add, 'The name of the murderer, on the other hand, varies. Some days she refers to him as Alfred, other days Gerald. She finds it difficult to separate the two.'

'Perhaps two people are involved,' she says.

The radiance of her flesh, the grandeur of her smile, the symmetry of her lips . . .

'*You still in here*?' my brother says. Knocking on the door, he opens it. 'You've been up here for hours.'

'Two.'

'I'm going out. I've told Mrs Hodges. She'll have your supper ready by seven. Is that your fucking homework?'

Having come in he looks down on the pad on which I have just inscribed 'the symmetry of her lips . . .'

'An essay on "Home Background". They assign the subject,' I tell him, covering it up, 'when they want to see what you get up to when you're out of school.'

Recognising the colour and shape of the paper he says, 'What are all these memos you leave around the house?'

'House?'

'In the fucking kitchen. The hall. On the stairs. I found one in the fucking john. Numbered. You and fucking numbers.'

'Reminders.'

'Of what?'

'Things I otherwise forget.'

'All it says on some is "Asshole".'

'School.'

'School?'

'Regression.'

'Regression?'

'Rather than pick a quarrel I write a memo.'

'"Cunt." That was another. You realise Mrs Hodges could easily find it. Maybe she has and hasn't said. She may not know what "cunt" is. Hodges will. He was in the army. He could think – I could think – it refers to her. Then we'll have the fucking hassle of finding another couple.'

'They'll never leave.'

'Why not?'

'They're on to a soft number.'

'Who do they refer to? Do you keep a record of all this crap?'

He's trying, once more, to look at the pad (I lying in bed, it propped on my knees).

'All I'm asking for is cooperation. If life is too easy we can make it hard.'

'How?'

'Any number of ways.'

He isn't keen to enumerate.

'I don't want you stuck up here all evening. Isn't there something else you can do? Two hours' homework is long enough.'

'Right.'

'I expect you to be asleep when I'm back.'

'What time are you coming?'

'Eleven.'

He's lying: the Rolls is in the street: I don't have to look. He's going to his flat. He won't even be back in the morning.

'Aren't any of your friends coming in this evening?'

'I wanted some time,' I tell him, 'to myself.'

'Too much fucking time. This room could do with ventilation.'

He's gone: an air of disquiet – impotence, frustration. I watch the rear door of the car – held open by the chauffeur – close behind his back.

His face gazes up. I wave, not sure, however, if he's waving too.

MEMO NINETEEN (19)

Everybody at Dover's is happy. The criterion of happiness Mrs Dover subscribes to is the capacity of everyone to smile. The 'dissidents', as she refers to them, who are unwilling or unable, she summons to her office – as, for instance, on this occasion when, removing the secretary and the typist from the scene and, now that Gerry is out of the house, transferring it from a school day to a

Friday evening (the cleaners, too, have gone), she enquires about my 'long expression', adding – referring to her flat at the top of the building – 'Come up to my room and make a cup of tea. I've got backache and I can't sit in this chair much longer.'

Mrs Dover is, unfortunately, a heavy smoker: it discolours (disfigures) what otherwise would be her surprisingly delicate hands – small for someone of such gross proportions. She goes to considerable lengths to disguise her bosom, wearing dresses which might be more suitably described as gowns: an encumbrance, a shelf, above which her head is mounted with its disarranged but never dishevelled hair (the pale blue eyes, the tiny mouth, inset with pearl-like teeth, beneath which is suspended, according to her cranial position, what varies between a double and occasionally a treble chin).

She is kindly, at the same time she is stern, her sternness a consequence of her kindliness. 'Do not take me for granted,' her look suggests: an injunction accompanying me as I follow her up the stairs – she turning off the lights as we ascend, as if foreclosing on the possibility of retreat, the two of us, finally, standing at her door, bringing with us, or so it feels, the day's atmosphere of dust and chalk and perspiration – an atmosphere (and the relative darkness of the landing) dispelled the moment she unlocks her door and switches on a light.

A smell of perfume comes out to the landing, the brightness of the light inside the comparatively narrow hall blinding my eyes, she turning off one switch and turning on another, announcing (exclaiming), 'I must get a shade for that lamp! I've been meaning to do so for ever so long! One very much needs a man to get things done. Living on one's own one soon forgets,' disappearing into a room beyond.

The furniture in the room in which she has left me is that of a long-established parlour: old, dilapidated, and strewn with cushions, one or two of which have burst.

'The kitchen's through there. Make one for me,' she calls, reappearing, moments later. 'Not found the tea? I take it one for you as well?' entering the kitchen, located on the opposite side of the room, returning after an interval with a tray, setting it down on a low table beside a couch. 'You'll have to show more initiative, Richard, if you're to make your mark in the way your brother has,' indicating, with the palm of her hand, I sit beside her. 'I don't suppose you do the washing-up, either?'

'I don't,' I tell her.

'In which case,' she says, 'you can pour it out. No sugar for me. I haven't had sugar since Mr Dover died.'

She indicates the walls of the room, decorated, excessively, with framed photographs, the majority of academic groups, youths and adults, in addition to a number of teams depicting one sport or another. On a sideboard stands the framed photograph of a solitary figure, Mr Dover, in mortarboard and gown, evidently taken in his youth.

'Nor have I decorated this place either,' drawing her cup to her and holding it in its saucer against her chest. 'Long in need, but I don't have the incentive. Now Mr Dover's gone.'

She offers me a smile, the school's contribution to the expressiveness of human life. 'Unlike the school which he'd wish me, as when alive, to keep spick and span.'

She drinks deeply and sets the cup and saucer down.

'How is your sister-in-law?' she enquires.

'Much the same.'

'Do you see any sign of improvement?'

'If anything, she's worse.'

'Close the curtains.' She indicates the windows which overlook the tree-lined road at the front of the building. 'I'm not one for being on view. Even if some of our neighbours are. The sights one sees occasionally up here. People assume they're not overlooked,' adding, 'I admired your sister-in-law. As I'm sure I've told you. I saw *Taken to Paradise* five times and I'd see it again, if I could, tomorrow. As for *Rachel* and *Each a Stranger*, those, too, if I had the chance. Films, as no doubt you're aware, go out of fashion, but some remain in the mind for years.' Waving at the curtains, she calls, 'Tug them harder. I should replace those, too, I'm afraid,' and when I return to my seat continues – casually, as she might have requested another cup of tea – 'This isn't a demand I make of everyone, but I wonder if you'd be dismayed if I asked you to rub my back? I can hardly reach round myself.'

'No,' I tell her, anticipating little else since the moment I started drafting the memo.

'I have something,' she says, 'you might rub on,' taking my hand and leading me to the door through which she first disappeared and which I discover opens into a bedroom: an uncurtained window looks out to the back of the house. In the centre of one wall is a double bed, facing it a desk and an upholstered chair. A bathroom and a dressing room open off on either side, the doors to both of which are open.

She groans as she sits on the bed and, bowing her head, releases a hook at the back of her dress. 'It's on the desk. I've put it out. If you go to the bathroom you'll find a towel.'

Returning – the bathroom as cluttered as the sitting room – I find her back is turned towards me, the dress unzipped, her arms drawn out.

'On either side of the spine. I'll show you the spot.'

From her shoulders she withdraws the straps of a slip and lowers that, like her dress, to her waist: an expanse of flesh is exposed to the evening light, the window, as I said, uncurtained, the tops of several plane trees visible outside.

'We mustn't feel immodest. After all,' she suggests, 'we've known each other so long,' unhooking the rear of the remaining garment before drawing that, too, down the length of her arms. 'As I'm sure your sister-in-law will tell you, a woman's lot is not to be envied. So many *things* we have to put on.'

One of her astonishingly delicate hands reaches round to indicate the area where I might apply the ointment.

'There,' she says, drawing herself upright on the bed.

She gasps at the first touch, bows her head, exposing the nape of her neck, and adds, 'I can't tell you, Richard, how relaxing that feels.'

Her back, at that first touch, is warm: when she moves to indicate I might apply the liniment lower, the skin, I discover, has a life of its own: its warmth comes to me: the declivities, the protrusions, the hollow of the spine, the swelling of the tendon either side, the shelving of her waist above her hips.

'We're bouncing,' she tells me, 'all over the place. You'll have to hold my shoulder.'

Her head sinks further forward: the liniment spreads its whiteness: each gyration of my hand is followed by a moan.

'Good.'

The scale and composure (the vastness: the depth, the width, the height), the whiteness of the flesh: for a while she doesn't speak. I place one hand across her shoulder, caressing with the other. Finally she says, 'Mind you don't spill on the cover,' and, drawing a cigarette from a packet by the bed, flicks a lighter, a cloud of smoke rising above her honey-coloured hair. Turning, smiling, she adds, 'Maybe to get rid of the smell you should wash your hands.'

When I return from the bathroom she is sitting, a dressing gown around her, on the edge of the bed, her legs swung over the side, stooping to fit her feet inside a pair of slippers.

'I'll get into something more comfortable,' she says. 'Pour yourself another cup of tea.'

I return to the sitting room and, not having drunk the first cup of tea, empty it in the kitchen and pour another, and am sitting drinking it when, still smoking, smiling, she comes back in.

MEMO TWENTY (20)

She doesn't invite me again for several weeks, scarcely acknowledging me in school. Only, one afternoon, encountering me in the school doorway, she says, abruptly, 'Come and have some tea. I'll give you the key. I'll be up in a minute.'

When she arrives she enters the bedroom without comment and a few moments later calls, 'You can make one later if you haven't by now.'

She is sitting on the bed in much the same position as she had been before, and, her back and shoulders bare, stubbing out a cigarette, adds, 'I'll have to have you come up more often.'

I hold her waist as I massage her back; as an alternative, I grasp her shoulder, gripping it beside her neck.

As I manoeuvre the liniment lower I release her shoulder and clasp her side. The weight of her subtended breast encloses my wrist. Sliding my hand upwards, my other busily engaged across her back, I hear Gerry coming up the stairs, followed by his cry, 'What the fuck are you doing in there? You're shaking my fucking ceiling!' the door opening, 'Maybe a change would be to your good.'

'Change to what?'

'Another school.'

'Why?'

'Dover's,' he says, 'is too enclosed. Too *privileged*. In a couple of years you'll be at university. Maybe you should be *branching out*. How about the American School?'

'It's full of fucking Americans,' I tell him.

'Or one of those Catholic, Jewish schools.'

'Don't you have to be one or the other?'

'Sure,' he says. 'We'll get you baptised. Believe me,' he waves his hand, 'they'll be glad to have you.'

'Those places are reductive,' I tell him. 'At this stage of evolution religion can only be seen as a symptom.'

'Sure.' A moment later, he adds, 'What of?'

'Regression.'

He couches his ear, not convinced of what he's heard.

'Evolution has evolved beyond that sort of crap,' I tell him.

He waits.

'Where do you pick up that sort of stuff?' he finally asks.

'I work it out,' I tell him.

'At Dover's.'

'I'm happy at Dover's.'

'You are?'

The thought hasn't struck him before.

'I don't like seeing you,' he says, 'immersed.'

'Immersed?'

'In just one thing.'

'What thing?'

'One *school*. Whatever you do in that fucking place.'

'You recommended it,' I tell him. 'How many schools did you look at before deciding?'

'Two.'

'You told me twelve.'

'I looked *at* twelve. I looked *into* two.'

'Fuck the American School. And fuck the Jewish one,' I tell him. 'Segregating children before they're born. What sort of fucking thing is that?'

'Another thing,' he says. 'This swearing.'

'I get it from you.'

'I don't swear,' he says, 'inside this house.'

'You swear all the fucking time,' I tell him.

'Jesus,' he says, 'so this is growing up? Give me dying every time.'

MEMO TWENTY-ONE (21)

I hang in at Dover's. Memos are memos: prospective events. Mrs Dover as undefined as no doubt she was to Mr Dover (they had no children, dedicating their lives – they alleged – to the welfare of the children of others).

I visit my sister-in-law at weekends. Gerry on occasion takes me in his Rolls. By preference, on my own, I travel by Greenline bus: one and a quarter hours north-eastwards out of London, beyond the suburbs, amongst the fields, the interval given over to adjusting my mind to what I'm about to encounter the other end.

It might have been a stroke of fate, not calculation (of that I can't be sure) which has made it possible to travel almost literally from door to door by single-decker (I prefer sitting at the front, looking over the driver's shoulder, or, occasionally, rearward and slightly to one side if there's no conductor occupying that seat himself): door to door from our home in Hampstead (catching the bus by Whitestone Pond) to Market Whelling. There's a ten-minute walk the other end down a winding lane to the battlemented gateposts, the metal gates of which are invariably open (a welcome sight) and beyond which the turreted outline of the house itself is visible above a line of distant trees. Farm fields sweep off on either side – a place, in its way, as exclusive as my brother's life, a strange compatibility between his choice of nuthouse and the way he chooses where we should live: when we come in the Rolls it's with a feeling we're the owners of the place (surging up the curving drive, no flunkeys, however, emerging from the door, only nutters, occasionally, like Martha herself).

Invariably my sister-in-law shows neither surprise nor pleasure at my appearance, a consistency of non-receptivity she sustains with Gerry, too. I sometimes wonder if she knows me – or him – at all. No doubt she is unaware of the mental gymnastics I am obliged to go through in order to confront her in a place like this, not she, however, but the other patients the disconcerting factor: I can't help feeling – the thought can't help expressing itself – that, taking into account the vagaries of human nature (a whole twentieth-century compendium to go through) it's not at all unlikely (the potential is there already) that I will end up in a place like this myself (Gerry more than halfway there already).

She is, in her fifties, beautiful to look at: more than beautiful, ethereal (not of this world): calm, composed – so self-contained – so, ideally what an autonomous, self-regulated human being should be. Even glancing at her, I am, frequently, reduced to tears. She sits in a cushioned, wickerwork chair, on a terrace, at the rear of the house, if it's sunny, placed there by an attendant – who, allegedly, 'adores' her – so serene, so abstracted, that often I'm reluctant to approach her. In the distance, a lake – a bank of sheep-mown grass sloping down towards it, a frieze of trees silhouetted, in a variegated pattern against the sky the other side: a place of serenity, of abstraction, as far from the world of Leighcroft Gardens as anything I can imagine.

My invariable response, once I have made my presence known ('It's Richard!' the blank, unvarying stare) is silently (vehemently) to enquire, 'Why don't we pack this in? Why don't you come back with me? Why not make a film? Why not be famous (once again)? Why not be my *sister*? Why not be my brother's wife?'

Her cheeks are plumper than in the past, her figure, if anything, stouter (enough, at least for me, to notice: so memorable her image on the screen): her mouth – her beautiful lips fuller (coarser, less refined: evidence of biting them – a pain I can't describe): the delicacy of her hands remains – reminding me, curiously, of the anachronistically delicate hands of Mrs Dover. Blue eyes, blonde hair (carefully tinted: Gerry hires a hairdresser to check her out each week). She pouts: her lips – her attendant, too, attends to these – are tinted red. Similarly, above her pale blue eyes with their thick blonde lashes, is a streak of eye shadow, spreading sideways and upwards in a quaintly quizzical, oriental fashion – an affectation of hers, or Gerry's, or the in-house attendant, I'm not sure which. She didn't look like this in the past: *then* an open, guileless, ingenuous expression – even, on occasion, faintly mocking (the eyebrows raised): generous, spontaneous: *glad*!

Her forehead retains its shape, even if the cheekbones are masked somewhat by the fullness of her cheeks: the fringes of her mouth are lined and, unmistakably, beneath her chin, a layer of fat – scarcely noticeable, but significant to me. Her skin is bronzed (so many hours has she sat in the sun): a light blue suit – silk, richly lustred – jacket, skirt, offsets the colour: her legs, like her figure, have retained their underlying shape. From a distance she presents an image of someone little more than half her age. 'What woman at her age – at *our* age – wouldn't want to look like that?' Gerry has often said. 'The *outside's* as good as it ever was. In many respects, a good deal better. Maturer. Firmer. She *looks* composed. She looks *enriched*. And yet,' he frowns, 'the inside, Rick, is *seriously* fucked up.'

We have an agreement, her husband and I, that Martha will be an 'open' subject. 'No hiding her in a cupboard,' he often says. 'Martha's as present in our lives as she ever was. No setting her aside. She's *with* us. One of the family. Don't either of us, Richard, ever forget it.'

We talk about her, as a consequence, scarcely at all: the declaration that she's 'one of us' is – and always has been – enough: our 'open' agreement is now a closed book. A ghost, her absence dominates the house, a given (if unmentioned) element of it. 'She's in our *thoughts*,' he says if – whenever – I bring the subject up: invariably when he fails to enquire how she is after one of my visits. A ghost, in effect, which resembles so little the figure that sits beside me on the terrace, staring at the lake, the distant trees (more potentially undiscovered bodies, 'culprits' passing invisibly to and fro). 'Suspects' have, recently, grown more elusive, and the 'corpses' she allegedly comes across more difficult to find: she will, on occasion, permission being given, take me across the grounds, indicating the places where we might, by constant searching, constant vigilance, come upon a 'clue': a broken twig, a trampled plant, a piece of paper beneath a tree, a footprint by a wall. 'They're cleverer, Ronald, than they ever were,' she often tells me, though even this mystery is beginning to elude her.

'Ronald' is one of her misnomers – one of many: I have long given up prompting her to my given name. 'Richard?' she will say, repeating it with a querulous look, adding, 'I knew it had an "r" in it. Not Ralph, then, Roland, after all?'

'Roderick, Robert, Rupert, Raymond' (odd she rarely hits on 'Richard') – even, occasionally, 'Ian' – no 'r' at all, the name of my (dead) nephew.

Poor Martha.

Poor Gerry.

Poor Ian.

Poor fucked-up Richard.

A star, its zenith: too close to the sun, the female Icarene, if she but knew it (the celluloid melting), not even aware she's taken off.

While we, her admirers, stand rooted to the spot.

Dear God, who has never answered my requests, this suffering in the name of 'free will' is beyond my ken. Does the fly sucked dry by the spider suffer from the same, the gazelle brought down by the tiger – its eyes alert, its body ripped apart – the fish crunched up by the shark – the cyclical horror of species devouring species upon which the whole of nature apparently subsists – benefit, like we do, from the graciousness, the generosity, the 'gift' of free will: or are we the 'material' of a self-devouring monster . . .? queries Audlin, aka Richard, Ronald, Roderick, etc., whenever he visits his alienated 'sister'.

She never will get well. Gerry's prognosis ('new drugs in the pipeline'), frequently – invariably absent-mindedly – repeated that she will, is intended to keep us 'going'. To keep *me* going, his own visits to Market Whelling growing – recently – increasingly infrequent. She will never know me as I am, nor will I ever know her as she was – other than the persona transposed from her movies (copies stored 'out of the way' in cardboard boxes in the attic: occasionally I climb up the ladder with a torch and lift a reel out, look at it, lifeless, wonder if it's deteriorating, and put it back. Gerry has plans to transfer all of them to new reels that we can store 'for the next generation: the generation,' he tells me, 'after you').

Will they want to know? Not as much as I do – and I'm an adjunct, scarcely functioning, if alive at all: a potential corpse, if not a murderer (lining up behind the trees, a 'nomen' with an 'r' in it, along with Ronald, Robert, Roderick, all the rest).

When I first used to visit her I had the impression (I had the *belief*) that, of all the people she *had* known, she knew me best: in her decline, I was, for a considerable period, her principal companion, not least when we came to England: the walks we shared searching for 'clues' – closer to her, at that time, than Gerry (his time taken up with 'work'). Closer, also, than her sister (who visited her only once, took one look and declared herself to be feeling 'that way, too'. 'Perhaps it's genetic!' she exclaimed. 'Our mother, after all, was very *odd*.'

'How odd?' I enquired.

'*Odd*,' she declared. 'She stayed married to our father all those years.').

I thought, furthermore, by being close, I might remind her – not only of who I was, but who she'd been: why she had come here; what, as an alternative, she had to live for (the resumption, for one thing, of her remarkable career). I would mention the titles of her movies, the stars she had appeared with (been fucked by, too, I assumed); spoke, too, of my own ambitions – or, rather, Gerry's ambitions for me – called her not only 'Martha' but 'Geraldine', even 'Matty', hoping to distract her from moving through the plots of half-forgotten movies, the titles of which, like my name – like, presumably, her own – meant little if anything to her. I had a camera (another prompt from Gerry) and took pictures of her sitting on the terrace, or in her room, walking down the staircase into the communal hall. 'I am,' I told her, 'your brother-in-law, who loves you very much,' to which invariably she responded, 'What law? Who says it?' (Even, on one occasion, 'Who passed it?') Little I say fails to disturb her. At times I wonder if my visiting her does any good, concluding, on several visits, I won't come again – to be mystified, days later, by an increasing desire to be with her, to see her (convinced, if I could find the right phrase, I could prompt her back to the person she's been).

Poor Geraldine.

Poor Martha.

Poor Matty.

Poor us.

(This when poverty isn't a problem.)

The fact of the matter was – the fact of the matter *is* – I scarcely know anyone else, she, other than Gerry, the person I'm closest to: a rake, a vocational voyeur, on one side, a nutter on the other.

MEMO TWENTY-TWO (22)

GREENLINE.

1. My brother never talks about his activities in the war.
2. I know he must have done something, having been mentioned in despatches – presumably having killed or crippled or disfigured someone on the way.
3. What he is clear about is that I should be grateful for what he and his generation have done on my behalf.
4. About the rest of his life he is loquacious.
5. Almost.
6. Or have I misjudged him?
7. I have seen Martha today, having only seen her a week ago. Gerry hasn't seen her for a month. We were going to Biarritz only this has been cancelled. Not only the film he's working on the cause, but he's quarrelled with the agent whose house we were going to borrow.
8. We live, always, in other people's pockets.
9. I have decided to make a virtue of being fucked up. It's done

my sister-in-law a power of good: people on hand, no requirement to earn a living: no requirement to do anything but solve mysteries for which no one gives a fuck.

10. When I tell Gerry I don't believe in 'politics' he hits the roof ('the bullshit panacea of the twentieth century like religion was to the nineteenth'). Everyone, I tell him, is active. I'd like to make a virtue of being pissed off.

11. A part of him is thinking, 'Is there something to be made from that? This is the first affirmative statement to have come from the creep, even if it's a negative one.'

    'What do you mean by that?' he says.

12. My brother rarely uses colloquialisms, except when he's worried about money (most of the time). Then he refers to stars as 'cunts', agents as 'toss-offs', and virtually everyone else as 'items I wouldn't piss on'.

    'All I'm saying,' I tell him, 'is maybe there's a virtue in what I am.'

    'Sure there's a virtue,' he says. 'There's strength and principle, too. On the other hand, nothing comes to he – or she – who sits and waits. And although that goes against contemporary mythology – vis-à-vis meditation, for instance – I can say it's true of my experience as well as of that of everyone who I happen to have observed. Activity generates comment and comment, in turn, generates thought. Thought, inevitably, generates action. This is the circle, Richard, we move in. This is the conclusion *I* have come to, after, I might tell you, a great deal of *thought*.'

    This is an observation, variations of which I have heard before and, although I can't identify its source, I doubt if it is one he has conjured up himself.

13. Or has he?

14. I have never seen my brother thinking.

15. In justifying myself am I inadvertently doing my brother down?

I glance at his dark eyes for a glimmer of awareness but all I see is apprehension which, over recent years, has come to characterise him more and more – not least, I'm convinced, when he's dealing with me. We've both, after all, got the abyss of Martha to fall into: a pit of incomprehension which awaits us both. If *she*'s gone down, why not one or both of us as well?

'It's only by opposing yourself to your equals, and particularly to those who are ostensibly more than your equals, that your own qualities are ever realised,' he says. 'You're shaped by what goes on around you, and if everything around you is defined by inactivity you end up . . .'

He intends to say 'like Martha', only Martha is more than even he would care to acknowledge (why she is like she is is 'inexplicable': a 'genetic aberration' the latest diagnosis – as revelatory as saying Hitler is the evidence of free will).

'As a bum,' he concludes.

16. The circles we are driven in.
17. (The continuum in which we live.)
18. 'Maybe I'm an observer,' I tell him.
19. To get him off the hook.
20. To help us retreat from familiar ground.
21. 'Observe from behind a camera,' he says. 'Make something from your observation. Artists *are* observers. The camera, which you object to, is as much a tool to a director as a brush is to a painter or a chisel to a sculptor. It doesn't invalidate what they do. I don't go in for your "anti-kinema" crap. It's your way,' he goes on, 'of getting back at me. I understand. But it's no way, Rick, of going about it.'

Maybe he concludes he's getting through.

He draws up a chair beside the bed.

'How's anyone to know what you're observing if you don't *demonstrate* your observations?'

'Maybe my observations are equated with inactivity,' I tell him.

'Sure.'

He waits, a demonstration by yours truly evidently underway.

'Inactivity,' he adds, 'is a lack of faith.'

'In what?'

'Anything.' He pulls his chair in closer: he's coming to the point: how many times have we sat like this, me sprawled on the bed, the putative invalid, he the exhorting visitor?

'Maybe there's nothing to have faith in,' I tell him.

Not a suggestion my brother likes: the evidence – the *material* – of faith is all around: take the house, take Mr & Mrs Hodges – take the camera he's bought me (and which I've used only once): take the paintings he's bought from penurious bums (and later sold at an inordinate profit).

Take the care he is exercising over me.

" " " " " " " Martha

(the astronomical cost of the Home he's found).

" " " " everything.

" " " " his job.

'There's everything to have faith in,' he says.

'I don't see it, Gerry,' I tell him.

'Take regard of your *perceptions*. Take regard,' he says, 'of the regard you hold them in.'

'Nothing adds up to anything,' I tell him.

'Am I nothing, Richard?' he asks.

'No.'

'Is Martha?'

'No.'

'Are you?'

I wait.

'How come we add up to nothing?'

He is showing a streak of commonsense (?).

'I hate to mention relevance,' he adds. 'Like,' he goes on, 'what we're doing here. The significance, for instance, of my talking to you.'

'What's relevance?' I ask him. 'What will Martha's madness add up to in a thousand years? What value the shit we live through now? I don't go in,' I conclude, 'for your thin-ice skaters.'

'What thin ice?'

He raises his head, gazing at me for several seconds, the caesarian fringe, greying at the edges, arrested on his brow.

'I'd like you to explain,' he says, 'the state of mind which, when surrounded by all this affluence, declares that there is no purpose in life that you care to respond to. Maybe you've been too much provided for. Maybe circumstances, derived from others, have allowed you the luxury to indulge yourself in negative thoughts and encouraged you, having nothing else to do, to feel sorry for yourself. Maybe affluence, Richard, is your problem.'

'I don't make a virtue of how I feel, even if you're inclined to,' I tell him. 'You ask me a question, I give you an answer. The next thing I know it's morality you're on about. What's so moral about making all this dough?'

'Maybe I should give it away,' he says.

He's suggested – indeed, offered (threatened) – this several times (a) as an indication that making money means nothing to him ('a means to an end'), (b) because it means nothing to him, giving it away would be a pointless exercise.

'I'm not an artist,' I tell him. 'If I were I'd be painting a picture.'

'Or making a film. The opportunities today for an apprentice film-maker were unheard of when I was young. Why,' he waves his arm, encompassing the room, the house, the heath, the whole of London, the entirety of the known and the unknowable universe, 'you had to kiss someone's ass for fifteen fucking years before you were allowed behind a camera, let alone a view through the eyepiece. They're making films in *schools*. I've been in schools where the kids are making films themselves.'

'Not Dover's.'

'Fuck Dover's.'

You see how early the process starts, the age's preoccupation with sentiment and action.

My brother applauds from the wings.

'Or write a book,' I tell him.

'Okay. Write a book.'

My brother is suspicious of – more than suspicious, positively detests – authors. For one thing, they're always after your money. For another, they're always preoccupied with something he has no time for. Themselves.

Which is why he hates to see me preoccupied in this way too.

Like the alcoholic genius two years back who burned him for twenty thousand dollars for writing a treatment of his early masterpiece in which he scarcely changed a single word – simply copied out the crap he'd written before, for which he'd only made fifty-four pounds, ten shillings and seven pence when the masterpiece was first published. 'I'll never employ an *author* again. Give me a *hack*, goddamit, every time.'

'Have you written a book?'

'No.'

'Do you intend to?'

'I haven't thought of it.'

'Why mention it?'

He is about to add, 'All these fucking memos around the fucking house,' for I can see the prospect of my writing a book so close to home disturbs him more than ever. For instance, he is currently in litigation with several characters in the US who are writing the life of his second wife. My brother wants Miss Geraldine O'Neill, at this stage of the proceedings, to be forgotten. He wants her to be forgotten while she's still alive – at the very least while she's off her head. The moment she is dead he has, I'm convinced, worked out the scenario for a first-class movie, in which case, if there are any books around, he will have to buy the rights: 'Let's burn the bastards now,' he says. 'In the long run, that way, we can save a lot of dough.'

'I could have said, "Or write a symphony".'

'You have to *train* to write a symphony. You have, for one thing, to learn the fucking piano. You have to have no training to write a book. Any asshole – and I've *known* some – can write a fucking book. The costs, for one thing,' he concludes, 'are *nothing*.'

He is thinking, no doubt, of my memo pads: he is thinking, 'This sonofabitch is going to write a book about Miss Geraldine O'Neill and how she was fucked up by her (present) husband and how all the blame can be laid at his door, the poor suffering bastard who's done everything to help her – and *him*: he'll create the shit-all scandal of all time for I'll hardly be able to sue my *brother* and, worst of all, say anything in public by way of litigation while my second wife is still alive.'

He is also (a secondary, though no less important function of his brain) reflecting, 'I can always buy the movie rights at cost, make him feel he's accomplished something independent of his brother, and show him I'm above all petty sentiment, even the inconvenience of being libelled.'

'I have a meeting.' He looks at his watch, a chronometer costing several thousand pounds – an early present, in their courtship, from Martha.

'Right.'

'We'll talk about this later.'

'Okay.'

'I mean that, Rick.'

'I'll be here.'

'I don't want you here. See a girlfriend. Get one to stay over one or two nights. I don't want you wanking here all evening.'

'Sure.'

'How about the fair-haired one who called last week?'

I can see he has a view to the fair-haired one himself: just as the fair-haired one had a view to him. 'Is that your *brother*?' she enquires, her pale blue eyes following Gerry out.

'I'll look forward to seeing her,' he tells me.

'I'll tell her.'

'Right.'

My brother skates off to his next assignment. Having paused by the bank, he swirls away. Faithless and unjustified as I am, I have to admire his grace. I have to admire his skill: his gyrations, his leaps and whirls – *his dancing and his speed are everything*.

THE BOOK

1

'I'm going, Martha,' I tell her.

She doesn't stir.

Neither does she move her hand, her habitual gesture – a casual, upward flick – enquiring and dismissive – when registering something of what is going on around her: a demonstration of 'as you were' or, even, conjecturely, '*understood*'.

She sits in her room as if she's waited here for hours, expectant (news of a fresh catastrophe outside: a 'crime' demanding her immediate detectorial presence). I've been told already she isn't well, Gerry instructing me on this visit, however, to tell her he'll be away 'for a month'.

In effect, five weeks (when he gives me the dates), coming into my room to inform me, the decision a torment to him (the ice getting thinner all the while, the speed required to keep ahead: one day, I know, the ice will crack: the strangulated cry, the outreaching hand, the desperate face as, caught irrevocably in his own momentum, he disappears – that grace, that dexterity: the 'perfect line' – for good).

An antidote to his anxiety (perplexity: letting go of those he loves), he suggests – surprisingly (the first time he has done so) – I travel with him (to New York, Los Angeles, back to New York). 'Maybe I should involve you in this production. Give you a break from Dover's, this house, a life which – my guess – isn't doing you an awful lot of good. I shan't, for instance, be taking Gavin. He's enough on his hands over here. You could do some useful work.'

'Like what?'

'Discuss the things I come up with.'

'Such as?'

'Money. Since you have no regard for it, detachment – yours – might be a help.'

'Waiting in hotels,' I tell him.

'Hell, no. There'll be a suite. I'd like you with me. All the time.'

A fresh – a novel – unexpected anxiety: an extension, no doubt, of the one he's shown before (via vexatiousness, exasperation, contempt) but this with a new intensity. What, for Christ's sake, is his brother up to?

'I'd hate to leave you on your own, even with Mr and Mrs Hodges. These trips to see Martha appear to be your only consistent social contact. Does she *insist* you see her?'

'No.'

'Does she tell you things I ought to know?'

'No different to the things she's said before.'

'Does she talk about us?'

I shake my head. 'I don't think she knows who I am. You,' I tell him, 'never come up. I wouldn't, either, if I wasn't there. She often calls me Ronald.'

'Ronald.' He stares at me for several seconds. 'As I say,' he says, 'I'd hate to leave you with Mr and Mrs Hodges.'

'And Martha.'

'And Martha.'

Mrs Hodges is, inimitably, the wife of Mr Hodges, who began his employment as a waiter on the old London, Midland and Scottish Railway: a dining car attendant, acquiring his NCO status during the Second World War in the Western Desert: incidental, this information, I have to confess, but, both by manner and appearance (stocky, barrel-chested, winged moustache), he lends formidable support to Mrs Hodges who is significantly bigger than himself: a Mrs Dover of the Domestic Front, with her own, authoritarian, dismissive flavour. My brother, in my view, was a sucker to hire them (accommodation provided – the basement – a salary to match): at the time he was determined (more than determined – vocationally inclined) to provide a *home*, a place fit to bring me up in after the life of itineracy which – an exact reflection of Martha's disturbance – he (we) had lived until then. In a sense, I suspect, my brother has never recovered from the war: seconded to the US Navy, he encountered a force of nature (the sea) and a societal enterprise (America) which have absorbed if not overwhelmed him ever since: subsequently, nothing has matched that expansiveness (I guess), not even Martha (though with her he had a try: films – or, rather, film-making – having little, if any interest, curiously, in the finished product, nor in the texts from which the films invariably derived: *the process is the purpose*).

As I say, a digression – but the thought of being the sole focus of Mr and Mrs Hodges' attention is more than my famous lack of resilience (resourcefulness, enterprise) will allow. Sufficient to say, however, that my disinclination to travel with and be in my brother's company all the while is matched by my disinclination to be in the diurnal presence of the domestic duo below: the formalised behaviour of the husband (mentally at attention all the while) and the ritualised dominion of the wife (everything in place, at the proper time – memos excluded, she not sure what to make of them: have they been written, for instance, by Gerry himself? Our writing is indistinguishable at times).

Having made my feelings clear – waiting in hotels, whether a suite or not – Gerry is (surprisingly) disinclined to press his point (what girls I'd have to witness passing through the bedroom, Gerry unable to endure twenty-four hours without a fuck). Five weeks! And me, seven and a half thousand miles, most of the time, from Mrs Dover, orgasmic interludes exclusively by hand. 'What's so different from home?' I might have asked, only, at Dover's, in Hampstead, at home, I catch sight of her every day (Saturdays and Sundays alone excluded).

Thereupon Gerry suggests I stay with one, or a succession, of my friends, or, conversely, one or other of my friends can stay with me.

'What friends?'

'Don't you have any friends?' (Enough bums pass through the house – none, he may have noticed, staying long.)

'None I'd spend *five weeks* with.'

'One week with each.'

'No, thanks.'

'I hate the thought,' he says, 'of you being on your own.'

'With the Hodges.'

'Fuck the Hodges. The Hodges are all right. *When*,' he says, 'we're here together.'

'Why not on my own?'

'You need . . .' he can't think of the word, 'a different *class* of person,' amending this, when he sees my look, 'a different *type*. A peer.'

'I thought you didn't go in for titles.'

'A *generational* peer.'

His patience, I can see, is running out.

Twenty-four hours later he comes back to the problem.

'Maybe you should go to Jimmy's.'

'Who's Jimmy?'

I'm lying – as usual on these occasions – in bed.

'Our brother.'

Patience still a premium.

'I thought you didn't like him.'

'I didn't say I didn't like him. I said we never got on.'

'Why not?'

'Chemical. Who knows? He pissed all over our father.'

'How?'

'He had no sympathy with his views. When he went bust he offered him no help. Not that I offered him much. At least,' he goes on, 'I *listened*.'

'What to?'

'*Him*, for fuck's sake.'

Not sure how obtuse I am.

'Jimmy, on the other hand,' he adds, 'thought he was a cunt.'

'Why?'

'How do I know? He thought he favoured me. As it was, unlike me, Jimmy had a very bad war.'

'How bad?'

'He fucked up early.'

'Early?'

'In France. Surrendered his men to, as it turned out, a smaller German force. Been kicking himself ever since. More than kicking . . .'

He waits: how much of this is Richard taking in?

'Did he know Hodges?'

'Why?'

Instantly suspicious.

'In the forces.'

'Hodges was in the desert. It was why I took him on. He hadn't fucked up. Fought at El Alamein and never looked back. Was personally recommended by Montgomery. As for Jimmy. He went off on his own. Up there he lives a very different life to the one we have down here. Nevertheless, he is your brother. Since there are only the three of us, and Martha, I'd say relatives, in our case, are thin on the ground. A pity to have discarded one.'

'I don't know him.'

'Every reason why you should. A wonderful opportunity to make a start. Don't let sentiments stand in the way.' He spreads out his hands. 'He'd be very pleased to have you.'

'You've *asked* him?'

'Sure.'

'When?'

'An hour ago.' He looks at his £10,000 (ten thousand) watch and adds, 'Two hours ago. The car can take you up.'

'I hate the fucking car. I feel an asshole sitting in the back.'

'Sit in the front.'

'Or the fucking boot. I hate the fucking thing.'

'Why?'

'It's not even earned. It's fucking rented. Apart from that, it looks pretentious.'

'It's the most beautiful machine in the world. A masterpiece of engineering. Eric will get you there in less than four hours.'

Eric is the chauffeur: a slim, obnoxious creep, who's fought in no wars, reveres my brother, thinks Martha has let him down, and despises me likewise. Gerry, where Eric is concerned, is life's generic force: no doubt he sees most of the women Gerry screws – on top of which 'Good old G', as he offensively calls him, gets him autographs from the stars, prefaced by the odious, 'To Eric'. The cunt.

'I can ask Jimmy to come and fetch you. He probably drives a Morris Ten. Or even rides a bike.'

'I don't know where he lives.'

'Up north.'

'Where up north?'

'How the fuck do I know? Some fucking place. I've never been.'

'But want me to go.'

'You,' he says, 'are a different proposition. On top of which, as I say, you're flesh and blood.'

More is conveyed than I ought to know: he stares at me intensely.

'He could arrange a school up there.'

'No, thanks.'

'You don't want to piss around for five weeks. You need some sort of focus.'

'I can write a book.'

'Schooling, at this stage, is all that counts.'

'Maybe I'm a genius and five weeks with someone you can't stand will turn me on. Make me appreciate what we have down here. What I have, for instance, with you.'

He's not over-fond of derision, either. 'Jimmy, despite his difficulties,' he says, 'maybe because of them, may very well give you a different perspective.'

'On what?'

'Anything you care to mention.'

'Like you.'

'Like me. Or you. All we have down here, as you suggest. I don't say – I've *never* said – this is the optimum way to live. It happens to be the way I've chosen. I never set out to be a producer.'

'What did you set out to be?'

He thinks back through the Navy and, after that, his career as an actor, and, before all that, to the prospects, which failed to materialise, of working with his father: taking over a textile firm of which, even before the war, Jimmy had washed his hands. 'Basically, all I wanted,' he says, 'was to have a good time. I played a lot of tennis.'

'*Tennis?*'

'I might have been a pro. Or the equivalent in those days. Tennis was a way – *the* way, at that time – to fuck a lot of girls. Short skirts, blouses. Sun . . .'

'Fucking, would you say, was your principal occupation?'

'Fucking, in those days, was barely understood. It was tied in with marriage, church, propriety. Nowadays it's an industry. Then, at that time – I'm talking of the thirties – to get your hand in a woman's pants required the skill of an engineer allied to that of a union convenor. It became, because it had to be, a way of life. Nowadays fucks hang out on trees. You can pull them down whenever you like.'

He may have gone too far: he looks at me (again) intensely.

'I am speaking as a brother.'

'I see.'

'It's not the sort of talk I'd recommend. You need a more civil parent than the sort that I provide. To be talking to a schoolboy as if he were a man may not do either of us a lot of good. *Jimmy* is civil. Apart from our misunderstandings – more my fault than his. He has written to me over the years, twice, maybe three times, with suggestions we might meet. I've always brushed him off.'

'Why?'

'I associate him with the past. Parochialism. Small-mindedness. On the other hand, would a small-minded man ask for a reconciliation? I'd say I've been stuck up. But, then, I never had the time. He's gone his way. I've gone mine.'

'What's his way?'

'He's the manager of an insurance office.'

'Christ.'

'A change from here.'

'Jesus.'

'He never had a child. His wife miscarried. Apart from that . . .' He shrugs.

'A pretty fuckless life.'

He doesn't like this, and says, 'Who are we to judge? Look at Martha. At least Jimmy's wife is still around. And, as far as I can tell, he doesn't fuck around like me.'

'I ought to go?'

'For what it's worth.'

The intensity continues.

'If I go,' I tell him, 'I'll make my own way. I don't like being carried by someone else.'

'Is that why you prefer Greenline to see Martha rather than going with Eric and me?'

'Yes.'

'You ought to tell her, incidentally, even if she fails to understand,' he says. 'Maybe *somewhere* she's aware of all that's going on.'

'You think so?'

'I *feel* so. Sometimes, out of nowhere, comes that funny fucking look. I've never mentioned it before. Maybe you've seen it, or she only does it with me. But suddenly, when I look away and then look back, I find her *looking* at me with this funny fucking expression.'

'What's funny?'

'As she looked before. Comprehending. As if all this . . . lunacy is a fucking act. A piece of dramaturgical skill. A way to escape from something which, as far as she's concerned, became too much.'

'All these *years*?'

Incredulous.

'I may be wrong.'

She's rumbled it.

Or not.

'Setting her hair on fire was an act? Coming down to dinner with people we didn't know with nothing on?'

I have to prove him wrong.

Mentally, I begin to count the occasions when she's threatened him with a knife.

'She's an actress. Maybe this is her way – her *definitive* way – as an actress, she chooses to express herself. I stress definitive. This is all-inclusive. An act to end all acts. Even the attempts at suicide.'

'I don't believe it.'

I have an ally in her, at last.

Or not.

'Sure,' he says. 'It may be me.'

Maybe a way, too, of getting me to go: curiosity, for one thing, about another brother: his relationship to *his* sister-in-law.

Have I agreed to go, or not? I can't remember.

'How do I tell him?'

'Who?'

'Jimmy. Tell him,' I add, 'I'm coming up.'

'I'll give you his work number, his home number. Ring him. He'll be delighted. He's always wanted a reconciliation.'

'Always?'

'I'll call him, after you've talked to him. He'll like it coming from you. You don't remember him?'

'Should I?'

'The last time he saw you you must have been nine. Seven. How many years ago? He was passing through London. He's passed through lots since, but never called.'

'Because of you.'

'I never had the time. I regret that now.'

'He screwed up with the Germans?'

'I had it easy. The Second Fleet. Like living in a city. He was on the front line. The Germans had the advantage. A prisoner of war. Not pleasant. It turned him in on himself. Incredibly aggressive. Faded now. It must have been what got at me. No way in. Hardly spoke. His wife had a hell of a time. What with that and my first marriage. And Ian . . .'

His thoughts float on: he hasn't thought this much about anything recently. Maybe I'm the answer. Much of his life – and Martha's, and Jimmy's – is behind him now: incredibly – exhilaratingly – most of mine is ahead. Okay? The right move? Who says? Putting his brother in the hands of an ex-POW who works in a provincial insurance office: exchange high society, he's thinking, for what? Am I putting my kid brother – *our* kid brother – out to dry? Am I putting our kid brother on the line?

He looks across.

Maybe not such a good move! Only, Richard, the asshole, has taken the bait: what the bait is, why he's taken it, for what purpose, only Richard can decide. A *brother* – unlike the current one: extension of flesh, antecedents – extension of the knowledge of where he's come from – with a view, perhaps, of *where he might go*.

Martha, when I tell her, says nothing: sitting in her room, looking out, from the ground floor, onto the terrace that runs across the back of the house, the windows to which are permanently locked: a privileged room (one of the best in the place: larger than most, its own bathroom as well as dressing room attached: my brother – or Martha – has spared nothing). She has a pencil in her hand – in both hands, for she holds it like a baseball bat, not so much to write with as to fend off (whatever she might be tempted, presumably, to write – too frightening the revelations she has to divulge). Her knuckles crested white – her delicate, sensitive, endearing hands. I love her so much I want, as always, to embrace her, tell her – reassure her – no crime has been committed (*no one* is involved: no victim, no culprit: none) – submitting to this temptation from time to time in the hope that love is what she's after: unconditional, unparalleled, unrestrained, otherwise undefined. Even my brother's suggestion this is faked makes sense – endearing her to me more: all this to conceal an inexpressible . . . what? Pain? Sure. True. Fact. I love my brother's second wife: lasciviousness, if it has been there (which I'd vigorously deny) has been transferred to the corpulent Mrs Dover, a travesty of the figure before me now . . .

Is that it?

When I try to take the pencil from her in order to hold her hand – unconditional attachment on her part, too – she resists by grasping hold of it more firmly.

'I'm going to Jimmy's,' I announce, then, 'James's. Gerry's brother,' and unable to think of any other description that might arouse her (will he, too, become another 'cause', another 'suspect'?) I add, 'I'll be away for several weeks. So will Gerry. He's coming down before he leaves. Both of us will keep in touch, on top of which I'll come back down – I'm going north – should you need me. Or ring each evening, if you like.'

She has a notepad by her feet; her dainty feet, the feet that were sung to in *Bachelor Folly*; the feet that danced in *Love Alive*; the feet around which the towel sensationally descended, after a bath, in *Happiness to Follow* (complaints from the Catholic Guild, amongst a lot of others, which were – equally sensationally – finally ignored).

On the pad are inscribed a number of circles, of varying diameter, none complete, like the striations cut by blades on ice.

There is no purpose in concealing it: I have often been tempted, in the presence of my sister-in-law, to carry on as if she isn't there:

laugh, move around, read, listen to her radio, turn on her television at which she is inclined to gaze for hours, irrespective of what's on the screen. Is all this a stratagem? I'd say – on reflection – definitely not. Yet . . . battier things have happened: would she keep up something so mundane if she wasn't genuinely out of her mind? But where? I'd say, far more, she was *in* it, lost, irretrievably, to those of us out here. Once the two of us sat watching *Finder's Keepers* in which she had a not inconsiderable part – the last film she made – with not a flicker of an eyelid on her part, abstraction – a vacuous detachment – sustained to the end (and, the screen blank, a long time beyond).

I stand at the permanently secured French windows and gaze out at the terrace, at the lawn, at the descending slope to the lake, at the silhouetted trees beyond (Collin's Wood: the *hours* we've hunted there for clues, suspects, reported bodies) and find my eyes are full of tears.

Why I cry I've no idea: I could have cried on numerous occasions, not least each time I leave her – she oblivious of my presence – looking back, expecting a wave, a glance, a last, remembered gesture. Her figure never stirs.

Nor does it now, with news of Gerry and my departures. Only when I conclude, 'For God's sake, they'll lock you up with her,' do the sobs subside and, turning back to the room, I see a look of consternation – as she might have examined an inanimate object sprung up in her path: the pencil in her left hand, the pad now on her knee, she has started to add to the circles on the sheet before her.

At some point, my back to her, she has stooped to the pad and picked it up.

I travel up the afternoon my brother leaves: I go with him and Eric to the airport. I've never seen my brother off anywhere before (he having offered to see me off at the station, I declining): a premonition of disaster – unexpected, alarming – disposes both of us to assume we'll never see each other again. Maybe it's caused by our unprecedented mutual departures, he going one way, I another – and for a significant length of time – but, equally unexpectedly, we embrace before he turns towards the reception lounge. We've embraced before – invariably on his departures and returns – but never as warmly, or as portentously as this: absurdly – what makes me do it? – I kiss his cheek.

More surprised (shaken) by this than by anything else, he glances back, once, before he disappears, gazing at me in the same curious fashion that has characterised Martha's reaction to seeing me cry. So absorbed by this response, in fact, that it's several seconds before he collects himself and raises his hand to wave.

It's as if he's suddenly *remembered something* – something pushed back, until now, to the rear of his mind. Then, with that skater's grace – that inimitable swiftness – he's gone (never, I morbidly reproach myself, to be seen again).

We return to the house to pick up Mr Hodges: my brother's idea. 'If I'm not to see you off, somebody has to. I'll ask Jack. I don't like the idea,' he insists, 'you going off on your own.'

'I'm often on my own.'

'Jack will come with you.'

'To *Jimmy*'s?'

'The fucking station.'

'As an ex-employee of the old LMS,' Hodges says, after he's climbed into the car (Mrs Hodges at the house door as well), 'I can't let you leave without a proper send off. Mr Audlin wouldn't like it. He gave me my instructions. It's more than my reputation would allow,' the NCO to the officer cadet.

He sits in front with Eric, I, an even bigger prick, behind.

'This was the terminus of the old LNER, the London and North Eastern Railway,' he says, as, despite my resistance, carrying my case, he leads the way to the platform (Eric, thank God, remaining with the car: what a fucking field day they'll have in the house with both of us away). 'It brings back memories, does this,' he finding me a first-class compartment. 'You'll go off as a gentleman, or I'll know the reason why.'

Asshole.

He's acquired the veneer of domestic subservience from films: not only an edge of self-consciousness but decrepitude. Was this the man commended for something in the desert? stout, square-shouldered, trim: a parody of what he's supposed to be.

The first-class compartment, thank God, is empty. 'It'll soon fill up,' he says, reluctant to see me sitting there alone, he anchored to the platform despite my suggestion he leave – remaining there, stoney-faced, looking for companions to board as well, almost soliciting a passing figure ('This carriage is empty, sir'). I bummed to the seat, the one compensation for this farcical departure the relief I feel when the train finally pulls out.

Hodges waves (he almost salutes), a robust stanchion to a domestic world I care little – so it feels – about: waves in an almost melancholic fashion, his hand hovering by his head, as if saying farewell to *everything*.

I wonder, as the train rumbles into a tunnel and I contemplate the brickwork passing outside – its crumbling texture a portent, I suspect, of the place that lies ahead – wonder what Hodges and Mrs Hodges make of Gerry and myself: 'respect', 'servitude', 'obedience' – qualities associated with military life: the axioms of the slave identifying with the interests of its master – the unspoken insolence of people who otherwise 'know their position': one of those 'traits', as Mrs Dover might call it, bringing up her school of gentlemen – and of which Martha, amongst her other 'absences', is blithely unaware: one of those mysteries which, so far, appear to have eluded her. Looking for 'traits' as opposed to 'clues' might task her more than her constant searches do already: not one of those mysteries she is here to solve, that being left to her disinterested half-brother-in-law.

Looking back on my home as I might, metaphorically, gaze back at it from the window of the train – currently concealed by tunnels and cuttings, and glimpses, as we trundle north, of stretches of London suburb – I have to conclude it resembles nothing more clearly than the stage-set of a film: an anachronistic one at that (still waiting to be 'shot'), the two stage managers busy in the basement, the two 'principals' active overhead (a minimal cast, a threadbare plot), a third, unresolved character, in the early stages of disintegration, hard to tell, reported in the wings (the Hodges, unlike Eric, who has driven out frequently to Market Whelling, scarcely familiar on her occasional 'home' trips, with Martha, at all). Why, I wonder, has Gerry gone to all this trouble, not least this fiction of creating a 'home'? (Home, *the* Home, is where Martha is – a not inconsiderable one, at that.) The furniture, for instance, you could find in LA, New York or Houston, or in those expensive service flats in South Kensington and Knightsbridge, scarcely distinguishable from that of a suite in an Intercontinental hotel. He may, for all I know, have hired it, like the Rolls – even though occasionally he asks me if there's anything I want 'by the way of decoration', casting his hand aimlessly at what he's put together as if his art director has somehow missed the plot: the house represents nothing more than a waiting room.

For whom? For what? Maybe for Martha to come back and tell us she wants to return to LA, Philadelphia – even Beaconsfield, for Christ's sake: anywhere, in any case, other than 'here'.

No doubt the writer who owned it before us had the best idea: everything in the house in *his* time, he told Gerry, was second-hand: 'Why pay bullshit prices for something that's going to be used in any case? I could furnish this twice over for what we'd pay out if all this was new,' my brother enquiring of me, after we've left the house on that first inspection, if we shouldn't buy the furniture as well.

'Why?' I ask.

'It looks so lived in.' He looks at me apprehensively. 'It's so much like a home.'

'It looks pissed on and shat on by that fucking cat,' I tell him, having stood on the animal as we came in the door (unconvinced, at that stage, my brother would buy it, his theory about 'community' announced only after we've moved in).

He may – more likely – have rented it, and not bought it at all: he may even, I often suspect, have rented his clothes: even the fucking pictures he alleges he sells: *everything*. Gerry is the sort of person over whom the average *rentier* hangs out his tongue.

The fact of the matter is – the truth of the matter is (any way you care to put it) – we are living on a film set, designed for a script which has yet to be written – a speculative venture on my brother's part uncharacteristic of his normal behaviour: ventures nothing without a scenario, at least a treatment, however schematic. 'This is for real,' he says, by way of explanation, on confirming we've 'taken' the house.

Its atmosphere, as a consequence of the motivation by which it came to be in our possession, is surreal: an atmosphere not unlike those constructs on the back lots of studios, or on the studio floor itself (half a sitting room; half a house; a façade without an interior, an interior without a façade: no wonder Martha went nuts): at any moment I expect a wall to be removed, a ceiling, or the floor: a camera to enter at the end of a crane: the feeling the whole time, even in my bedroom (which I have made, for this reason, as anonymous as I can: of no interest to anyone), is of being 'shot', what we've said, done, not said, not done – perhaps in some other location – being repeated.

Yet, as in Mount Street, Curzon Street, Berkeley Square, Putney or Beaconsfield, not to mention the Scottish Castle, occasional (borrowed) apartments in New York, Tangier and Paris, it is nothing new: all that is unexpected is the inappropriateness (the *provenance*) of the setting. My brother does not operate naturally in a house like this (a curious element of our 'scenario', for instance, is that he looks more *at home* in the institutional atmosphere of Whelling Hall: a place, revealingly, designed – certainly equipped – for lunatics: he *operates* there as if he *were* at home, relaxed, convivial, laid back – as if, at long last, he knows precisely not only where but *who* he is). Maybe it's not unlike the shore establishments he visited or lived in in the navy; or maybe it's its implicit air of 'class' – however parodied, trivialised, adapted – something recognised from an earlier life. Certainly Hampstead is *foreign* to him – as it is, indeed, to me. Certainly, too, I can't imagine Martha living there. If Gerry's intention is – or was – to show me how hopelessly equipped we are to live in a house and look after a problem as intractable as his second wife he couldn't have picked a better setting than Leighcroft Gardens NW3. Our 'home' wouldn't be 'complete' with Martha (the hopeless project he's working on) so much as torn apart.

The train slips over a river: distracted by the change of scenery – urban displaced by rural (a herd of cows) – I go along to the dining car. Maybe everyone is travelling *into* London this time of the day (not inappropriate I should be moving in the opposite direction), for the interior is deserted: a girl sits at a table diagonally opposite, her male companion with his back to me. I catch her eye in a manner Gerry, in his less brotherly, more avuncular, *companionable* mood, would undoubtedly have recommended. She reminds me, strangely, of Martha.

England is dead: is that why Martha came here, to match her condition to a place as un-American, in this respect, as any? As it goes, I go – scratching, in her case, amongst the ruins, oblivious of what, in reality, she's scratching for: death itself, presumably, in one form or another. The place – like Whelling Hall – has the air of a haunted palace: which is probably why Gerry sets up his camera with an air not only of fatigue but frustration – certainly disappointment. He'd prefer – much prefer – to be back in the States where you can set up a camera at ease. 'Only the sane go nuts, so watch them,' Martha might have said, warranting her decision not only to go but to arrive, not only to arrive but to stay. But for her I wouldn't be heading north – gazing at a girl's remarkable – sensuous, sensitive – face (pale skin, pale eyes, dark hair) over a man's anonymous right shoulder: she is facing backwards, I forwards: symbolism of a sort suggested there.

'Nothing matters' a positive statement (at that moment): a nihilist's affirmative creed (something counts, if it doesn't add up): there is, otherwise (I morbidly reflect) no will to survive, merely an anxiety to preserve form (Hodges, Eric – the latter's peaked cap which even my brother draws a line at, insisting he doesn't wear it – just the pleated-pocket uniform – when he's around – and Mrs Dover and her privately funded pupils): the scruples and the certainty of class, the knowledge that nothing, least of all death, gets out of hand: no blood, no wound, no pain – merely the fictional enterprise on which, for instance, my sister-in-law is engaged.

I eat the toast, I drink the tea, I bite the piece of cake I've ordered. Looking out of the window I consider how many miles away, across the fields, is Market Whelling: she, too, presumably, will be having tea, dreaming of (embalmed in) vicarage lawns, village greens, suspects, corpses, 'solutions' which fail to emerge anywhere but there.

None of the clues, however, 'add up': killings go on unabated: circles beget circles: nothing breaks out. Lines curve and return to their source – the source, I'm convinced, of my own misanthropy. Nothing, however much I might have wished it, is ascertainable, meaningful (correct), complete.

The girl, smiling in consideration of what her partner has or has not said, looks over again: her lips move: her eyes return to him. A curl dances by her cheek: she raises her hand, signalling chastisement, she curious to see, however, its effect on me.

I've seen my brother do it two hundred thousand times and know how well I do it now: with a tutor like Gerry, where women are involved, it would need a genius to fail.

I smile.

A faint discoloration rises to her cheek and – God help me – she is looking at my *hands*.

Her companion, aware of this intrusion, glances across his shoulder.

He is much older than she is: I allow my gaze to encounter his – blank, uncomprehending – then, unblinking, return it to the girl's.

A moment later, placing money on the table, rising, he takes her arm and departs along the carriage.

Her figure – legs, waist, hips, thighs, shoulders, head – I follow to the door.

Moments later – I can scarcely believe it – she reappears: returning down the carriage to her table, she retrieves a handkerchief from the seat (I am working wonders), glances across and, as she straightens, I rise and, indicating my table, enquire, 'Fancy some tea?'

'No, thanks.'

'You've had some.'

Observation, not enquiry.

My brother's tactic: face adversity, with women, with a broadening smile.

'I have.'

'It's more refreshing this side.'

I indicate my table.

Wit is man's first defensive gesture: an observation borrowed from my brother, it, in turn, borrowed no doubt from someone else: probably the author who screwed him for twenty thousand for a treatment as unusable as one he might have written himself.

'Really?'

'Also,' I suggest, 'a different view.'

'Yes.'

I don't know whether she's agreeing the tea is more refreshing and the view superior to the one on the other side of the carriage, or that she will sit down: anonymous fields fly past on either side.

Until I step round the table and draw out the chair she is unsure herself.

She sits, lifting back her hair with either hand.

This, for me, is an indescribable success: flicking swiftly through the shoals of women I have encountered, I reflect that not one have I ever approached, or been approached by, who hasn't known precisely who I am (that one identity static: a brother). For an instant, my confidence deserts me: returning to my chair I catch a glimpse of myself in the carriage window (darkened by, first, a cutting, then trees outside) and am jolted into smiling once again by the discovery that it is Gerry who is standing there: if not him exactly, a more engaging, younger self. I smile the Audlin smile, preface to many self-exculpating explanations: tall, lean, dark-haired, caesarian-fringed, caesarian-featured. Grandeur, ascendancy: style: what more could a woman want – dressed in a suit purchased for me and insisted upon on the re-introduction of me to the family (the northern branch): dark, sober (a vertical, faint-red striation), which, by its anonymity, draws attention to my shirt – blue – and my diagonally-striped pink and grey tie – as well as, of course, to my, once again, smiling features? Charm, as any thin-ice skater knows, is more than two-thirds of any battle: speed, lightness: grace.

I place my hands before me as I sit at the table and casually rearrange the cup and saucer and plates – the milk jug, the cutlery, the sugar-bowl: these, my hands suggest, will not intrude upon or invalidate any subsequent refreshment. Handing her a napkin (from several on the table) which – her gaze still on my hands – she takes, I keeping my movements to a minimum as a hypnotist might before his subject, until, clenching them beneath my chin, I make an observation about the weather, summoning (as I do so) the waiter with a glance.

He, approaching the table, gazes at the girl with a not dissimilar fascination, which obliges me to repeat the order twice.

Her hair, dark, but with a reddish tinge, hangs to her shoulders; her eyes are hazel (on closer observation) – a hybrid colour, somewhat like her hair, her mouth broad, thin-lipped: she is, if not of my age, a little older, mature, like me, before her time.

I order two more teas and confirm, 'We don't have to eat them,' adding, 'either,' and watch her smile, 'but it gives us an excuse for sitting here. It's far less cramped than the compartments and we have a wider view,' indicating the length of the carriage which gives us a broader perspective of where we're going, where we've been, as well as of where we are.

Before she has sat at the table she has glanced along the carriage, reassuring herself, I assume, she hasn't been followed. 'I'm going to visit a relative,' I tell her, and begin to unfold my story, surprised at the alacrity with which I do so, and the pleasure – the extraordinary relief – I experience in recounting it. 'Someone I don't recall. A half-brother,' the whole – or nearly the whole – of my history, as an aside, laconically slipping out. 'And you?' I conclude, anxious not to bore her.

At this final enquiry she glances once again behind her and announces she is returning from a trip to London. 'We go every two or three months. To the theatre, to visit friends. To see exhibitions.'

I have refrained from identifying my brother's job; nor have I mentioned the situation of his wife – casualness the keynote of my account. It's as if my gifts – my precocity, as Gerry would be inclined to call it – have, for the first time, been brought into focus: I feel exhilarated and, at the same time, wholly in control, no longer an apologist for, or a victim of, events.

Even when her companion returns – someone she has described as a 'cousin' – a few seconds after our second tea has been served, and approaches the table, asking, since evidently he can think of nothing else to say, 'Are you all right?' her look is scarcely turned aside, she responding (every confidence in her manner), 'I came across a friend.'

Our names, amusingly, have not been exchanged.

'Will you be long?' he enquires.

'Not very.' Her gaze returns to the table: not someone to get on the wrong side of.

Having watched his approach down the length of the carriage –

the darkening of his look as he reaches the table – I watch his long departure: tall, darker than myself, elegantly suited, these trips to London, I assume, are, or have been, his idea.

'My name, by the way,' she says, 'is Martha.'

The coincidence – stated so abruptly, and, because of the previous incident, conspiratorially – unnerves me (is this another of Gerry's 'plots'?). Or – more weirdly – one of Martha's?

'You look surprised.'

'It's the same name,' I tell her, 'as a relative. In fact, my brother's wife.'

'I see.'

She waits.

No further explanation forthcoming, she adds, 'I always think it odd.'

'Odd?'

'Old-fashioned.'

'I like it.'

'You do?'

'I like it very much. My name,' I go on, 'is Richard.'

'I like that, too.'

'You do?'

She nods. 'Dick has a reassuring sound.' She smiles. 'Do you abbreviate it?' Still smiling.

'Sometimes Rick. Or Rickie.'

'Rick. It rhymes. Relevant in your case, too, I take it?'

Laughter, for a while, absorbs us both.

'My second name is Armitage.'

'Scottish?'

'Is it?'

'I've no idea. Mine,' I tell her, 'is Audlin.'

'I know someone called Audlin.'

'Could be a relative.'

She doesn't reply.

'Are you at college?'

'Will be soon.'

Dismissing it, she waves her hand. 'And you?'

'Sure.'

'What do you study?'

'Sanskrit.'

'Sanskrit.'

'I might switch,' I tell her, 'to something else.'

'Such as?'

'I haven't decided.'

Why I pick Sanskrit I have no idea. Lying, in the Audlin household, comes easily to hand: there it's anodyned as 'imagination'.

'Grand.'

The word comes out with a flattened vowel: the suggestion of something solid, reliable.

Gazing across the table I isolate her face: why, with its pale skin and dark hair, hazel eyes, I identify it with *my* Martha I've no idea; something of the same aura, the same glow: something of the same unwitting confidence: an emissary, or so it feels, from another world. And the inflection of the voice: the interrogative stress on the final word.

'Film-making, for instance,' I suggest.

'Are you interested in films?' Her eyes refocus with this fresh enquiry.

'My family are.'

'How?'

Trump card: play it now or later?

'My brother is a producer.'

'Really?'

Not much excitement there: someone picking up a book and, having opened it, closing it with a snap.

'I find films boring,' she adds.

'You do?'

'I find them shallow.'

'Shallow.'

'Superficial.'

Why hadn't I told her that?

'Slight.'

Maybe I should have said 'psychology'. Advisory work with the CIA. From Martha's preoccupation with murder I might have chosen anything: precocity, I could have told her (not far from the mark) sets me apart.

'I'm at that stage,' I tell her, 'I could move in almost any direction.'

'Life's pretty useless, don't you think?' she says.

'Sure.'

'Yet you intend to do something with it.'

'I could, on the other hand, just bum around.'

No wonder Gerry's favourite epithet: arsehole, asshole: having pre-empted my occupation, I find it impossible to retreat.

'Everything,' she says, 'is so arranged.'

'Prescribed.'

'I'm very much drawn,' she says, 'to the philosophy of despair.'

Even that's been canonized.

'It seems closest to *reality*,' she adds.

That stress, again, on the final word, its truculent, trailing, interrogative flavour.

'Me, too. I think,' I tell her, 'of little else.'

'How can you think of nothing?' she says. 'Nothing, by definition, is not thinking at all.'

'Sure.'

'I do not think, therefore I am not.'

'That's a thought,' I tell her.

'So it is.'

'All you do,' I suggest, 'is sensate.'

'Precisely.'

Her eyes, more evenly, examine mine. The tea, I'm aware, has been left untouched. I am conscious of her hand upon the table: it toys with a napkin, then sets it down.

'Which is why I agreed to sit at this table.'

'Consciousness, your consciousness,' I tell her, 'informs me now.'

'It's sensation alone,' she says, 'that is speaking, no objectivity of any sort involved.'

Her look, throughout this exchange, has scarcely faltered: mine, I assume, is flickering up and down: her hand, her mouth, her eyes: the untouched tea. Even, occasionally, the view outside. A town has passed. A second.

We are moving through a landscape in which factories have appeared. We have been talking, it feels, for hours: the strangeness of the encounter is paralleled by an even greater strangeness visible outside: yet all this is, I conclude, leading to *familiarity*.

'You realise,' she says, 'I'm pissing you about?'

Her smile – radiant: more than radiant: *ethereal* – has reappeared.

'Probably,' she tells me, 'you're still at school.'

'Right.'

'Sanskrit bullshit.'

'Correct.'

'I'm pissed off, too.'

'Why?'

'You're the expert.'

Trembling in my legs beneath the table.

'Are you,' she goes on, 'as feckless as you seem?'

'I am.'

She extends her hand. 'My *cousin* does not like me talking to strangers. My one inclination is to talk to no one else. I shall have to leave.'

'Maybe,' I tell her,' we'll meet again.'

'I doubt it.'

'You can't be sure.'

'No,' she says. 'You can't be sure. But then, in that case, we shan't be strangers.'

Extending her hand further for me to shake, she rises.

'You American?' she asks.

'I've lived there for a while,' I tell her.

'Quite a while,' she says, 'I think.'

My hand, after a further, firmer clasp, is suddenly released: tossed back, it feels, in my direction.

'It must be pretty boring living here.'

'It is.'

'Boredom is something of a way of life with me. I like,' she tells me, 'pissing you about. Doesn't seem much else to do, otherwise, don't you think?'

'Sure.'

'Everything, wouldn't you say, is posthumous?' she says.

'Right.'

'So where is the life we had before? You realise,' she adds, 'we've ceased to fake?'

'Have we?'

'I think so.'

'Strange pickup,' I tell her, 'on a train.'

'Won't lead anywhere,' she says.

'It might.'

'No chance.'

'We might get off at the same station,' I tell her.

'Like the Audlin I know might be your brother,' she says.

And she's gone, the waiter approaching, we the last two in the carriage.

'Finished, sir?' he says.

'We have,' I tell him.

'You can stay, if you like,' he says, as he begins to clear, I having watched her down the length of the carriage: slim, composed, a mirror image, her persona, to my personum: the door slides to behind her back.

I sit at the cleared table in the deserted carriage and watch the landscape change: a river: collieries: headgears, slagheaps: strands of stagnant water: a feeling of being enclosed by – let's face it – something of an artefact: manmade, unyielding: dour. Bleak.

The waiter, passing through, confirms my destination.

I return to the compartment to retrieve my case: an impression, as I pass along the corridor, of disparate elements outside: brick, stone, metal: people.

Yellow fumes, at one point, rise in the air – then darkness as the train runs beneath the canopy of a station.

2

A woman recognises me as I emerge at the end of the platform: I have an impression of her waving, I glancing round to confirm it's to me – catching sight of my recent companion passing with her partner, she looking in the direction of the woman before disappearing beyond the barrier.

The woman is wearing a green coat with a dark fur collar: the colour of her stockings is light, her shoes conspicuously high-heeled (doesn't want to be found too short), her hair cut in a cowl-like fashion around a tautly-featured face: sharp, inquisitive, birdlike (censorious, opinionated, engagingly engaged).

My other sister!

'Richard!' An exclamation which suggests involuntary involvement, raising her cheek to be laid against mine, a squealing sound – appropriate to her person – accompanying the gesture. 'I'm Clare!' with which, I can see, she's more than delighted. Placing her arm in mine, and adding, 'I have the car outside. James is at work but over the moon at your coming.'

I am looking for my fellow passenger and her companion but they have not reappeared – aware, at the same time, of the pressure of my half-sister-in-law's arm (exuding a sense of confederacy, warmth), the daintiness of her grip, her gloved hand resting in the region of my wrist – and of a feeling I associate unmistakably with rapacity – voraciousness: strength (stoicism): with curiosity, solidity: frustration.

We cross the station forecourt, my attention still on the crowd ahead: no sign of that by now familiar figure. We approach a car of conventional appearance, she having signalled she might take my suitcase (Gerry has suggested two: I have insisted one: 'Only five weeks,' I had told him. 'Five weeks,' he has said, 'can be a long time.'), I resisting her offer (such dainty hands, such – despite the volume and the cut of her coat – a delicate figure), she raising the car boot to announce, 'You have so little luggage! Travelling *light* is a thing with you as well. Does *Gerry*?'

'Not at all,' I tell her, wondering how close they've been.

Opening the passenger door she adds, 'You can drive if you like.'

'I don't have a licence,' I tell her, passing before her, getting inside, examining the crowd through the windscreen.

'Of course!' she slipping in behind the wheel, revealing, as she does so – I am speedily distracted – first one knee, then the other below the fur trim of her coat.

With extraordinary alacrity she starts the vehicle and steers it down a cobbled ramp into what looks like a city square.

'You're so much *older* than I'd imagined,' I wearing an overcoat, one of Gerry's, too large for me (and long ago discarded), which, to a degree, bulks out my figure. 'Though I recognised you, Richard, well enough. That Audlin look is not easily mistaken.'

The carefully made-up face, the mouth: a sense of self-possession: the thin lines bracketing the lips suggesting, above all, a disposition to humour: the delicacy of the ears, visible beneath the cowl of tinted, auburn hair: the profile as she gazes forward full of animation: the sudden, if almost absent-minded gesture with which, after negotiating a set of traffic lights, her hand releases the wheel and tugs down her skirt, the stockinged sheen conspicuous in the shadow: I am forgetting the girl on the train.

The fact of the matter is my sister-in-law is something of a flirt: her instinctive regard for her body in relationship to the one she is with.

In, I estimate, her late forties (in reality, her middle fifties), sensually preserved – self-acclamation, self-appreciation written, I suspect, all over her: I admire her gloves – leather, the seams raised, dyed a diaphanous green – anticipating the receptivity of the hand inside, the way – the provocative way – she grips the wheel: as potent a foil to Mrs Dover as any I might have imagined: I shall, I decide, stay here for ever.

We drive through slow-moving traffic, stopping, starting: the movements of her hands on the wheel (the car is automatic): the movements of her high-heeled shoe on and off the pedal (the other immobile at its side): the raising and lowering of her knee alternately exposed and concealed beneath the fur of her coat: how wonderful! (how wonderful. Do I have the same effect on her?).

In concert with all this, her scent: invigorating and at the same time soporific: I wonder what my brother – my, as yet, un-reacquainted-with half-brother – makes of this: is he aware of the wife he has let loose on the streets? Does he appreciate what a *woman* he's got? Someone, I reflect (glancing across), not unlike a child – conscious, however, of her mystique, performer and audience, it seems, in one.

She is, meanwhile, pointing, things out: a church (a cathedral), a town hall, a county hall, a court of law, an art gallery ('we might go there') – she is, she tells me, driving 'the long way round' – a theatre ('we must *definitely* go there. I so *love* the theatre, don't you?').

'Not much,' (dragged there too frequently by Gerry to see a 'star' or even, God help us, a 'character actor').

'In that case, Richard, I must teach you,' she says (she has, I'm convinced, a tutorial nature). 'I'm a *friend* of the theatre, and enjoy it so much. Also of the art gallery, though I go less frequently there. Are you interested in art?'

'Not much.'

The truculence ('honesty') prompts her to turn her head: she smiles: a galvanising expression: my heart leaps up: I'd love the theatre and visit any number of exhibitions if that smile – and, God help me, that *laugh* – came with us.

'You mustn't think of us as country cousins. We do have a *life* up here,' she says.

'I'm sure.'

'What *do* you like, Richard?'

'Like?'

'By way of *living*.'

'Being on my own.'

'Not much fun!' She glances across again.

'The stage I'm going through,' I tell her.

'We can soon put a stop to that!'

The galvanic smile and laugh again – deep, antagonistic, challenging.

We cross a bridge: a surge of dark brown water, fringed by yellow foam: barges moored on one side: a row of buildings, several stories high, dominates the other: mills, warehouses: smoke hangs in the air. The perfume evident in the car is countered by a sombre smell, reality, of a sort, intruding.

'Not a great deal to admire. *At first glance*. Once you get to *know* the place, however, there's a great deal to be said for it. Particularly the people. They are very warm. Unlike so many in London. You, of course, excepted!'

She knows I know she knows I'm aware she knows how to turn me on: the lapdog expression I assume I must be giving her, anxiety appeased.

'I've been so looking forward to you coming.'

'Why?'

'We were so lacking in contact before. James is so keen to make up with Gerry.'

'So is Gerry with James,' I tell her.

A startled glance: not so much reassurance as surprise – prompting (almost) the enquiry, 'What is Gerry up to?'

Gerry never has a motive which, at first sight, is apparent: a thin-ice skater is always focused up ahead: the potential of the ice to take his weight, the speed required to get across: the cracks, the sound of, drive him on – those and the perverse ambition to skate on thinness, oblivion destined to overtake him.

No wonder he has sent me onto 'safe ice': he must be having qualms (what about, I can't be sure: 'what am I tossing this kid into?'), measuring all this, too, with Martha's eyes: the blank, unyielding, incomprehending stare ('nothing there for him, either, poor mutt. Maybe Jimmy will do the trick' – if not, more nearly, his wife).

'Not a great deal to admire.' She indicates the view of what, presumably, are the outskirts of the town: semi-detached houses, gardens, a factory, a garage, fields: I like the inconsequentiality, however: the sight of all this does me good: nothing here – its one virtue – *counts*: a common – a stretch of heathland – the road opening out on either side, the glimpse of cooling towers in the distance (a ship, its funnels sinking below the skyline), the road, moments later, lined by hedges, winding uphill, surmounting a crest, the view – *a* view – of hills, wooded, low down.

At the foot of a steeper hill, surmounted by a clump of pines, stands a stone house of recent construction, the earth surrounding it – the rudiments of a garden – bare.

'We've been here only three months,' she says. 'James's idea. Though it's too far out of town for me. However, several of our friends are keen and are thinking of moving out as well.' She waves her arm at the hill, the car circuiting an asphalt area at the front of the house and drawing up at a pillared porch.

The door is approached by shallow steps.

'More modest than the one you're used to,' she adds.

'Not at all,' I tell her. 'Ours is semi-detached.'

'Several times the price of this one.'

'I've really,' I tell her, 'no idea.'

The car stops. She is getting out: a glimpse of the inside of her leg, then, in a cloud of scent, she's gone, the boot released from inside the vehicle. A moment later she is tugging out the case, I rushing round to take it from her. I'm aware of the slightness of her figure at the same moment as I am of her remarkable strength – or, if not strength, tenacity – grasping her arm and then, involuntarily, her waist as I wrest it from her.

'No, really,' I'm telling her, at which she laughs.

'I can see you're as *determined* as Gerry,' she says, leading the way to the door, opening it, calling, 'We're back!' no response, however, coming from the hallway or from the rooms on either side, or from the staircase mounting overhead. The barking of a dog comes from the rear of the house – not, I have to confess, a sound I welcome. 'It looks as though Mrs Jenkins has slipped out. She may have gone to the village. She *was* preparing supper. And getting your room ready. Though I'd already seen to that.'

She has gone through to what, evidently, is the kitchen at the rear and, scarcely commensurate with the sound it is making, an animal little larger than a cat comes out. Its friendly intentions and scuffling on the polished wooden floor are evidenced, I presume, by the agitation of its tail. 'This is Snuffy. He's not ours. We're looking after him for one or two days,' stooping, stroking the diminutive head, the front of her coat, having been unbuttoned, opening. A suit of jacket and skirt is revealed inside, a blouse visible within the collar of the jacket. 'We can go in there,' the dog, living up to its name, slavering and snuffling over my shoes, the door she's indicated opening into a room of a not inconsiderable size: heavily, if not lavishly furnished, its windowed interior is further illuminated by a large coal fire: a settee of considerable proportions stands directly before it, armchairs, of similar proportions, on either side. A corresponding room across the hall is furnished, I see, through its partly opened door, with a dining-table of similarly ambitious proportions: 'entertaining' is the word that springs to mind, I experience a first hint of disappointment.

My suitcase, for some reason, is still in my hand (a suggestion, I assume, I am about to go, though what I might have been anticipating

I've no idea: something older, more decrepit, more abandoned, even: less explicit, less defined). The place smells of novelty, the atmosphere that of a scarcely-lived-in hotel: only the dog lends a touch – a tenuous touch (apart from her) – of animation. Clare, the remarkable woman who appears to shrink – at least, to diminish against the excesses of the furniture and the pristine walls and ceiling. Through two windows the car and driveway are visible and, through a window in the adjacent wall, which is also occupied by the fireplace, the as-yet-to-be completed garden: partially outlined paths and rudimentary flowerbeds, schematically set out with plants: a lawn has only recently been laid out, the divisions between the sods still visible. 'We've been trying to hurry it along since we knew you were coming. Why not come up and look at your room?'

She alone, I reflect, is the saving grace, following her to the stairs, ignoring the dog. Her coat abandoned in the hall, I scrutinise her waist, her hips, her calves: where the stairs divide in opposite directions she glances back and, recognising my response, extends her hand: I immediately feel the warmth of her fingers. 'It must make you nervous, but there's no need to be,' she says.

A room looks out to the back of the house: a bed – a double bed – a desk, a chair, an easy chair, a television set, a radio and a record player: more equipment than in my room at home. The interior, like the rest of the house, smells of paint.

Through the window a view of the pine-crowned hill overlooking the house: a herd of cattle, in single file, has been released and threads its way across it.

A door opens into a bathroom. I set the suitcase down.

I can't, for that instant, recall the reason I've come, and look to her for an answer.

This she must have recognised: there she is, a house designed to go mad in, and she as lively as a bird: a pretty, persuasive, pertinacious presence, smiling at my unease.

'You are, I hope, going to like it, Richard?'

Much effort has been deployed, she standing beside me, still holding my hand.

'Dinner – supper – whatever you call it, has already been prepared.' She indicates the room as something I might, with a little encouragement, soon get used to. 'James will be home and we'll have it together. We thought an evening in, for your first. In the meantime, is there anything I can get you? Why don't we have some tea?'

I am reluctant to release her hand, she, I suspect, reluctant to release mine also.

'I had some on the train.'

'I can show you round the rest of the house,' she adds.

'I'd prefer to stay up here.'

'There's so *much* I'd like to ask you.'

Still we stand, fingers intertwined.

'Such as?'

'Your interests. What you'd like to do. What *we* should do to facilitate your studies. We don't want you to fall behind. All manner of things! Just to get to know you! Are you interested, for instance, in following Gerry into films?'

'No.'

The promptness of my response closes the subject down.

'Gerry tells us,' she says, 'you often write.'

'Write?'

'You're always making notes.' She laughs, a trilling declamatory sound, faintly instructive, starting briskly and ending abruptly. 'Perhaps you will with us.'

The strangeness of our standing there, absorbing one another: I scarcely know her, yet fusion, of a peculiar nature, is underway.

'Why don't we go downstairs and sit? *I*,' she tells me, 'would like some tea.'

Releasing our hands we descend to the kitchen: from there – fully if not ideally equipped and looking out to a terrace at the back of the house (and that strangely-crested hill) – we return to the room at the front.

Only once in the kitchen, as if to renew contact, has she drawn me to her – to indicate a 'gazebo' being built where the pasture on the hill comes down to the garden, the division marked by a recently planted hedge.

Now we sit apart, she on the settee, a coffee table before her, on which she has arranged her tea (a cup for me, should I change my mind, I having carried the tray in for her), I in one of the easy chairs at an angle to her.

There is something dispossessed, I conclude, in my nature, subliminal in London, more explicit here. There is only one way of our being together: she is describing her and my half-brother's life in the town, and all I am conscious of is the way her skirt rides over her knee, of the suspension of one leg across the other, of the delicacy of the foot, the high-heeled shoe, loosely attached, dangling in the air (an invitation, almost, to remove it).

I watch her lips, her hands, her eyes, her hair, oblivious of all but the *tone* of what she says: meetings are analysed, people described, projects taken up, explained, dismissed: I am enclosed by intrigue, plotting, defamation.

Conviviality, humour, charm – and something little short of triviality.

My remoteness is a challenge.

'Are you all right?' she finally asks.

She pats the settee beneath one hand, replacing her tea on the table.

'You're such a long way away over there,' she adds.

With the same casualness as, at the station, she took my arm, she takes my hand as I sit.

'I want you to feel at home,' she concludes, enclosing my hand in both of hers.

I am enclosed, too, by that cloud of scent, absorbed by the lines at the corners of her mouth, by the way she simultaneously smiles and frowns: the endless digressions from a narrative which takes her back, continually, to, 'Where was I? Oh, *yes*! This will fascinate you, coming from *London*,' resuming a previously abandoned account.

I also observe, close to, the line of her thigh: the way her skirt moves as she talks, her leg swinging freely, indispensable, so it seems, to her speech.

Examine, too, her fingers, clenched around mine: the petal-shaped nails, lacquered, and each, curiously, with a character of its own: the thumb (curled back), the forefinger, which, to stress a point, occasionally stiffens – and examine where our fingers actually touch: the colour, the lightness, the warmth against mine.

'I feel we've been here hours,' she suddenly exclaims, glancing at a watch. 'I shall have to switch on dinner. Normally I'd have asked Mrs Jenkins to stay, but I thought, on your first evening, we might be alone. James will be back almost any time now. The odd thing is,' she adds, examining my hand held in hers, 'I feel we've known each other for *ages*. I feel so at *home*, my dear, with you!' reaching across to kiss my cheek, I, as she withdraws, kissing hers.

Moments later she is taking the tray, refusing my offer to help, and is saying, 'I'm going to change. Maybe you should take a shower. I'm sure you must be sticky after the train,' calling from the hall, 'All I can say is I'm so *glad* you're here.'

I remain in my room, unpacking, after I've had a shower, conscious, all the while, of her movements in the house – first in a room along the landing, then on the stairs, then at a phone in the hall (the echo of her voice), then, finally, of her activities in the kitchen.

The landscape, meanwhile, has darkened outside: a car comes up the drive: moments later I hear the front door slam, the dog barking, then a male voice calls, 'I'm back!'

An answering response from the rear of the house.

After a conversation, first in the kitchen, then in the hall, footsteps sound from the stairs, I turning to face the door.

My half-brother is my half-brother's brother: stockier, darker, less caesarian (the profile – Gerry's – of a hawk), this an (imagined)

Neroic presence, portly, almost, fuller-faced, the features – and figure – of someone, dark-suited, quietly, soberly, going to seed (scarcely a fit companion for the woman below): nevertheless, to some degree, a *brother*: the shadows beneath the eyes, the balding crown of the head, the pouching around the mouth, the rotundity of the belly: a conventional, if not self-consciously conventional man, tailored to needs not necessarily – perhaps even antipathetic to – his own. Yet three and a half years in a German prison camp (if I've got it right), emerging estranged, transformed, eerily subdued, returning to a life that had gone on adequately without him: eyes, undeniably, like Gerry's (presumably mine, too: how *sharply* had Clare glanced at me: the same, undoubtedly, but different): the same thickness of the lashes, the eyebrows, unlike Gerry's, greying, his hair cropped short and almost white: a sombre, vulgarised, stouter version of his brother, the expression that of someone emerging from a cave: secrets, incommunicable, characterise his look: someone I am *half* close to: something between us not quite there.

He shakes my hand, staring, demandingly, into my eyes: an immediate, urgent, unguarded look: '*Do I know?*' I feel him enquire, though what the knowledge is I've no idea.

Things, I have heard earlier, have been carried across the hall, presumably to the dining room.

'It's so good to meet you, Richard,' he says, 'after all this time. You were only so high the last time I saw you,' releasing my hand to indicate a minimal height from the floor. 'I'd have recognised you, however, just the same. You have something of the family's, certainly *Gerry*'s look,' this final observation bringing a flush to his cheeks. 'How *is* Martha, by the way?' an enquiry, curiously, not made by his wife (too preoccupied, conceivably, describing her own affairs).

'The same,' I tell him, unsure how much he knows. 'I don't think she'll much improve.'

'Always live in hope,' he says, grasping my hand more firmly before releasing it. 'Sorry I wasn't at the station. Got everything you want?' Glancing round, the sound – an amazing sound – of what I assume to be his wife singing (melodiously, lightly, fluently) in the house below.

'Everything,' I tell him, and gesture at the room. 'It's good.'

'Anything else, you'll let us know. You're free to come and go as you choose. I'm sure Clare must have told you,' adding, 'I'll just wash up and meet you downstairs.'

And is gone.

She examines my gaze as I return to the hall, she passing through once more from the kitchen: she is wearing a dress, cut modestly at the neck and buttoned down the front: her shoes, flat-heeled, make less of a feature of her legs. Her face, presumably freshly made up, is that of a child. 'Go all right?' she asks, gesturing upstairs.

'Fine.'

'He's so pleased you're here. I do hope nothing will spoil it. After all, he is your brother.'

Her eyes cloud briefly with concern.

'Half.'

'But that's a lot!'

I am seated in the sitting room when James (as she persists in calling him) returns, playing with the dog which, evidently, is to be removed tomorrow. He wears a cardigan, slacks and slippers, and evidently, too, has had a shower: he gleams – beams – to some degree a different (pleasanter, more likeable) man, casual, unforced: he strokes the dog, its yapping scarcely a distraction. Maybe this was the original version which went to war – the informal officer (not suited to the job) before the inopportune surrender, something *active*, nevertheless, forceful, even, going on beneath the surface, yet scarcely showing at all.

He pours a drink, insists on pouring me one ('You'll like this: only sherry. First evening, and that'), handing me the glass as his wife, my half-sister-in-law, comes in.

She is – 'James' is startled – radiant: she glows – her voice, her face, her manner – sitting in the chair opposite me, 'James' taking his place, after handing her a glass, on the settee. 'Here's to your visit.' He raises his own glass: we drink. Her eyes meet mine across the width of the hearthrug.

This, I reflect, is provincial life.

'Gerry,' James enquires, 'is busy in New York? Is he often away from home?' he adds.

'He's making an effort,' I tell him, 'to be at home as often as he can. This trip, he says, is unavoidable. Financing the films he makes is difficult from London. He suggested, on this occasion, I went with him.'

'Weren't you inclined?' a measure of relief in Clare's enquiry.

'Living in hotels I've done before. I prefer to be . . .' I'm about to add, 'at home', but continue, 'here,' smiling: the lightness of my voice, the amicability of my expression: somehow the sound of her singing has settled everything. 'Otherwise he's anxious to sustain at least the semblance of a home.'

'Gerry has had his difficulties,' James declares, reconciliation, of a sort, evident in his voice. 'With Martha, too, of course. And Ian.'

'Ian,' Clare involuntarily responds.

'And Ian,' James confirms. He waits to see what effect this might have had, if not on me, on her. 'Do, by the way,' he says, 'call me James. Or Jimmy, if you like. Gerry does. That was my name at home. Though Clare doesn't like it.'

'Jimmy is such a diminutive,' she says. 'And James is such a lovely name,' she adds. '*Do* call me Clare,' she concludes, with a laugh.

Bonded to her in such an immediate (and unexpected) way, I take care to moderate my look, glancing at James and announcing, 'James – and Clare – sound fine to me.'

'I know he's anxious to do his best for you,' James says. 'We all have our difficulties, but his have been particularly onerous, as you must be aware. Martha must be a great burden. A wife is of great importance to a man.'

'So is a husband to a wife,' Clare says.

'So he is,' James says, and smiles.

Small, even teeth, which may not be his own.

Another wartime loss.

'I'm sure Richard doesn't wish to be burdened, too,' Clare says. 'Particularly on his first evening.'

'I don't mind at all,' I tell her, before James can interrupt – as genially disposed to her, in this instance, as discretion will allow. 'He often talks of his problems but I don't think I'm much reassurance.'

'Really? Not even *brotherliness*?' Clare replies, something other than enquiry in her voice. The dog has nestled in the chair beside her: her neatly-tapered, manicured hand caresses its head. 'Friendship,' she adds, 'of the most intimate kind. I'm sure you must offer him something.'

'It's not really "friend's talk",' I tell her. 'Gerry's keen to keep Martha away from gossip, local or otherwise, and what he would value most would be talking to another man.'

'There's always this friend Gavin we hear so much about,' she says.

'He's more a working relationship,' I tell her.

The bearded creep: I classify the diminutive, balding, dark-eyed, opportunistic Gavin in the same category as Eric: 'Eric without the uniform,' I tell Gerry who, unperturbed, invariably rejoins, 'Gavin is the best, most trustworthy colleague I've ever had.'

The shit.

'The poor, wretched woman,' James has said. 'I know what it's like to be out of your mind. I've seen men consumed in that way on several occasions. Possessed or dispossessed, it's hard to tell.'

The observation, made almost privately – provocatively – is left hanging in the air.

'Though it could be a relief,' he suddenly goes on, 'to discuss these things with members of the family. I gather Gerry has told you something of our past.'

'A little,' I tell him, and wonder – no doubt as he and Clare do – how much.

'I needn't go into it this evening, but estrangement between the two of us is not something I've sought,' James says. 'It's been forced on us, I guess, by circumstance. Gerry always was a high-flier and took a more frivolous view of the family. Particularly of our father who, in my opinion, was a self-destructive, obtuse old man. He ruined his company, when he might well have saved it. Why, I know several of his former employees even now . . .'

He stares at me for several seconds.

A telephone rings in the hall and Clare gets up, sets down her glass, glances pointedly at me, and passes in a cloud of scent.

'It's Mrs Jenkins,' she calls, 'checking on dinner,' returning to the room to add, 'It'll be ready in one or two minutes. Though I can always keep it hot if you want to talk.'

Anxiety in both of them, I conclude: no doubt, before my arrival, they have discussed at length the significance of my visit. Much they might wish to enquire about, curiosity aroused by the unusual circumstances surrounding my presence.

'I thought it might be Gerry,' she goes on. 'He said he'd call from New York.'

'He's had hardly time to get there,' James says.

'It takes,' she says, 'as long as that?'

'When did he leave?' he asks, and adds, 'On top of which he has people to see.' To me, he enquires, 'The two of you get on well, I take it?'

Less enquiry than declaration.

'Fairly,' I tell him.

'A big gap in age.'

He waits for me to concede.

'More like a father, wouldn't you say?'

'Not after the description of *our* father,' I tell him, at which he laughs, suddenly, immensely, uncontainably pleased: he gazes at me for a while in silence, beaming: his eyes are almost wickedly alight.

'It's interesting to examine the past,' he says. 'At a certain age it's inevitable. I'm two years older than Gerry and have had a head start, though not in respect of what he may have told you.'

'Mainly about our father and my mother,' I tell him.

'Would you like,' he says, 'another drink?'

He is on his feet, taking Clare's glass, then mine, and crosses to the cabinet behind the door.

'Did you know my mother?' I ask.

'Scarcely at all. I was estranged from the family at the time. It was something in which I didn't encourage Clare to take an interest.'

Smiling at me, she raises her glass.

'Better times, Richard,' she says, and drinks.

'To better times,' I tell her.

A short while later we go into dinner. I talk, by request, about Dover's (Mrs Dover, Mr Dover RIP), my friends: in no time at all we are back with the past – in this instance, the recent past: James' job – which he unenthusiastically sketches in ('of no interest, but it keeps me off the street. Keeps *us* off the street,' laughing, glancing at Clare).

She and I sit opposite one another, either side of the table (sufficient to accommodate a dozen), James at the end between us.

I watch her eyes, her mouth, her neatness – the *precision* of her lips: her minimal appetite. I watch particularly that part of her with which I have recently come into contact, her hands: neat, delicate, also precise, marvelling that they and I have been absorbed so swiftly into the normality of the house.

'I have a secret, too,' James says, the meal coming to an end, I unsure what the previous secret might have been. 'I've taken up writing in middle age. Gerry may have told you. I was always reluctant to tell him. I wanted the Audlin name to establish itself without, or, rather, *before* his intervention. If it all works out I can sell him one of my books.'

He examines me keenly, something of the expression of a younger man.

'What sort of books?' I enquire.

'Detective novels!'

In reaching for my glass I knock it over: the stain spreads slowly across the cloth.

'I'll clean it!' Clare is already on her feet: a napkin is dabbed at the liquid. 'Really,' she says, 'it's of no account. We're always spilling something.'

'I've startled you,' James says, and laughs, regarding the red stain, however, in a melancholic fashion.

As if there aren't enough corpses and culprits in the family already.

'Martha,' I tell him, once the problem on the table has been resolved, 'is fond of detective novels. Or was. She doesn't read them now but assumes she's living one. Sometimes,' I add, 'as a victim-to-be, other times as someone looking for clues. Bodies and searches are her principal preoccupation. At least,' I pause, glancing at Clare, uncertain how far I might go. Almost involuntarily, it would seem, if we were sitting closer, she might have stretched out her hand to mine. 'She's endeavouring to solve a mystery the enormity of which she can't divulge and the elucidation of which absorbs her, seemingly, every second.'

'Mystery?' James says. 'What mystery?'

'The philosophical mystery which no one feels is relevant any more,' I tell him. '"What can I know? What might I hope for? What might I do?" More relevant to me is what *do* I know. What *does* it mean? Does meaning *have* worth? Does language *make* sense?'

They are gazing at me with mutual apprehension: the telephone rings. Clare, after dismissing it with a wave of her hand, rises with, 'It might be Gerry,' and is gone. Moments later her voice announces,

'We're having dinner. I'll ring later,' and is back in the room, explaining, 'A friend,' and then to me, '*Not* Gerry.'

'My own mysteries,' James says, 'are more modest, if not mundane. Who killed whom, and when.' He glances at Clare. 'More to do with provincial life of a distinctly, if not oppressively, urban nature. No vicarage or village green. Murder in the manager's office. The effect of *work* on the human mind. Who wouldn't care *not* to kill their boss?'

He laughs once again, in the same melancholic fashion: maybe he's aware of how dull this venture sounds, the perversity in persisting in writing 'mysteries' part of the purpose in writing them at all.

'Have they been published?'

'Not yet.'

'Will they be?'

'I've written seven. Apart from rejection slips, I've received two letters from publishers expressing an initial interest and suggesting – at least, one of them – I expand the range of my subject. However, apart from writing about the war, about which no one, any longer, has any interest, I don't have very much choice. *Clare* enjoys them.'

She smiles: *don't*, her look suggests, discourage him.

'I don't know why they haven't been published,' she tells me. 'They're as good as any other. Just because it's an insurance office. That's where murders, you'd think, *ought* to take place.'

Passion, of a sort, is suggested, displaced or organic, hard to tell.

'I'd like to read one,' I tell him.

'They're nothing.' James dismisses them with a wave of his hand. 'These things are invariably for older people. Youngsters, nowadays, scarcely read at all.' He pauses before concluding, 'I'll let you look at one.'

'He writes them in office hours,' Clare says. 'So in a way he's paid to write them.'

She laughs, lightly, engagingly: the same trilling, interrogative sound I associate with the other, younger, Martha: how swiftly *she*, I reflect, has been forgotten.

'Oh, they know me.' James is smiling: an ingenuous expression which evokes something, I assume, of the intimacy of their relationship. 'When I *retire*, which I hope will be before long, I'll be able to write them all the time. Apply myself in a way I haven't been able to do before.'

The only purpose to, the only justification of, my being here, I conclude, is his wife: what she holds out to me. The warmth and directness she represents reverberate through my mind (oscillate with the force of her physical presence). What happened earlier, however, before James' arrival, may very well not occur again.

'As it is,' my half-brother gestures at the room, our meal at an end – served, in its various stages, by Clare, despite my offers to help – 'most of our *recent* time has been taken up with this. I thought to move into a new house before I retired. If the worst comes to the worst, after retirement, we can sell it off. By then its value will have increased. This,' he gestures at the room again, 'has absorbed us for the past four years. Finding the site. The architect. Getting permission. It's two years since I completed a piece of fiction. Though I'm glad to say I've started something new. Writing prompts you, after all, to the thought of another life. Certainly, in my case, *different* to the one I have at present.'

Still Clare watches us, gauging my reaction, a suggestion in her look of 'don't disillusion the man', I recalling the sensation of my hand between hers, a receptivity implied that needn't stop there: 'complicity', her look declares.

We return to the sitting room, each of us tired – if not exhausted – by the events of the day. Further conversation about the house, the history of its building, the current search for a landscape gardener, the previous one having died.

'That was a shock. No mystery there. Heart.'

Grief animates Clare's face, my one impulse to go to her.

'Mortality.' My half-brother is in a reflective phase. 'It's at this stage, Richard, one takes it into account. Looking back, on the one hand, then looking ahead to measure the distance. The house, to that extent, is a relevant statement. I could walk out of it tomorrow and not come back, for all of its *significance*. Since there's nowhere of greater significance to walk *to*, the only relevance I'm aware of, since we built the place, is to stay.'

He glances at Clare for confirmation: the first dispassionate look I've seen him give her.

'What do you say?' he asks her.

'I'm content with it.' She doesn't return his look. 'Particularly since we went to so much trouble. To me it's neither good nor bad. I *preferred* where we were before. Draughty. And a fortune to heat. And more rooms than we knew what to do with,' glancing at me. 'An old mill-owner's house on the edge of town. Stone and, in the basement, very damp.'

'It *was* cold,' James concedes. 'It did have character, however.'

'Which is what I'm saying.'

Her look, finally, engages his.

'I'm agreeing,' he says, a sudden intimacy between them.

Shortly after that it's decided it's time to go to bed, Clare, prompted by James ('Has Richard got everything he wants?'), accompanying me to my room, standing at the door and announcing, 'If there *is* anything you'll let us know.'

'Maybe,' I tell her, 'I should kiss you goodnight.'

Not a suggestion she responds to: nevertheless, crossing the floor I kiss her cheek. 'Thank you for making me so welcome,' I tell her.

'Goodnight,' she says, smiling, and goes, her door – I assume it is *their* door – closing along the landing.

Her perfume, the slightness of her figure, her radiant look: it's as if she's still in the room.

For an hour, or longer, I lie back on the bed, falling asleep finally only to be woken almost immediately by Clare, in a nightgown, tugging at my arm.

Light streams in from the landing.

'It's Gerry.'

'Where?'

'On the *phone*.'

In the hall, looking back up the stairs, I see her standing, blurred, in her nightgown, gazing down: I can't identify the meaning of her expression: inconvenience, irritation, doubt – or excitation.

'Are you okay?' he asks me in my ear.

'Do you know what time it is?'

'Clare says you've settled in.'

James, no doubt, is awake as well, if not disturbed by the light in the hall.

'They're a remarkable couple,' he adds.

'Are they?'

'Don't you agree?' He's drunk, or close to it. 'I've misread them in the past. Not appreciated them for what they are. Did I tell you they had a miscarriage years ago? It brought them together with a shared sense of loss. The opposite of what happened to me when Ian died.'

'How's work?'

'Work?'

'Business.'

'Fine.' He waits: expensive, too, this distance. 'Just as well you didn't come. All they do over here is talk. The one word for it.'

'Bullshit.'

'Right.'

'And drink.'

'Some drinking! Too much at stake on this occasion, Rick.'

There are sounds of voices at the other end. 'I ought to go. I wanted to know our kid was okay.'

'Which one?'

'Both of you, God dammit. All three. Apologies for not ringing sooner. I'll call again in a couple of days. Be *friendly*.'

'Friendly?'

'With Jimmy.'

'Sure.'

'And Clare.'

'And Clare.'

'And me.'

'And you.'

'*I* want to be friendly. *They* want to be friendly. None of this fucking highbrow stuff with you. They're simple, ordinary, straightforward people.'

'Who?'

'For fuck's sake, Richard!'

He waits again.

'They *are* straightforward people. They live in the fucking provinces.'

'Sure.'

'This could be a much needed healing of the past.' He covers the phone the other end, he and the voices abruptly cut off: the sound of mid-Atlantic waves is followed by, 'Maybe I should go. Good to hear your news, and lots and lots of love.'

'Sure.'

'I mean it, Rick.'

He sounds further away than ever.

'Right.'

'Give my love to Jimmy.'

'It's James.'

'James?'

'It's James over here, not Jimmy.'

'Give my love to *James*.'

'Right.'

'And to Clare. She *is* still called Clare, I take it?'

'Sure.'

'Don't want to sound too fucking informal.'

'No.'

'And lots of love, of course, to you.'

'You've said that once.'

'Lots of love to you, *asshole*!'

'And to you.'

'Remember how much I love you.'

'I believe you do.'

He waits again: I wouldn't be surprised if he isn't crying: not him so much as the Whiskey Sour.

'This is a big thing for me. You and Jimmy.'

'Me and James.'

'You and James. And Clare.'

'Right.'

'See you, Richard,' he says, and goes.

I allow the purr to remain in my ear, evoking an image of Gerry at the other end: what time in New York? Maybe early evening. A bar. Someone's apartment. Maybe someone's bed, he knows more people there than he does in London.

I'm aware of the dog around my feet and when I reach the landing Clare is waiting by my door.

'Everything all right?'

'Fine.'

She picks up the dog and says, 'He apologised for ringing late. It was the first opportunity he said he'd had. It was good of him to call.'

'It was.'

'He really cares about you, Richard.'

'I know.'

'*Really*.'

The dog snuffles at her face: it – her face – is pale in the light from the landing: she is, I realise, wearing no make-up: an older face, marked by lines which give it gravity, bleakness – a softness, however, in the eyes, a look of appeal, if not entreaty.

'I know he does,' I tell her. 'I'm sorry it disturbed you. He could have rung in the morning.'

'He wanted to be sure. Times between there and here are always confusing.'

A hint of something not exclusive: delaying her departure she has put the dog down and stepped inside the door.

I kiss her cheek.

A moment later she has drawn away.

'Snuffy!' she calls from the darkness of the landing, the dog scampering off along the bare wood floor.

The scratching of its nails: I hear a bark.

She has a *strategy*, I am thinking. Something she has planned. Not childlike, childish, or child-anything: that is *me*, at this end, I conclude.

3

The following day my half-brother has left for work by the time I get up. Clare is busy with someone downstairs: two places for breakfast have been set on the dining room table. Moments later she appears – wearing a suit: trousers, jacket, low-heeled shoes (practicality, it appears, her theme). She has, she informs me, taken Snuffy back to his owner.

Perhaps I am here to replace the dog, a more articulate distraction: I've grown half-inclined to its presence by now.

'I've been out walking,' she further informs me. 'I often walk early. James is frequently at work by seven.'

'Seven?'

Earlier than Gerry when he's not shooting.

'He likes to get in before the others. He gets more done in that time, he says, than the rest of the day.'

'Particularly when he's writing.'

'Particularly when he's writing!' She laughs, examining me, however, with an enquiring expression. 'I wondered if you'd like to go into town,' she adds. 'After, of course, you've had your breakfast. There's *so* much I can show you. Mrs Jenkins, meanwhile, is in charge round here.'

A woman, at this point, emerges from the kitchen: stout, companionable, middle-aged: she shows little, if any interest in me – a deference with visitors indistinguishable from indifference which I immediately associate with the contempt shown to the same by

Mrs Hodges: she remains at a distance, prohibiting the shaking of hands. Thus does she show, I assume, she knows her place – a mental genuflexion which Clare scarcely appears, if at all, to notice: 'We're clearing up from last night,' she says, as the woman turns away. 'Normally we have breakfast in the kitchen.'

'Let's have it there, in that case,' I tell her.

'Oh, there's much clearing-up to be done today,' she says, and adds, 'I'll bring the tea. Or do you prefer coffee?'

We sit facing one another, James' empty chair between us, its significance, as she talks – resuming her conversation of the day before – receding. 'We can look in at the theatre. I often have coffee there on a morning.'

A vacuum cleaner is audible in the sitting room across the hall. What does Mrs Jenkins – like Mrs Hodges (like Mrs Dover) – *really* think?

Clare gets up and closes the door.

I like her: I like her beyond her increasingly obvious appeal: an animation which, for much of the time, in the past, has been suppressed, certainly confined – if not by marriage, or a house, or even a job (she has, at one time, she tells me, worked for James herself, as well as for 'one or two others') – by a 'consensus' she has found it hard to confront, let alone deny. Maybe I see too much of myself in her: despite the formality of her appearance, and a subtler application of make-up, I'm aware of an effervescence – restless, trustful, yet something less than naive – certainly not, by Gerry's definition, provincial.

My immediate instinct is to offer her help: of what kind, however, I can't be sure: I'm more confused than she is, she further along the road to what might, for both of us, be defined as 'emancipation'.

'Perhaps you'd prefer to potter round here,' she concludes.

'Town,' I tell her, 'is fine.'

We drive in the car: not her car, she insists. 'It's James's. He drives mine, which is smaller and easier to park. A peculiar arrangement.

We often go on holidays, or have done, by car. Then, of course, we always take his. Always this country. He hates abroad.'

She has changed, in the interval, into a dress and jacket, the hem of the former, unlike her skirt of the previous day, halfway down her calves. Something in her manner – her tone of voice, her bearing – restricts the intimacy which had characterised her earlier – *our* earlier – behaviour.

Once clear of the heathland we descend to the buildings familiar from the day before, the town spread out disjointedly across the bed of a valley, a nexus of taller structures at its centre: a tower, a steeple, a dome. Somewhere, amongst it all, presumably, is James: at his desk, in his office, possibly, by this time, writing his 'thriller'.

'Let's try the art gallery! They have such lovely pictures. I'll show you my favourite.'

We walk a great deal (the facilities for parking restricted): she is, I conclude, exorcising, or distracting, a greater intent. At one point she takes my hand (we are crossing a road) and for a while (on the other side) walk with our arms swinging between us, an immediacy in her manner, frivolous, thoughtless, undemanding.

At the gallery we look at a lot of paintings which have no interest for me whatsoever (works by several of the artists once 'owned' – or rented – by Gerry): contemporary art, I tell her, has been suborned by photography.

'What does "suborned" mean?' she enquires.

I disclaim, to her amusement, all knowledge of the word.

I delight, not in the pictures, but in her regard for them. They might easily have been dogs, or cats – or even people: or, at one instance, our reflections in the glass: she, me, the room and the pictures behind: we might easily, I conclude, have been a mother and son. 'Don't you like it?' she enquires of one particular representation – of what, precisely, I'm not at all sure: a phalanx of colours that 'represents' nothing but itself: she is, I realise, one of those people who take 'things' at the level of their intentions.

'Sure.'

'You're a difficult person to please. You realise that?' she says.

We are in a room with one other person: he, attracted by her voice – its charm, its lightness, its alertness – glances across: an elderly figure, he moves unobtrusively closer.

'Not really.'

'Last night, for instance,' she is moving me away, taking my arm, 'I thought you very *good*, but I also thought we bored you.'

'Not at all,' I tell her.

'It must seem,' she pauses, 'very dull up here.'

'Dull?'

'After all that glamour.'

'Glamour?'

'Gerry's *life*.' She shakes my arm with irritation.

'I find it novel. Unexpected. Enlightening, even,' I tell her.

'I suppose that's to do with Gerry, too.'

'Gerry?'

'He brought you up amongst adults. There were never any children about.'

We are leaving the gallery and returning to the street.

I link my arm through hers. 'I like being with you,' I tell her.

'You do?'

'Much.'

I attempt to take her hand, for her to resist.

'I feel so under scrutiny,' she says.

'From me?'

'The way you look.'

'Which is how?'

'As if you're *thinking*.'

'I am.'

'Instead of *being*.'

She has thought about this, I assume, a great deal: not in reference to me but in relation to something more oppressive.

'We're *being* now,' I tell her, re-taking her arm.

'Are we?'

'I like it.'

'I like it, too.'

'No judgement of any sort,' I tell her, 'is involved. Other,' I go on, 'than I like you very much.'

'Perhaps that,' she says, 'we should dampen down.'

She is wearing a plainly-fashioned coat, brown, unlike the one of the previous day, and expressing, like the rest of her clothes, practicality and little else.

'I am dampened down,' I tell her.

'I'm very easily taken in by people,' she says.

'How?'

'I see their good points. James always sees the bad.'

We are walking briskly: there's somewhere else she's decided to go.

'He didn't strike me that way,' I tell her. 'Not least,' I go on, 'in his attitude to me.'

'He's keen – very keen – to make a go of things,' she says. 'I wouldn't wish to spoil it.'

'How could you spoil it? Surely,' I ask her, 'it's all the same thing?'

'Not really.'

I glance across: it's as if, at that moment, she's talking to herself. 'I don't see any point to things. Or, rather, I do, but I can't sustain it. I often see things as the *sum* of what's been taken away. Those paintings I like. But they don't, when it comes down to it, make you happy.'

'What makes you happy?' I ask her.

'I don't like to confess it,' she says, 'but being with you. I felt it the moment I met you at the station. Not *family*. Though that as well. Something else.'

'Maybe that's okay.'

'It doesn't *feel* okay.'

'Why not?'

'I'm old enough to be your mother.'

'Maybe,' I tell her, 'you see me as a son.'

She has, I realise, begun to cry.

'Maybe we shouldn't talk about it,' I suggest. 'I wouldn't wish to disappoint you.'

'Oh, but you don't,' she says. 'It's quite the reverse. I have your identity *confused*,' she adds. 'I haven't felt so *well* for quite some time. James gets so wearied with the way I am.'

'Gerry with me, too,' I tell her.

She has stopped to dry her eyes.

'He worries about you a great deal, I know,' she says. 'He doesn't wish you to go the same way as Martha.'

'Why should I?' I ask.

'No reason at all,' she says, briskly. 'It's just that he finds you very reserved. Not reserved. *Withdrawn*.'

'Has he told you that?'

'It's what he *infers*. "See if you can bring him out," he said.'

We walk for a while in silence: her tears have long since dried.

'Maybe I shouldn't have told you,' she adds.

'It's nothing new,' I tell her.

'Maybe it'll help you to understand.'

'Do you find me withdrawn?' I ask.

'Not at all!' she tells me.

She is examining the shop windows, abstracted, contained.

'Here we are!' she suddenly exclaims, and gestures to the opening to a cobbled yard: having released my arm, she now re-takes it.

At the end of the alley we emerge in the forecourt of a theatre: of Edwardian design, it has recently been refurbished.

We examine the notices outside, then, at her suggestion, enter the foyer. The atmosphere intrigues her: the red, deep-piled, carpeted stairs, the polished hardwood banisters, the shining brasswork, the overhead chandelier: the photographs (several of Gerry's confrères), the posters (names from several of his credits, too): an air of expectancy and – I have to face it – *enjoyment* (how do you get pleasure from all those inflated bums?). She makes enquiries about a performance to which, threading her arm in mine, she draws my attention. She books three seats. 'Once! Just once!' she pleads. 'I'm sure you'll like it. I've seen it twice, in previous productions, and loved it more the second!'

A musical.

'We can always leave at the interval.' She laughs. 'But by then I know you'll be hooked!'

Her despondency of only a short while before has disappeared: mercurial, guileless: strength, I conclude, as well as charm; vulnerability as well as frankness.

What would the poets have made of such an occasion?

Not much.

I'm aware of someone whose moods change, vicariously, from minute to minute – she dancing (almost, from toe to toe) as she walks beside me in the street.

'Let's have coffee! We could have had it at the theatre. They have a marvellous restaurant but I know somewhere just as nice!'

'Coffee' turns out to be an early lunch; early lunch is followed by a walk in a nearby square where she is interested in showing me the houses – Georgian, a Victorian church at its centre. 'I so wanted James to buy a house here, though none was available at the time. Most are converted into flats. I wouldn't wish to live in one of those. What I like about our present home is its *independence*. Created by ourselves. Unique. So like James! Do you like independence?'

Maybe, with James, she means something else: the same withdrawal she anticipated in me.

'Yes,' I tell her.

Conviviality turned, once more, into guilelessness: a charm, a candour, of which, I assume, my half-brother is enamoured, too.

As we return in the car she enquires if there's anything else I'd like to do. 'I don't want to take up *all* your time. Perhaps you'd like to wander on your own?'

'Later,' I tell her.

At intervals we have encountered people she knows: an intensified burst of animation exceeding anything she has previously shown (a corresponding feeling in me that I slow her down), she introducing me with a delight which intrigues whoever we stop or whoever, more frequently, stops her: 'Clare!'

She is an exceedingly popular person (I conclude), as welcome an element in other people's lives as she is, at present, in mine (an 'authenticity' about her difficult to ignore or discount): I am, even at this point, reluctant to leave her.

As we reach the car she announces we'll drive back (once more) 'the long way round', and leave the town by a different route to the one we left by the previous day, or the one by which we entered that morning.

'There's James' office.'

She indicates a building overlooking the river: a renovated warehouse, conceivably, or a mill.

'We could call on him, if you like. I'm sure he wouldn't mind.'

'Won't we interrupt his writing?'

'Not a bit!' She laughs. 'He works far harder than anyone I know. Don't be taken in by his diffidence where work is concerned. He's sometimes not home until after nine. Other times away for several days. Not while you're with us, however. Maybe,' she concludes, 'we'll leave it till later.'

We pass through countryside characterised by wooded hills, occasional villages and, finally, a lake. We draw up in a lane beside it. 'There's a lovely walk from here. Not for today. But I'd love to show you. Do you like the country?'

'Not much.' (Better, I reflect, than, 'No.')

'Why not?'

'I associate it with Martha. When we first arrived she was enamoured of country cottages, villages, rectories. We'd spend hours together searching.'

'For what?'

'Clues. I thought it was a game.' I shrug. 'To keep me amused. *Gerry* thought the countryside would soothe her. She'd already started cracking up before we left, though it was put down at the time to a sense of humour. She was noted for her comedy, you know. Irony, at least. An unusual commodity over there.'

'She had a *wonderful* sense of fun, I know.'

'How do you know?'

'From her films. I scarcely knew her in person. I only met her twice. Each time on passing through London. She was a very *comedic* person. And very emotional. I liked her very much.'

'She became fixated on crime,' I tell her. 'I thought there was a practical reason why she took me on those walks. Dark glasses. Headscarf. Scruffy clothes. I was *embarrassed* at times to be with her. I assumed she was doing it to keep me occupied while Gerry was *working*. Setting up his films. Then I began to suspect there was something going on which was to do with who she was. A personality. I'd had all that in LA, and it had somehow faded over here. For a while no one knew where she was. In Beaconsfield, even, near the studio. Then it got out. People hounding her. Hanging around the house. It all seemed logical, if odd. Which is what life had been with her and Gerry from the start. He was overshadowed by her. Though, of course, I knew he adored her. How he adored her. He went practically nuts when she first cracked up. It was put down to her *eccentricity*. As you say, her sense of fun.'

'He still does admire her, I know,' she says.

She gazes at the surface of the lake, I wondering, at this point, if I might contradict her: her hand, releasing the wheel, encloses mine.

'Poor Richard,' she says.

It's a moment, had I chosen it to be so, when I might have leaned across – and who knows what next might have happened? Maybe she has brought us here with this in mind – at least, to test out (and reject) its probability.

'I don't feel bad about it at all,' I tell her.

'That's good.'

'I feel more concerned for her than Gerry does.'

'I'm sure that isn't true.'

'He's exhausted by it. Not that he doesn't care.'

'He cares a lot. As you say,' her gaze reverts to the lake, 'he's had a long time to endure it. Plus all the intrusion he's had to deal with. That, at least, to a large extent, is behind you. There's the occasional journalist, he tells me. Parasites,' she concludes, 'of course.'

'Most,' I tell her.

'How awful.'

We sit in silence, her hand on mine: the lake, the trees, the hedge enclosing the lane itself.

'Not much more,' I tell her, 'to be done. The doctors' diagnosis is she'll never change. Dementia, at her age, invariably gets worse.'

Her grip tightens, involuntarily, as if she's afflicted by another thought: it's almost, for an instant, as if Martha is beside me.

'We have to bear up under these tragedies,' she says. Glancing across, her expression full of affection, she adds, 'We have to count ourselves fortunate in other ways.'

'I'm not complaining,' I tell her. 'Where Martha's concerned, all I want is the best.'

This isn't precisely what I'd meant to say, nor, I suspect, is it precisely what she'd inferred: in a sense, it would have been better to have been brought up by her and James (I'm reflecting), their relationship with my father and his second wife no doubt prohibiting it.

'Let's go home,' she says. 'We've had a full day.'

Mrs Jenkins has gone by the time we return. The house is silent.

'What would you like to do now?' she says. 'I usually have a rest in the afternoon.'

'I'll have a rest, too,' I tell her, a strange formality in place now we're in the house alone.

'If there's anything you want in the kitchen, use it,' she says, 'as you would your own. Or anything else, for that matter,' she adds.

I go up to my room, stare out at the hill at the back, observe the herd of cows, and lie down on the bed. Not much comes to me by way of reflection: the girl on the train the previous day has been subsumed by everything that's followed: even enquiring about her has slipped from my mind. Mentally I prepare a memo, uncertain what I'll inscribe.

What was my (our) father like, the one person we have in common? Only the conflicting and possibly perjured views of my half-brothers to guide me. His ghost – a metaphysical as well as metaphorical presence – hovers, in a mutilated fashion, above the house: somewhere out there, in the town, is the site of his mill – *one* of his mills – located, evidently, in a tributary valley.

Within moments, however, I'm thinking of her: lying on another bed, only a few feet – a few yards – away.

The telephone rings: I hear her voice coming from what I presume must be her bedroom.

Moments later she is standing in the door.

She is wearing a housecoat: flowered, reaching below her knees. Her feet are bare.

'I wondered,' she says, 'if you were all right?'

I raise myself on one elbow.

She stands with one hand on the handle of the door.

'I really appreciate the time you've given me,' I tell her.

'It's been a great pleasure, Richard,' she says. 'Is there anything more I can get you?'

Perfume drifts in: it envelops the room.

'You've done everything,' I tell her.

'I'll leave you to rest,' she says. 'I, too, enjoyed today so much,' and is gone, closing the door behind her.

I assume, for a while, she has returned to her room.

Resolution, of a peculiar nature, takes place in the form of another memo.

Equally resolutely, I set it aside.

The tension between our two rooms feels like a third, connecting, compulsive, dynamic presence.

I get off the bed and open the door.

I walk along the landing to the front of the house. There are, I've discovered, five bedrooms, a storeroom, and a second bathroom. All the doors, but one, are closed: inside I glimpse what must be the corner of her bed.

She is, when I look in further, sitting on the bed, her back to the door: two windows look out to the front of the house.

She has removed her housecoat and is wearing a slip. Her head is bowed, examining the telephone receiver in her hand.

She slowly replaces it, I remaining in the door.

Seconds extend themselves, it feels, to minutes.

Only then, finally, does she raise her head: she examines the view at the front of the house.

I have gone too far to go back, I decide.

The telephone rings.

She starts, but doesn't answer it, the sound also coming from the hall.

'Come in,' she says, suddenly, 'if you like.'

Reality and prospect uneasily combine.

'Perhaps,' she adds, 'you should get undressed. Do you know much about all this? It's mechanical,' she continues. 'At least, to begin with. I'll show you the procedures, and you can take it from there.'

She has thought about this, I assume, for some time, confirming a decision taken, probably, as we were walking round the town, or while sitting by the lake.

The 'mechanics' she applies in a practical (and, I now realise, a characteristic) fashion, first in explaining her 'function' and then extemporising mine.

'It may end, on your part, prematurely,' she goes on, applying first her hand and finally her mouth.

Her prognosis is correct.

'Which doesn't prevent you, Richard, from doing the same for me.'

The afternoon, what remains of it, passes swiftly. By the time James returns supper – or dinner – is being prepared. He is in an avuncular mood, listening to our activities of the day, excluding the final significant one, with a smile. 'Do you think,' he enquires, 'you'll like it here?'

'I will,' I tell him.

'If there's anything we haven't thought of, you only have to tell us.'

'I will,' I confirm.

'I can't tell you,' he says, 'what it means to have you with us.'

'I appreciate it, too,' I tell him.

'Anything,' he concludes, 'on the telly? I usually flake out this time of the day.'

Indeed, a little later, after supper, we are sitting, the three of us, watching the screen, Clare beside him on the settee, he finally, head dropping, falling asleep.

We exchange glances across his body.

'You go up,' she says, 'if you like. This is what usually happens. If,' she goes on, 'we don't have people in. At some point,' she lowers her voice, 'I wake him.'

And later when, evidently having roused him – several telephone calls taken in the hall below – I hear them come up to their room, the sobriety of his voice, her lighter, effervescent, almost frivolous one.

Moments later, knocking, she puts her head around the door.

'Goodnight, dear,' she says. 'Thank you so much for the day.'

'Thank *you*,' I tell her.

'Oh, we mustn't set too much by it. There's still some time ahead.'

'Thank you, all the same,' I say.

'I think,' she says, leaning further in and lowering her voice, 'there may have been much which you knew already.'

And is gone.

Perhaps I have – not unsurprisingly – misjudged her: not only mercurial but deceptive: even the sobriety might be applied – beneath all I've seen, a different woman entirely: someone methodical, composed – even (the thought occurs to me for the first time) vengeful.

With this confusion I go to sleep.

4

Two weeks pass: so much occurs yet little is retained (memos and/or number obsession abandoned), events succeeding, and precipitating, one another with a speed I rarely appreciate and can scarcely comprehend. Not least of my observations is that my half-brother knows, if not is in collusion with, what goes on – daily and vicariously – in the countryside as well as in various rooms of the house.

James' lack of curiosity dominates (for me) the mood prevailing in the place – a mood with so many subtleties and changes (receiving the sanitised version of our activities each evening with a credulity which beggars belief).

'Does he know?' I ask her (my efforts to satisfy her efforts to delay my equivalent satisfaction improving by the hour).

She draws back from where we are lying: our engagements invariably take place in the afternoon when Mrs Jenkins isn't around, our impatience for her to complete her domestic chores and depart often obliging us to occupy ourselves with visits to the town (one evening, not memorable, with James to the theatre, Clare's enthusiasm for the occasion genuine enough).

'Why should he know?' she asks.

'Surely he's aware?'

'He would have mentioned it if he was.'

'Maybe not,' I tell her. 'It might be too difficult. He may be hurt. How, for instance, might he bring it up?'

'Does he *look* hurt?' she asks.

'No,' I tell her. I shake my head.

There's a formality about our relationship, in the presence of others, which I can only assume – I'm convinced – is an unmistakable signal of what we are up to: the sort of formality which engages couples in the company of other couples doing precisely the same thing: visitors to the house, in the evening, or friends or acquaintances we encounter in the street (at the theatre: more than a dozen there), look from me to her and back again, the blankness of expression sufficient an indication that 'relative', in my case, doesn't fit the bill. Only occasionally does she, not James, give an account of the curious gap in ages between my half-brother and myself.

'The fact of the matter is,' she says, after a significant silence from both of us, 'it wouldn't matter a great deal if he did.'

'Why not?'

'The war immobilised him,' she says, and adds, 'in that way.'

'To what extent?' I ask.

'To the extent of those activities that absorb both of us at present.'

I'm about to enquire, if that's the case, how come they conceived a child?

'When I did conceive,' she adds, 'it was by another man.'

'What other man?'

For a while she doesn't respond.

'The child I did conceive,' she finally (almost formally) declares, 'was by Gerry.'

We're lying on the bed and this brings me, after several seconds, to a sitting position.

'Does he know?'

'Who?'

'James,' I add. 'Or Gerry.'

'Of course.'

'It was acknowledged?'

'Naturally.'

Sitting there, gazing out at the half-completed garden: no significant steps have been taken to complete it since my arrival.

'Why "naturally"?'

'At the time we thought it was the only way I might conceive,' she says.

'Is that why James and Gerry quarrelled?'

'Partly.'

'Our father's objectionable nature an excuse?' I ask.

'*After* the event,' she says. 'We were, for a time, quite friendly. Gerry, James and I. As you might imagine, for such an arrangement to take place.'

'Did Martha know?'

'It was before Martha's time.'

'Did Gerry's first wife know?'

'Their relationship was over at the time. What with the death of Ian . . .'

'Now me,' I say after a considerable silence, a hardness – indeed, a harshness – in her I've only briefly glimpsed before.

'Yes.'

'Why are you telling me?'

Another casualty of war, I am beginning to reflect.

'I thought you'd asked.'

'If James knows about us.'

'Probably.' She adds, 'We've never been involved, in that way, since the first years of our marriage.'

'Why have you never left?'

'I love him.'

'Really?'

'Really.' She pauses, lying there, her head against the pillow: her body, exposed, takes on a different texture: something coarser, cruder, even brutal: her arms are raised behind her head.

She examines me with a smile.

'Keep it in the family?' I enquire.

'That *was* the idea,' she says.

A measure, too, I reflect, of how much James loves her.

'And this?'

'The same idea,' she says, 'as well.'

'Does Gerry assume we'll get involved?'

'You'll have to ask him. All he *mentioned* was your reserve. Your *aloofness*. His perplexity about what he should do for the best. He cares. I think, at times, he gives you the impression he doesn't. As it is,' she lowers her arms, taking my hand between both of hers – a by now familiar, if not habitual gesture, 'he's aware of his inadequacies as a parent.'

'A parent?'

'A surrogate. So are we all,' she says, and adds, 'You're our mutual responsibility.'

'This your way of expressing it.'

I withdraw my hand.

'This,' she says, 'was not expected. The first time at the station I realised I had a problem.'

'Really?'

'For most years of my marriage I haven't functioned as a woman. As, no doubt, you're finding out.'

'I'd have thought, if anything, the reverse,' I tell her.

'Frustration builds up. More, in your case, than I was aware. I simply feel James, if he does know, would not resent it. He's even, in the past, *after* Gerry, acknowledged the likelihood of my going off with someone else. I've always reassured him otherwise. He's responded by giving me all the freedom I want.'

We are silent once again.

I lie back on the bed: my immediate reaction is to go to sleep, to blot it out. Instead, I enquire, 'We've all three fucked you over the years?'

'Male potency, at your age, *biologically*, is at its peak,' she says. 'I wouldn't have believed so *much* was possible. *I*'m post-menopausal. A peculiar freedom. Not that I wouldn't have welcomed it, before, even though, after the miscarriage, I couldn't conceive.'

I am reassessing what I imagine Gerry – and James, and she – might have planned. Was much of this foreseen? Is this part of a broader agenda? Is this what Gerry means by an 'expansive education' (a phrase used after our interview at Dover's)? Is he diverting responsibility for my well-being – my upbringing – away from himself (a justifiable desire, even in my eyes: he has, after all, done his whack) to other, equally well – if not better-placed members of the family? Is this our father's legacy (i.e., liability) being more equitably shared out – handed on from one half-brother to another (neither's exclusive responsibility) – handed on, in a curiously similar way, from one sister-in-law to another, with Martha lunacy, with Clare, presumably, lasciviousness the problem?

'James must know,' I tell her.

I get up from the bed: she likes to watch me, I've discovered, getting dressed (I, similarly, her undressing).

'Why?'

'Simply what we *don't* say to one another. So much of what we might have said has been conveyed in other ways.'

She spreads out her hands: I haven't troubled to retrieve my clothes and take a peculiar delight in allowing her to examine me: a nakedness which knows no bounds (free – in a curious way – as she has suggested).

In much the same fashion she has, almost instructionally, allowed me, perversely, to examine her, for she is more conscious of the signs of ageing – insisting on a realism, in this respect, I shy away from: her thighs, her waist, her breasts, her neck: all these, at different times, she has disavowed with 'don't look at me so *intensely*,' and, 'you mustn't *see* precisely what is going on.'

Yet there is only one place I have minutely (to her consternation and yet subsequent delight: her strangely, consistent, ambivalent response) explored – with the intensity, for instance, she is examining me now.

She is drawing up a *bottom line*: she is seeing how the debit and the credit balance: she is, prompted by my misgivings and her revelations, assessing the account.

'You could divorce James and marry me. That way we'd both be satisfied,' I tell her.

'You're far too young.'

'Not for long.'

She smiles. 'James and I are far too old to change. We've been through this, after all, with Gerry.'

'The circumstances,' I tell her, 'are different. Flexibility as opposed to rigidity is now the rule. Modern times!' I finally exclaim.

I am pleased, smiling – but, unaccountably, not knowing why.

Moments later I reflect that my pleasure is the result of perceiving that this latest news can bring this relationship to a close.

'I seem to have been manoeuvred into a situation in which I am the innocent party.'

'Not *so* innocent, Rick,' she says.

The first time the abbreviation (she must have heard it from Gerry) has been used.

'*Innocent*,' I insist.

'Nothing is that clear,' she says. 'Nevertheless, I may have handled this quite badly. Each of us has injuries of which we rarely speak, or, perhaps, are unable to. In our case, none of this was expected. Gerry's intention was to give you a break. Provide you with a root you didn't know you had. However imperfect. It's only right he should hand you on to us. Shortly,' she goes on, 'you'll leave. All this,' she gestures round, 'will vanish. Whether your self-enclosure will have ended I can't be sure. Undoubtedly, you'll be *different*. As for James, his injuries go deeper than you imagine. He was brutalised by the war, and was in a way lucky to survive it. Luck equates with brutalisation. What should he, what should *we* make of that?'

'Doesn't this,' I ask her, 'make it worse?'

'He hasn't told you, I know, but it was he who introduced Martha to detective stories.'

She waits for my surprise to express itself.

'We met her and Gerry shortly after they married. Over here. James bought Martha several books to read on the plane going back. She became addicted. Not a cause, of course, but a symptom. She rang several times asking him to send her more. We didn't realise, neither did Gerry, that deterioration was already taking place. He thought her turning down offers she would normally have agreed to was a newfound heightening of her ambition, an integrity he connected with their marriage.'

Still I am standing there, her eyes following my body up and down.

'It was part of the blame James took on himself. Part of the blame Gerry thought he should bear. If it hadn't been that obsession, however, it would undoubtedly have been another. Ironically, it brought her to England. And you came with her. That, too, James feels responsible for. It helps to countenance what's happened here. Apart from this,' she gestures to me, 'we're happy. He leaves me to my friends, I leave him to his work. And his detective stories. As you might guess, they have an additional significance to, and justification for, him now. Not something he'd be inclined to mention. I hope you'll treat this with discretion.'

'Would *Gerry* mind me knowing?'

'I suppose, in sending you here, he's opening his book.'

'Book?'

'His past. Something only partly opened till now. His wartime marriage, his first wife pregnant at the time. He was far too young. She was much older. And the war. The war did for them both, in a peculiar way. He and James,' she concludes.

This aspect of Gerry I'm not familiar with – the tennis-playing tyro, of his own description, the liaison affair with the American Fleet: for a while both of us are silent.

'What will you do,' I finally enquire, 'when I'm gone?'

'Bit by bit,' she says, 'I shall get back to normal. This has never happened to me before. What will *you* do?'

'I've no idea.'

She watches me in silence once again.

'Normality, I imagine,' she suddenly announces, 'is why we're living here and not in London. James, much earlier, had the chance, with his insurance work, but decided to stay where he was. This place, after the war, was the only one he had any contact with. Gerry went off to America, where he'd been, in any case, several times before. That's partly, of course, what broke up his marriage. America. It went to his head. Ian dying shortly after. Maybe James, for his part, wanted to come to terms with his past.' Again she gestures round: the new house, the town: the countryside: the hill. 'It all, in some way, *added up*. Or seemed to, at the time. No wonder he took on insurance.'

She laughs: lightly, her habitual, trilling, affectionate sound (the other deep, antagonistic, challenging).

'Has he come to terms with it?'

'What do you think?'

'I don't know him well enough.'

'I'm not sure anyone does. Not even me. It may be what keeps us going.'

We are sitting downstairs, still talking, when James returns, an unexpected conviviality persisting throughout the evening: several friends drop by. I go up early to my room.

I feel a new warmth for James: the temporary nature of our arrangement: the strange detachment I associate with both he and Clare: our mutual involvement at the same time as our partial disregard: the deployment of sexuality to convivial ends in a situation – and an environment – which would normally preclude it: the *insurance* manager in his office overlooking the river (once an industrial scene) preoccupied with 'mysteries' – murders, unreasonable deaths: his teenage 'brother' in consort with his wife (his unspoken acquiescence): the inclusivity of 'family' life.

Much of the time we spend in the car, travelling into and out of town or around the countryside, a companionship characterised by silence, on my part, and something singularly the reverse on hers: she 'chatters' ceaselessly, irrespective of whether I'm listening or not. These 'outside' activities – cafés, restaurants, shops (even, once more, the two of us – a matinée – the theatre) – occupy, invariably, the first half of the day. The second half – Mrs Jenkins having completed her chores and gone – in bed, or in an alternative location. We often simply lie and talk, on our backs, holding hands, a Hansel and Gretel in an altogether original setting, certainly an unexpected, not to say unlikely one. Her voice, irrespective of what she's saying, calms me, disposing me to untroubled reflection. I am – the phrase occurs – moving into myself, ingesting, so it feels, an element of her, something which occupies, then fills up a void which I knew to be there but could never locate. It's as if, I tell her, *she* is fucking me, a less than mutual yet nevertheless desirable avocation: I feel, I tell her, she is *instilling* herself, transposing herself as an otherwise insatiable spirit: love flows in as I flow out, onto her hand, into her mouth, into *her*: fulfilment of an obscure and, because of that, of a resonant nature.

'I can't help wondering what I'll do when I've gone,' I tell her (thinking exclusively of me, not of her).

'Carry on as you were,' she says. 'But more, as you would put it, *fulfilled*. In any case,' we are lying once more on the bed, 'you can, and must, come up again. I may even come down and visit you. It would be nice to be shown round London by someone as sympathetic as yourself. This,' she gestures to both of us, 'needn't come to an end. It will,' she concludes, 'be more intermittent.'

We go to the cinema occasionally, in the evenings, with James, Clare driving 'his' (bigger) car – the one we use during the day – I sitting, at his insistence, in front, he in the back where, I assume, he watches both of us, conjugating his wife and his half-brother, no doubt, in novel ways.

In the cinema we sit with Clare between us, her hand

occasionally drifting to mine, our arms compressed against each other's, my fingers, intermittently, touching her thigh. She has, over the weeks, taken to experimenting with her underwear, disappearing into the bathroom with her latest purchases, to re-emerge, shorn of her outer clothing, dressed in something approaching a convivial style. She lives, she tells me, an 'appropriate' life: a philosophical, if not a religious affirmation, irrespective of the mores by which 'appropriateness' is measured. I, too, am seduced by an 'appropriate' regime, in the belief that (so this is what Gerry has been getting up to all these years) it begs the principal questions at the same time as it assumes it's answering them. We 'collude' in her choice of underwear – and her engaging way of displaying it – in the same way as we 'collude' in everything else: collusion, after all, is what binds us together (all four of us, if we include Gerry; all five, if we include Martha – oblivious or not): less a family than a household, a ménage, the common element – to which I mentally return all the time – a father I didn't know and who, about his fatherliness, my two half-brothers are divided. 'He was,' James announces one evening, from the back of the car (returning from a film whose explicitness, unanticipated when we went in, has dismayed us), 'a great womaniser. It's one of the things I had against him. He wronged our mother. Gerry's and mine. In that respect Gerry derives much of his nature from him, whereas I was so much – perhaps too much, in this respect only – like her. I *acquiesced*.'

It's a word that prompts Clare into ceaseless chatter (referring to the film), the word, however – a relevant confession as well as a critique, I can't help thinking – hanging in the air like a physical presence: accompanying us, even, from the darkness outside into the lighted porch, the hall, the sitting room, where the suggestion is made that we have a drink.

'Why don't you stay with Richard tonight, Clare?' James suddenly, amazingly suggests, handing out the drinks as casually as he might a round of cards. 'I don't want to handicap you in any way.' Clare avoiding my expression – avoiding looking at me at all. 'Good God,' he goes on, 'this is nothing to what went on in the camps. This, whatever Gerry might think, is a *liberal* house, not least in the freedom we bestow on one another. Surely you've told Richard I'm impotent? I genuinely and sincerely do not mind. Marriage – *our* marriage – is built on firmer ground than exclusivity, or anything like. We are, after all, realists, if nothing else. And Richard is a far more rewarding and appropriate partner than anyone we know. Anyone other than in the family.'

It's an invitation we don't accede to (conceivably James' intention): it introduces an element of circumspection to our encounters: as the prospective close of the visit approaches I suggest we work towards a conclusion which, I tell her, 'decides itself' (phone calls every three or four days from Gerry, reassurances, heartfelt, at either end). 'One morning I'll get up and know it's time to leave,' I add. 'I should, after all this time, see Martha.' Phone calls there, too, she listening silently the other end, prompted by her attendant, I hearing only her heavy, suspenseful breathing. 'I have to see her. I feel guilty if I don't. Guilty, too, about leaving here. Guilty, too, about staying. Guilty about *everything*!'

Yet neither Clare nor James appear to mind my indecision; it's as if my involvement with his wife fortifies James in ways that, like everything else, are unexpected: he exudes charm as well as complicity, encouragement as well as – a curious phenomenon – an increased confidence in himself: 'I think I'll send out all seven books again, possibly to an agent, something I haven't tried before. They'll know more about these things than I do. No more insisting I'm a one-man band. Or you,' he adds, jocularly, to Clare, 'a one-man woman. What a delight,' he concludes to me, 'to have you with us.'

Reluctance becomes associated with my inability to leave – until, without warning (consistent with everything else in this venture), Gerry arrives.

He appears one evening, no warning given, tanned, to a degree (more time in LA than New York), bearing presents, curiosity as well as unease evident in his manner, apprehension as well as the expectancy of, by his arrival, promoting pleasure.

God's gift to whom, for what, and why?

'Good God!'

James' voice comes from the hall after he's gone out to answer the ringing of the bell, the lights of a vehicle arriving and departing preceding the sound.

'Gerry!'

It's an announcement – we are watching television – which brings Clare to her feet: moments later she, too, is in the hall, I following, catching sight of Gerry embracing (reunited with) his brother, then transferring the same gesture to his sister-in-law.

He looks across her shoulder; or, more nearly, above her head: the warmth of her response – and James's – I see less as a challenge to than an endorsement of myself.

'I got back this morning and thought I'd come straight on up. Didn't wish to prepare you in case I didn't make it. In addition, I wanted to see *precisely*,' he glances at James, 'how everything is.'

'Dandy,' James replies.

'Fine,' Clare joins in – with an exuberance novel even for her. 'Richard,' she goes on, 'has been so good to us.'

The preposition I'm not sure I have heard: 'to' or 'for'?

'For us,' James concurs.

Gerry looks well (he says the same about me: 'Mature, by God! He's grown two years!' embracing me as he enters the room). 'He's grown a couple of feet, as well. Is this the *youth* I left behind? How long have I been away?' Holding me, finally, at arm's length. 'An unmistakable improvement, James!' he calls over his shoulder, his brother, as if the sole beneficiary of this encounter, standing in the door, Clare with her arm – amazingly – around her husband's waist (already beginning our delayed departure). 'Wonders, Clare, will never cease. Rick's positively pleased to see me!'

'Surprised,' I tell him. 'No warning.'

'None needed, Richard,' James says from the door: the room – the house – has been abandoned, his manner suggests, to the two of us, he and Clare, their work done, retiring.

'How long are you staying?' Clare, releasing James, is entering the room.

'Overnight. If that's convenient. I have to be in London tomorrow. I had to make a diversion to Market Whelling.'

Of course: Eric: the Rolls: maybe, even, he's driven him up and gone into town to find a hotel, Gerry unsure of his reception.

'How is Martha?' James enquires.

'She wasn't aware I'd gone. Or even I was there. No different from before. You've spoken to her several times,' he adds to me.

'Spoken,' I tell him. 'Not received.'

'I'm sure she takes it in. Takes *you* in, if she doesn't me.'

He is looking to James, oddly, for confirmation.

'Have you eaten?' Clare enquires.

'On the train.'

'Drink?' James says.

'Now you're talking, Jimmy!'

A strange, synthesised, mid-Atlantic accent: he is still somewhere out there, above the waves.

'It's so good to see you all together!' The unspoken question: will I be going back with him?

I've already decided not – concluding I could scarcely leave without a moment (at least) with her – even, stay with her and James for ever.

Gerry, however, is impatient to go (on the phone several times before we retire to bed: 'I'll pay for the calls!' dismissed by his brother).

They are disappointed he is determined to leave (so early) and finally he postpones his departure until the afternoon (further calls until, James having delayed his own departure: 'No more calls, Jimmy! Let's sit and talk!').

A résumé of his time in the States. 'It'd be so much easier if we *lived* over there. But,' spreading out his arms, 'not possible. Apart from Martha, I want Rick to grow up in a non-violent place,' followed by a résumé, by Clare, of our time together. As she accounts for one visit to town, then another, one trip round the countryside, then a second, a visit to the theatre, the prospect of another, a unique, mid-morning visit ('to take him by surprise') to James's office (he delighted to receive us: enthusiastic, engagingly shy introductions to his staff), Gerry's eyes flick from her to me and back again, his lecher's *animus* ignited, he finally reaching the point where he interrupts, 'I hope he wasn't a bore, Clare. He scarcely says two words to me, and neither are repeatable. I thought much of the time he'd either be studying or go off on his own.'

'He's been nothing but involved,' Clare says.

'Involved?' He looks at me less with surprise than consternation.

'We'll be sorry to see him go.'

'Let him stay.' He spreads out his hands: nothing, his gesture suggests, could be so simple.

'For good?' She smiles.

'As long as he wants. As long,' he says, 'as he *studies*. Dover's have given him work to do while he is here. I suppose he hasn't looked at it.'

'All of it,' she says, glancing at me (half of it is true). 'He's so often *writing* in his room.'

'Not his fucking memos?'

'I don't think so.' She looks at me again.

'Our house is full of memos. He has, what I call, memomania. That and fucking numbers. *Everything* has to be written down, particularly if it didn't happen. And if it didn't happen, dated.'

He is looking at me for confirmation.

'No memos here, Gerry,' James confirms.

Gerry flicks out his arm. 'He's free to choose. He won't wish me to stay. There's Martha, of course. He's the only one she responds to.'

'Hardly at all,' I tell him.

'Hardly at all,' he says, 'is more than she does with me. I can never raise a flicker. I think she thinks I'm another goon. Or one of the fucking doctors.'

'That's not a good way, surely, to talk about her?'

Clare, I can see, is shaken: Gerry is here for sympathy – see how badly he has been badly done to – and inadvertently discloses the obscene environment I've been brought up in.

'After all these years?' He shrugs, glances at me, and adds, 'What would you prefer?'

'I'll come back,' I say, 'in one or two days.'

'Make it a week. I've so much to do I'll hardly be there. Though sooner, of course, if you like.'

'A week,' I tell him.

'Fine by me.' And looking up at James he adds, 'Not fucked up your schedule, I take it?'

'Not at all,' James says. 'If anything enhanced.'

'Let's have a talk, James.' Gerry suddenly rises. 'How about your garden?'

'Are you interested in gardens?' James enquires.

'Not at all,' he tells him. 'Yours looks like a battlefield. On the way in or on the way out?'

'In,' James says. 'We're looking for a designer. The previous one died.'

'Fortunate for him, I'd say,' Gerry says as he follows his brother out.

Some time later we observe them walking along the half-completed footpaths, Gerry's arm companionably in James's, Clare relieved to see the warmth between them, which, knowing Gerry – and James – I believe is real enough.

'Poor James,' she says, as she watches them from the window. 'He so *wants* to be at one with Gerry. Despite all he says, he so admires him, yet hasn't found a way to tell him. Gerry's so abrasive, and, as you can see, *obscene*. I'd practically forgotten. Life appears to have coarsened him. I'm sorry to see how much.'

'A thin-ice skater,' I tell her.

'What is one of those?'

'Just as you sum up Gerry.'

The younger of the two brothers is preoccupied: despite his exuberance, his mind is on other things: *serious* other things. I've rarely seen him both so present and so distant.

'Jet lag,' Clare suggests when I point it out.

'That, too,' I tell her.

'A thirteen-hour flight from LA, then Market Whelling. The train up here. He mustn't have stopped for twenty-four hours.'

'He's used to moving,' I tell her. 'It's when he's standing still you have to worry. Surely you must have noticed.'

'No,' she says. She shakes her head.

'Earlier,' I tell her. 'When you first knew him.'

'No,' she says again and I see she, too, must love him. 'So what are they talking about?' she adds.

'Us,' I suggest.

'Us?'

'Me. You. How we are together. He's bound to enquire.'

'I hardly think so.'

'Why not?'

'Their looks.' She adds, 'They would have looked quite different.'

'How?'

'*Different*. After all, I know them both.'

I am conscious, in that instant, of someone I scarcely know: an awareness that has come and gone over the previous weeks: one moment she is the woman with whom I have struck an immediate accord, the next someone eerily overseeing not only her life but mine.

'In that case, they are re-acquainting themselves,' I tell her, 'with one another.'

'That's far more likely,' she says. 'On the other hand, I'm not sure what we ought to do. Carry on without them, or wait for them to finish. Mrs Jenkins I've given the day off.'

In the end she busies herself in the kitchen, I propped up against the wall, disinclined to sit (arms folded, feet crossed), gazing out at the garden at the back – that area least traversed by my two half-brothers.

'We're strangers, aren't we?' she says, reading my thoughts. '*Half* a relationship with James, and no connection with me, other than through marriage.'

'Isn't that just as well?' I ask.

'Fortuitous,' she says. 'I might easily have married someone else. In which case we wouldn't have met.'

'Chance.'

'Chance,' she says, and adds, 'Does *everything* hang on that? It trivialises all of it,' she concludes.

We chatter on, dispossessed, waiting for the conversation in the garden to end.

At one point we hear the two brothers come in the front door and go upstairs, returning a little later and entering the sitting room, James, surprised not to find us there, calling, 'Clare?' with an alertness I've never heard before, the two of us returning to the hall. 'There you are,' he says. 'We were *talking*! The past! A hell of a lot to get through, neither of us inclined to stop.'

Gerry is sitting with a drink, glancing up as we come in: his interest is focused on Clare, examining her with, I reflect, something little short of admiration.

'We could do with a week, just to cover part of it,' James adds. 'And well worth the trouble.'

'Maybe we should take a week. Go away together. The four of us,' Gerry says. 'Clare, I haven't a doubt, would have a lot to contribute. And Rick could write us up in his memos.'

'Why do you go *on* about it?' Clare says. 'There've been no memos here.'

'Just as well. I'm glad to hear it,' Gerry says.

'He's sent off his work to Dover's each week and they've returned it, marked, the next. Otherwise,' she adds, 'he's kept quite busy.'

'I'm sure he has,' Gerry says, gratified – intrigued – to have aroused her. 'Have a drink.'

We go out to lunch, taking Gerry's luggage – a holdall and a briefcase – with us. In a restaurant overlooking the river – where Clare appears to know everyone at the other tables, and where James, not she, we discover, occasionally has lunch – Gerry says, 'We must do this more often. I can't tell you how *fulfilled* I feel, after all these years, to have the four of us together. Martha would have made it perfect. Even then . . .' The thought trails off, he waiting for one of us to complete it.

No one does.

'It's a privilege having you come at all,' James says. 'When was the last time?' he adds to Clare. 'We were trying to work it out.'

Dates are suggested, my mood abstracted: three adults, one juvenile, not, for the juvenile, a positive mix.

'Things must change,' Gerry is saying. '*I* must change. Less work, more people. Less people than more *family*. The problem, otherwise, is the more you do the more you are obliged to. I delegate as much as I can but unless you're looking down their throats nothing,' he concludes, 'gets done.'

We drive to the station to see him off: a delegation of three figures standing by the carriage door in which he's framed, his earlier anxiety, it seems to me, returning, glancing at me swiftly, then away: how much – and what – has passed between him and his brother I've no idea.

Then he's gone, the train gliding out, a glimpse of his figure as he moves to his seat (a pang within me that I'm not going with him), his final call, 'See you in a week's time, Rick' – and James is saying, 'I'll walk to the office from here. See what they're up to without me,' and he, too, is gone, disappearing through the crowd outside the station.

We return to the house.

James, when he comes in that evening, glances enquiringly from one to the other of us, then looks away, evidently satisfied, no postmortem required: whatever has passed between him and Gerry appears to have done no harm.

'I should think the reverse,' Clare tells me, later, looking in my room. 'I've never seen him so enlivened.'

The week passes – work sent off, at a brisker rate, to Dover's: a protracted, almost elegiac farewell, my half-brother, on two evenings, leaving us to ourselves, only insisting the three of us should remain together on the one before I leave. We have a meal at home which concludes with his declaration, 'If you only have one more night . . .' Clare declining the suggestion she should spend it with me. 'We have,' she says, 'spent so much time together.' This her way of preparing for our separation. I, for that night, spending much of it awake, she coming into the room at an early hour and announcing, 'I couldn't sleep, either,' a Hansel and Gretel still, if of an indeterminable age.

At the station, showing the same discretion, James says his farewell at the barrier, declaring, 'You go ahead,' the two of us embracing by the carriage door. 'You'll write, I assume,' she says. 'If only a memo.'

'Sure,' I tell her.

'It'll seem an empty place without you.' She gestures round. 'The town. The house. Your room. I don't think I could bear to go in knowing you won't be there.'

'That's bound to pass,' I tell her.

'You'll know it's always there.' She backs off across the platform. Perhaps James is watching, hard to tell.

'I can always ring,' I tell her.

'I'd love to hear your voice.'

'Yours, too. You,' I tell her, 'ring me. We can, if you like, ring each day.'

A whistle blows.

I step inside the door.

'Goodbye, my dear,' she says, eyes glistening now with tears.

5

It's been arranged that Eric meets me at the station – only, I manage to avoid him: not easy, with one exit from the platform. I see him waiting at the opposite end, *in uniform* (cap as well), and when all the passengers have drifted off I wait for him to inspect the carriages, ducking his head as he passes each one, finally enquiring of an attendant, I, ducking, too, exiting the train at the barrier end and disappearing in the crowd outside.

One sanitised situation exchanged for another: the first-class carriage, the back seat of the Rolls. I walk until my arm aches with the weight of my case (I've come away with more things – Clare's wilful presents (invariably clothes) – than those with which I started), then catch a bus, getting off in Camden Town, prospecting whether to tube or taxi the remainder of the way to Hampstead, savouring, as I do, the sense of freedom – of no one knowing who or where I am. Eric, meanwhile, on the phone, enquiring if he's been given the wrong train time, even the wrong station.

Free!

Gerry's fault: only Martha accepts me as I am: that quizzical smile which animates her features when she listens to me speak, I gazing at her, full of expectation, convinced, at any moment, she will *come alive*.

Over all these years, I have, I conclude, learned nothing.

Indolence intruding, I catch a taxi to Leighcroft Gardens: where else can I go with my residual allowance (thrust in my hand by

Gerry before departing, a similar, if significantly larger, disbursement to James and Clare, I assume)?

The house, when I arrive, appears not only empty but deserted.

The curtains have gone and, as I confirm from the front steps, the furniture too.

Confused, the taxi having departed, I wonder if I've come to the wrong address (the lock's been changed: my key doesn't fit).

I step back to the street, look at the façade, at those on either side, and confirm (a) this *is* it, and (b) the place *is* empty: even the curtains from my room have gone, as well as – I go round to the side door – Mr and Mrs Hodges from the basement.

A feeling of exhilaration gives way to alarm: free! liberated! Where, however, do I go?

Back to Clare and James; on the other hand, I have no money.

The day is drawing to a close: a notion of catching a cab to Gerry's West End office (the grinning Gavin in charge, who pays the fare) I reject on the realisation, by the time I arrive, there'll be no one there.

I could, alternatively, call one of my (few) friends (juveniles, without exception); that, too, feels undesirable: if I am alone why not remain alone? Returning to the front door to check again that my key won't fit the lock, glancing in obliquely at the window (how *bereft* the place looks: suddenly retrospectively, it has possessed a great deal of charm – even if most of the furniture was rented: Gerry, like Clare, *galvanises* everything around him) re-descending to the pavement where my suitcase stands like a discarded adjunct of the house itself.

A part of me, I conclude, has been removed: whether a good or a relevant part, or a redundant one, I can't, for that moment, decide. I wander down the Gardens in the direction of the Heath, remember a favoured spot in the nearby Gainsborough Gardens – a treed and shrubbed enclosure within a circle of Edwardian mansions – and, finding a bench facing, through the trees and beyond the houses, the setting sun, sit there to reflect on my situation.

Not only has the familiar gone but an element I relied on: Gerry, like so much else, I have taken for granted: whatever his shortcomings, he has always – if, at times, from a considerable distance – been a constant provider.

The enclosure of trees and shrubs – around a lawn: a one-time tennis court visible against its otherwise sloping contours – darkens: the sky reddens, then fades beyond the turret-like extrusions of the houses: the grandiose (irregular) façades, the sombre brickwork and glowing paintwork and plaster surrounds (what care people take in providing themselves with a home: what consideration). The air is still, the sky clear: a not inappropriate night to spend in the open.

Slotting the suitcase beneath the bench I lie along the bench itself, Gerry's overcoat beneath my head, my arms folded. After a while, as lights go on in the houses, and the air grows chill, I remove several bulkier items from the suitcase, my Clare-purchased dressing gown amongst them, and arrange these beneath my head, drawing the overcoat on and, grateful for its more than ample size, sink my face inside its collar.

Surprisingly, I fall asleep, waking to note I have been asleep, sinking into oblivion once again before, at some early hour of the morning, waking to the hardness of the bench and wondering if it wouldn't be more comfortable on the grass.

Sounds in the surrounding shrubs have woken me: at first I assume a bird, then a rat, then a cat – a dog: an animal walking out from the densest shadow and, after pausing to glance in my direction, moving across the grass, something hanging from its mouth: a loping animal – bowed head and strangulated tail – which, as I focus on its shape, I recognise as a fox.

High up, a solitary light is burning in one of the houses and I imagine a similar light burning, high up, in ours: my room. Isolation feels, suddenly, less like freedom than rejection. I recall the warmth of Clare's body, its texture, its smoothness, its embracing, intoxicating charm.

What, I wonder, would she think of this?

I turn on my back, contemplate the stars (visible through a thickening haze): the darkness, the hardness of the bench: what would it be like knowing, out there, there wasn't an anchor – like the several I am blessed with: even Martha, even her – my thoughts caravaning northwards: what would it be like to be like this for ever: what would it be like if no one gave a fuck?

This is me, legs curled within the constraints of the bench, shrouded in an overcoat of Gerry's, one which, at some time, has enclosed him too, my seigneurial half-brother – my other half-brother, their respective spouses – and my own, cataclysmic, generational *gap*.

Light comes up amongst the bushes, descends over the houses. Aircraft, at intervals, lumber overhead. The need to urinate (defecate): hunger. I realise how little I appreciated having a home: somewhere to eat, something to be known in – gazing at the houses opposite, envious of their location: a part as well as apart: unity, composure.

Birds sing; a vehicle passes on a nearby road, the Gardens otherwise silent. Lights flicker from the aircraft overhead. A feeling of desolation envelops me: what has Gerry organised on my (on our) behalf? Where was Eric instructed to take me? Where, have they concluded, might I be now?

Shuffled (like this) between locations: one fortuitous exercise followed by another. What have they intended? What new locale has Gerry found? Why, so swiftly, without warning, has he abandoned not only 'home' but 'community'? Where do James (and Clare) feature in the plan? Why have none of them told me? What, if anything, am I supposed to have done?

Abandonment, on my part, can be brought to an end in a moment: a phone call, a walk, a ride – a ring on someone's door – and this hiatus will be over. Love knows no bounds, but then neither does hate – or vacuity – and that greater emptiness above my head: despite my reflections I am still lying down.

A milk float circles the Gardens, invisible beyond the shrubs: a blackbird darts off with its startled chatter: someone else's life begins: expectancy, on the one hand; containment, on the other: lost or found, I am still in Gerry's pocket (or James's, or Clare's): as for Martha, she might as well be sitting by me (a constant preoccupation, a constant companion), presence or absence, to me, the same.

In limbo: suspended: time out: have I told Gerry, has he assumed, the memoranda are for her, copies left on each of my visits, a résumé of life-without-her, she and I united by a reality described exclusively by me: the mystery we live by, the as-yet-to-be-recognised corpses, suspects, culprits, the account that she and I must live by, both of us assembled, cast as an amalgam – a residue of someone else's life?

I relieve myself amongst the bushes: when the milk float has gone I collect a bottle and a loaf of bread in waxed paper left on a doorstep and move off through a gate in the direction of the Heath.

I haven't been up this early for a long time (a lot to be said for it), things moving without me, I a piece of refuse delayed, in the stream, by an overhanging branch a moment before, being dragged on – finding another bench at the summit of a knoll, a pine tree overhead and a view – a low perspective – of the City, the light flooding from my left where it throws into shadow several ponds fringed, on their opposite banks, by houses, trees, lawns . . .

I drink the milk, eat a slice of bread, possess an inordinate desire to abandon the suitcase which, so far, I've carried with me: a documented life to be documented yet – a rabid, faithless, faded account: a protean journey in search of a life other than that prescribed by circumstance (or nature) – the grass descending the slope below me, the reflection of trees in the bird-strewn surface of the ponds – and me – eating bread (white, sliced), drinking milk, aware of traffic descending the road I've crossed to my right: everything – Gerry included – going on without me: something in which I play a minimal, if not a non-existent part.

An omission in the midst of an otherwise featureless story, an embryo grown up in the company of *halves*: nothing to claim me, measure me (retain me: retrieve me, restore me).

The amount of money I have will get me, by taxi, to Gerry's West End office: I've been there once or twice before: if he's not there, Gavin will be. If not him, someone who can book me into a room, re-introduce me to a life which I have, temporarily, at least, abandoned. Beneath those roofs, those chimneys, behind those windows, in those vehicles, in those gardens: beneath those trees, conceivably on this bench, the containment of an apprehension greater than even I can imagine: like a wall, holding back a sea, an ocean. A maelstrom.

I decide to walk, discarding the half-empty bottle, the opened loaf of bread, ruminating on what I envisage as a return to fiction, the scenario Gerry has put about as my (and Martha's, peripherally his own) existence: a scenario still waiting to be completed, set in motion: transferred to film . . . catching a bus at South End Green, which takes me to the West End: a second bus to the end of Oxford Street from where I make my way through Grosvenor Square to Grosvenor Street and Gerry's office.

Closed.

I sit in the square and contemplate the pigeons (the winged eagle suspended over what at one time might have been my embassy). I am free, eclipsed, on the loose, secured – the remnant of a story put about by someone else (a mystery and, as yet, something little short of murder), something other than my own creation, something more than I would have wished. At liberty. *Not* free.

The traffic intensifies around the perimeter of the square, the shadows lightening on one side, disappearing on the other, the embassy a bulwark traversing the two.

Sometime later I try the door in Grosvenor Street again: suites of offices in what may have been built as an apartment block, conceivably a house, Gerry's on the first floor: suitcase in hand, dishevelled, a parody of the occupant of the office – dressed in his overcoat – I present myself at the reception desk: Susan (or

Samantha), of whom I have heard much (but too little): blonde, pleasantly-featured (my brother picks them well, dropouts from Cheltenham Ladies or Roedean – disillusioned if they aren't quickly 'cast'): her startled (horrified) expression, embarrassment and consternation unevenly mixed. I wonder, for a moment, if she recalls my name (she has been to the house on several occasions), but moments later she exclaims, 'Richard!' followed by a glance at the door leading to the corridor behind her back – rising, formalising the occasion, coming round the desk, shaking my hand, my suitcase by now on the floor beside me. 'Gerry'll be *so* pleased. He's been up half the night.'

'Is he in?'

'Not yet.' She adds, 'Gavin is. He's on the phone. Second door on the left,' indicating the passage before concluding, 'Leave your suitcase. I'll look after it. Here, I'll show you,' and is knocking on the door before I've scarcely had time to follow, Gavin seated behind my brother's desk, beyond him two tall windows which look out to the now busy street below: a pugnacious, dark-eyed, bald-headed, bearded, comparatively tiny figure (two ears conspicuously projecting from a rock-like head): he stands, the phone to his ear, the flow of his conversation uninterrupted, his eyes trumphantly, eerily, fixed on me: 'Here,' he says, and adds, 'Your fucking *brother*. He's just walked in the fucking door.'

Framed posters of my brother's 'triumphs' in uniform ranks on every wall: some of these he's had at home – before removing them on grounds of 'ostentation': not so here (American *and* British releases announcing an area of variable achievement (occasional embarrassment) which only a lunatic would disown): the logo 'A Gerry Audlin Production' dominates all. Maybe I'm too sensitive to it.

'*Richard*. He's standing *in front of me*.'

He hands the phone across the desk: a figure disproportionate to the dynamism it allegedly contains.

'Speak,' he tells me. 'He's been up all night,' laughing – uneven teeth – as I announce, 'Hi, how are you?'

I don't hear the initial remark, only the calmer, '*Where have you been?*'

'Home.'

'Which home?'

'Precisely.'

'Eric was at the station.'

'I missed him.'

'Why not ring?'

'I wanted time to think.'

'What about?'

'Why the house was empty.'

'I intended telling you, if you'd just done as I'd planned.'

'Why I wasn't told there was a plan.'

'You were *told* that Eric would meet you at the station. Can you *imagine* how he's been? He feels he fucked up and it was all his fault.'

'You sound more concerned about him than you do about me.'

Silence at the other end.

Silence at this end, too, I decide.

I glance at Gavin – who takes a shine to sitting behind Gerry's desk – he back in the chair, the busy street beyond: picking his teeth, pleased with the scene he's created (another scenario): under a pseudonym, he's written several of Gerry's early films, dated 'thrillers', this, evidently, a new one.

He nods: 'give him shit', his look suggests, 'like he gives me. Only *you* can do it!'

'The house,' my brother finally says, 'is sold.'

'Who to?'

'Does it matter?'

'That fast?'

'No faster than it was bought.'

'It seems fated to fast purchases,' I tell him, he no thin-ice merchant for nothing.

'We have a flat.'

He doesn't use 'apartment', which he knows I hate: I've seen too many of them.

'Where?'

'Down the road.'

'Which road?'

'*This* road.'

'Where are you speaking from?' a sudden (alarming) impression he's in the next room.

'*Grosvenor* Street.'

'I don't like living in town,' I tell him, wondering if he might not come through the door.

'It's temporary,' he says.

'What isn't?'

Telephones ring behind me: everything – but everything – everything with my half-brother's on the move.

Gavin, the demon associate, smiles – or, if not smiles, laughs – his mouth, his large, irregularly-toothed mouth open: expectancy, elation.

'I'll go up to James's. And Clare's.'

'No need.'

'Have you cancelled Dover's?'

'Not yet.'

'I'd like to stay.'

'I'd prefer you to leave.'

'What about the *community*?'

'Fuck the community.'

'What about the Hodges?'

'Fuck the Hodges. They've been screwing money out of the housekeeping behind my back.'

So money, I conclude, is now our problem.

'It's the deceit,' he adds. 'The lack of trust.'

'I must have come across that somewhere. It slips my mind at present. *Trust* . . .'

'Stay where you are. I'm coming over. Where have you been all night?' he asks.

'Gainsborough Gardens.'

'Who with?'

'Alone.'

Gavin, thrust back in Gerry's chair, listens with calming interest.

'Whose house?'

'On a bench.'

'Whose bench?'

'In the Gardens.'

'*In* the gardens?'

He finds this difficult, if not impossible, to comprehend.

'On a bench, in the Gardens. I borrowed a bottle of milk and a loaf of bread.'

Maybe he's stopped listening: all I hear is his breathing: he's excited: if he's screwed me, I can screw him.

Or maybe he was in the midst of giving Gavin a bollocking – hence Gavin's look of unrelieved pleasure, not least at being interrupted, not least at hearing Gerry being pissed around by me.

'Ask Gavin to send out for some breakfast. Don't move. Hand him back.'

After Gavin's put the phone down, picking up another and saying, 'No calls,' he indicates a chair by the desk, or, alternatively, a facsimile of one of the couches we had at Leighcroft Gardens: there are two of them, one on either side of the office.

I sit by the desk.

'You pissed up on purpose' less question (Gavin's) than pleasured statement.

'Sort of.'

'He's been pissing himself in ways I've never seen.'

'Such as?'

I dislike Gavin the more I see of him: the process continues unabated: 'One of the *family*,' Gerry has told me. 'Not *my* family,' I told him.

He folds his hands behind his head, relishing every second. 'If he ever has occasion to call the police to his house – or flat – you can be pretty fucking sure they'll refuse to come. He's had a squad car down practically every fucking street throughout the fucking night. He had you down as kidnapped.'

'Why's he sold the house?'

'He didn't tell you?'

I shake my head.

'He was about to exchange when he left for New York. He got an offer he couldn't refuse.'

'And didn't tell me.'

'You know Gerry. Doesn't like decisions being questioned. Pisses on you, otherwise, for fucking hours.'

'Don't you get on with him any longer?'

'Sure.'

Releasing one hand, he gestures round: the other cradles the rear of his head.

'I do his pissing for him,' he says.

'Indispensable.'

'I am.'

Hands lowered, leaning forward, fists beneath his chin. He adds, 'Something to eat? I'll ask Sam.'

'No, thanks.'

'Coffee?'

I shake my head.

'Something stronger?'

'No, thanks.'

'Gerry and I go back a long way.'

'So do he and I.'

'We go back even longer.'

'I'm his brother.'

'Half.'

Why fight over him? I wonder: 'the precocious shit,' his eyes give out, his mind prospecting something else.

'He really cares about you,' he adds.

'I know.'

'*Really*. These cunts round here . . .' he shakes his head. 'He doesn't give a fuck. That's why he's successful. Give a fuck in this game you're finished. He will *never* be finished. It's been a privilege to watch him. Know what he is? *Elegant*. The reason he's elegant is because he can afford it. The reason he can afford it is because he doesn't care. What the philosophers call a phenomenologist. Only one like him. He has all the other fuckers scratching their heads. *They* care. Can't make him out. The point for him is there is no point. You can't get a sharper view than that. Not cleaner. Not neater. He never deviates for a second. Unadulterated pointlessness.'

Releasing his head from his fisted hands, smiling – his large, uneven teeth carnivorously on display – he says, 'You can't get a purer *existence* than that.'

A telephone – one of several on the desk – rings, despite his instructions it shouldn't.

'Put him on,' he says, having picked it up, covering the phone to add, 'We've been waiting for this all week.'

'*Wonderful!*' he continues, uncovering it. 'Why not? We had an agreement. Who gives a fuck? Cut his balls off. Stuff them down his fucking throat. Because . . . because . . . because,' eyes flashing, smilingly, at me, 'because, if you'll fucking listen, he'll never need them in this life again. Because Gerry, I can tell you . . . Gerry, I can tell you . . . because, you cunt, it's what you *said*. Your word isn't worth a piece of shit. *Anybody*'s shit. You can tell that to that arsehole, too. *He* knows. *You* know. *I* know. *Gerry* knows . . . Go fuck yourself, you prick!'

Putting the phone down he gives a howl of laughter.

'They'll fry that cunt,' he says. 'This is normal day-to-day business, Rick. See what I say about Gerry and *care*? We've pissed over that guy from several thousand feet. He doesn't like it one fucking second. Gerry – *Gerry* – will be *pleased*.'

We sit on either side of the desk, silent for a while, I prospecting him, he prospecting something else.

'I mean . . .'

Nothing for a while emerges while he considers what to say.

'The *one* thing – the *two* things – Gerry cares about are you and Martha. Oh, and this shit-arsed brother you've been to see. All this . . .' he waves his arm. 'You heard that call.'

'He'd sell us all,' I tell him, 'for a film.'

'No way!'

Offence, for the first time, registers on his gnomic face.

'There are sides – *a* side – of Gerry you've never seen. And nothing to do with here at all.'

His hands are spread-eagled – small, short-fingered – as if to frame my face.

'Like what?'

'Like *he* would have to tell you. Not me.'

'Why's he never come clean?'

'It's nothing to do with cleanliness,' he says. 'There's no word for it. Take it from me. You and Martha are the most precious things he has. How is she, by the way?'

'I haven't seen her. Recently,' I say, and wonder if I shouldn't have gone to Market Whelling first. No doubt Gerry's rung there to see if I have.

'She lays great store by you, as well.'

'She doesn't know me.'

'Don't you believe it.'

'Have you seen her?'

'Gerry's convinced she takes everything in.'

'I see no sign of it,' I tell him.

'Maybe you're not looking,' he says.

'No one could look harder,' I tell him.

Putting up his hands to fend me off, he says, 'Give me someone who's more attached to Martha than you are. You are *examplary*, Richard.'

The door has opened behind me: an affectionate embrace before I rise or turn, Gerry's cheek beside my own: a distinct smell of his deodorant.

'Half the fucking night I've been driving round with Eric.'

'With the *Rolls*?'

'*With the Rolls*.'

'Did you go to Leighcroft Gardens?'

'We went there first.'

'We must have missed one another.'

'It's not the only place we went.'

He's hauled me to my feet. 'Fuck knows what I've been thinking half the fucking night.'

He has recently showered, the smell of soap and scent particularly strong: the hair – homely, upright, thickly-textured: the suit, the tie, the shirt: his face, if grave, suggests no dark night of introspection so much as a couple of hours on the telephone (feet up).

He cares. He cares, he cares. As Gavin says. For someone who cares about nothing he cares a lot.

'You've gone out of your way,' I tell him, 'to fuck me up,' so rare an occurrence – the tears – he glances (for blame) at Gavin.

'What's Gavin been saying to you?' he says – Gavin having already cleared the chair for Gerry's occupation.

'How much you care,' I tell him.

'Would I be pissing round thinking you'd been kidnapped,' he says, 'if I didn't?'

'Kidnapped?'

'Someone in my position. Or fallen off a train. How would *we* know if you didn't ring? I've called every fucking hospital. Every taxi rank. *Eric*'s aged ten years in the past ten hours.'

'The platform,' I say, 'was crowded.'

'He says it wasn't.'

'So what?'

'*So what*?'

'I missed him.'

'Half the office have been ringing round. Your friends. Who *are* your friends? I should have their numbers. Sam was here until midnight. Gavin. I *forced* them to go home.'

He is dressed with some care, for going out: lunch, certainly: someone entertaining, after. Phones ring, feet pass to and fro: energy, initiative: thrift.

'Iverson rang,' Gavin announces.

'Fuck him.'

'So we did.'

'Good.'

'That's what I said.'

'Who to?'

'Richard.'

'We'll have him running the office yet.'

'Give him time.'

'Give him time.' Gerry beams: seeing me here is part of his victory: house sold, no ransom paid. The kid precisely where he wants him.

'Where are we living?' I ask.

'We're booked in at Claridges, for fuck's sake. Where do you think?'

That, too, a part of our Gerry and Martha past.

'I've no idea,' I tell him. Tears, drying, are inexplicably replenished.

'Maybe I should leave you two to talk,' Gavin says.

'We are talking,' Gerry says. 'Maybe you can tell him. All I want for him is the best.'

'Had you sold the house when you came up to Jimmy's?' I'm surprised, myself, that James is in the diminutive.

'I had an offer. I confirmed it from New York.'

'The night you rang up, after I'd arrived.'

'The night I rang up.'

'And never said.'

'What was the point? You'd only have worried.'

'Like I am now.'

'There is no need to worry. We have,' he tells me, 'a place to live. Gavin likes it. Somewhere,' he adds, 'where we can start again. I don't like – I never liked – the exclusiveness of Hampstead. I don't like,' he concludes, 'living in a suburb.'

'Hampstead is a village. A *community*,' I tell him.

'All those fucking trees?' He looks to Gavin for confirmation (Gavin, with his four kids and three previous wives somewhere down the line, lives in Putney – where we tried to live for a while ourselves – selling the house, God help us, to Gavin. No doubt for a killing: Gavin has a great deal to be ungrateful for: the inverted world we live in). 'All that *grass*. All those fucking *flowers*? Down here we're in the middle of things.'

'*Your* things.'

'*Our* things. This is where they happen.' He looks to Gavin again, who merely shakes his head. 'This, Gav, after being up half the fucking night.'

He examines me as he might a creature flown in from another planet. 'Gavin told me *all* night,' I tell him.

'Half the fucking night *is* night,' he says. 'The other half is day. All I'm trying to do,' he adds, spreading out his arms (so that's where Gavin gets the mannerism from), a fresh exudation of scent and deodorant flooding the room, 'is what is best for you. I'm trying,' he goes on, 'to keep you on the ball.'

'What ball?'

'*This* fucking ball. The ball where fucking things happen.'

He turns to the door.

'Leave your suitcase. One of the girls can bring it across.'

'Girls?'

'Anyone can bring it over. *Someone* will bring it over.'

'When?'

'When I've shown you the place I've found. The fucking paradise I've discovered.'

Exhaustion, defeat: despair: I have a choice as we take the lift to the floor below (another addictive habit of his: I might have known: he dislikes *stairs*: something to do with his time in the navy?), orders flung out on either side, over his back, across his shoulder. In the street, having taken my arm to leave the building, he releases me. 'Don't you like it?' He signals the street itself as if that, too, he's hired. 'Handel lived round here.'

'Like Freud in Hampstead.'

'He hardly lived there a fucking year.'

He's taken my arm again: we enter a door between two shops, mount stairs from a darkened hallway: the building exudes wealth of an anonymous nature: this, everything tells me, is not for me: is, more startlingly, not for us. Is Gerry, I'm suddenly obliged to consider, cracking up, precipitated into actions without consulting anyone involved? Am I in the company of a suitable companion to his crazy wife?

Yet the apartment we walk into (another lift, after a mezzanine floor) at the top of the building is both light and spacious: views to the south and north: the roofs of the façades opposite (Handel's presumably somewhere amongst them) the rear of a mews behind. The most curious thing – it isn't furnished: parquet floors, bare walls, curtainless windows.

He hasn't committed us to it yet.

'This it?'

His other, private address – his 'screwing-hole', as Gavin inelegantly refers to it – is nearby: there he's had his shower and dressed: there he's lived, I assume since leaving Leighcroft Gardens.

'A lease, in this case, not a freehold.'

'Can't afford the freehold?'

'It's not available,' he says.

It confirms, if anything does, he's mad: a mid-Atlantic junkie run out of cash: a foot on either continent and nothing in between.

'It's no comparison to Leighcroft.'

'Fuck Leighcroft. Why do you go on about that place?' he says. 'Out in the fucking suburbs, miles from anywhere,' he adds.

'You *sold* me on the place,' I tell him.

'Now I'm selling you on this.'

'Handel lived two hundred years ago.'

'Fuck Handel,' he says.

Up against it, he has no time.

'It was,' I tell him, 'a place I liked.'

'A place you hibernated in,' he says. 'A place in which you went to ground. All those memos. All those numbers. Obsessional, for Christ's sake.' He taps his head: unusual, for him, he's genuinely frightened.

We are in 'international' space again.

I feel it circulate around me: characterless rooms, vacuous walls, anonymous furniture (when it arrives): tarmacked streets, flagged pavements, uniform façades: impersonal (I am reporting from a distance: I am what I would be if I wasn't around).

'This is your room.'

He strides along a passageway to a flight of stairs: narrow, neat, like you'd find aboard a yacht. He says as I follow, 'This place gets us into a livelier part of town. No driving in and out each day.'

Eric, too, no doubt, for the chop. Not all bad news. I wonder if he's realised.

I don't accede to his invitation to mount the stairs.

'You said you liked driving in and out. Gave you time to think.'

'Think?'

'What goes on in normal people's heads.'

'Okay. It was. I'm not a stand-still merchant.'

Say that again.

'Does Martha know?'

'Why should she?'

'You were keeping a room at Leighcroft for her.'

'She'll have one here.'

'She'll go nuts in a place like this.'

'She's nuts already.'

'So are you. Thinking I would like it.'

Tears, embarrassingly, reappear: Clare, I conclude, must have opened me up: all I can think of is crawling home to her.

'Once the furniture's in you'll like it.'

'What furniture?'

'The stuff I've bought.'

'Hired.'

'Hired. It's still *bought*. Paid for. Most of it up front.'

'What about the furniture we had?'

'All right for a house. Not for an apartment.'

He adds, after a moment, 'Not for a flat.'

'This,' I tell him, 'is like a dream.'

'I knew you'd come round to it.'

More than pleased, he manages a smile.

'A nightmare.'

'This trip up north hasn't done you,' he says, 'much good.'

'Was it intended to?' I ask him.

'Okay. I didn't *consult*. If I had, we'd still be arguing at Leighcroft.'

'I liked Leighcroft.'

'Why do you keep bringing up that fucking place? All I heard was, "How long do we stay in this fucking hole?"'

'When we started. When,' I tell him, 'we first moved in.'

'You resist – shall I tell you? – *change*. The *principle* on which the *whole* of my life is based. *Advancement*. *Challenge!* You resist,' he finally tells me, 'doing anything at all!'

Clearly James has not told him about Clare.

Or has he?

'I'll die,' I tell him, 'in a place like this. I don't like what it's doing to me.'

We have returned to the central room: soulless, empty.

We stand, marooned, in the centre of the floor, gleaming wood on every side, the murmur of traffic several floors below (the emptiness, even, of the sky).

'Did *Jimmy*,' he asks, 'talk about me?'

'In the most commendable fashion,' I tell him.

'What the fuck does that mean?'

'With admiration. Regret for the past. Hope for the future.'

'And Clare?'

'She, too. Even more. They're two,' I tell him, 'of your greatest fans. And Martha's. James doesn't show it, but evidently he's very proud of you.'

He gazes at me, in that instant, as he might at Gavin. As if, without saying, he's concluded he can't trust him another inch.

'They haven't seen Martha for fifteen years.'

'That long?'

He can't be sure (he doesn't care): suspicion dominates his thoughts, colours his features: a reddening in the region of his neck extending to his cheeks, his forehead: I've rarely seen him so ill-at-ease. Even his fragrance appears to fade.

'Since we can't or don't live here, where do we live,' I ask, 'in the meantime?'

'I've borrowed a place in Chelsea.'

'Chelsea?'

'Close to the river. You'll like it.'

He's moving me around like a piece on a board. The thought – the awful thought – occurs: he's run out of cash (and credit) *entirely*: the lease on this place must be short indeed (it may even be in the name of Gavin).

He watches me busily shaking my head.

'What's the matter with Chelsea?'

'What's the matter with anywhere?'

'I'll give you the keys. We'll get you a cab. You'll like it. It belongs to a friend. I haven't committed to this place yet,' he adds.

'Lose it.'

'Think about it.'

'I've thought.'

'No hurry.'

'What about school?'

'You're too fucking bright for school. Dover used to say it was like having an adult in her class. You walked all round her. So she said. They never taught you a thing, she felt.'

'I liked her.'

'As sure as hell she didn't like me.'

'She blames you for fucking up Martha.'

'Me?' He appears, for the first time, shocked. Alarmed. 'She – *Martha* – was nuts when I met her. At the time it seemed like stardom. Who she was. *Dynamic*.'

'I just feel lost.'

'Lost?'

'I haven't a home. I don't *belong*. Nothing is real. It's all *passing through*. *I*'m passing through. We never stop.'

The thin-ice skater wheels again.

Rocks back on his heels: 'You still have me. You still have Martha. You still have Jimmy – and Clare – for fuck's sake, Rick!'

'I just want somewhere,' I tell him, 'where I'm known for five consecutive minutes.'

'You are known. Gavin knows you. *Jimmy* knows you. We *all* know you.'

He is beside himself with rage: mercurial: he's never still a single second: 'the ungrateful cunt,' he's thinking. 'I'm not his fucking *father*. Martha is not his fucking *mother*. What does he fucking want? Can't he see we're *all* orphans?'

Only, he says, 'I'll come to Chelsea with you.'

'No, thanks.'

'We'll get you a crammer. Get you into Oxford. I know one or two people there.'

'Fuck Oxford.'

'Or Cambridge.'

'Fuck Cambridge.'

'Yale.'

'Fuck Yale,' I tell him. 'I'm not going to a fucking college.'

No point, his manner suggests, pursuing it at present: Chelsea enough to be going on with: get the sonofabitch out of the fucking street, Handel or no Handel: get him out of his half-brother's coif-fured hair.

'I'll get back early this evening. We'll have supper together.'

'Don't bring Eric.'

'He's gone.'

'Gone?'

'I don't need him any more.'

Since when? *Last night!*

'Because of me?'

'I can travel more easily by cab. I don't need a car. He and the Rolls came together.'

He's pissed-out, I'm sure, in New York. And LA. Twice before he's been broke – on both occasions breaking the one rule he's adhered to from the start: use *only* other people's money – like, I assume, he used Martha's (paying her back later).

Or did he?

Have we?

What do we owe?

Who do we owe?

Some time later I'm sitting in the back of a cab, an address written for me on a piece of paper (the Gerry Audlin logo on top) – watching the streets of Belgravia give way to Sloane Square and, from the shopping conduit of the King's Road, turn south towards the river.

He's seen a guide book once again: a plaque to Oscar Wilde along the street, another one to Whistler: the key lets me into a white-tiled hall, hung with reproductions (of Ravenna mosaics): broad, full of light (the building several stories high). A lift is available to the second floor: ignoring it, I choose the thickly-carpeted stairs, the ascending walls hung with (Victorian) reproductions: Alma-Tadema, Leighton: the place, if nothing else, has other-than-Gerry aspirations.

A formidable door which requires two keys to release it (the stairs winding overhead): the lift clicks and moans behind my back: ahead an even more thickly-carpeted hallway, stairs ascending in a spiral, a room, beyond, of considerable proportions illuminated by a large, single-paned window: a view across roofs to Westminster: immediately below, the rear of a military museum (vehicles and guns mounted in the forecourt). From the back of this interior rooms overlook the Chelsea botanical garden: somewhere to the left the river.

The rooms are sparsely but expensively furnished: paintings (abstract, of no distinction) hang, less on than from the walls – large, overbearing. Stairs, in the principal room, lead to a gallery, its rear wall lined with books: once a studio, its function has long since been abandoned.

It exudes ease, informality, composure: rooms I might, other than the paintings, have put together myself: the view reassures, the height and breadth of the window, the expanse of sky, the movement of cloud and birds and aircraft: the distant fluttering of a flag: the irregularity of the horizon. This I wouldn't mind living in (I decide), though what I'd do here I have no idea: someone else's conception, not mine, let alone Gerry's: few signs, for instance, of the owner's occupation: clothes in the principal bedroom at the head of the stairs, several scripts (Gerry has been here, I calculate, several days), a smaller bedroom at the rear which I assume – the furniture impersonal here – is mine. A bathroom, tiled, generously provisioned with towels and toiletries (not Gerry's either).

This, I conclude, for what it's worth, is 'home'.

I get a bath and, refreshed, wander to the kitchen: two fridges, one large, one small, both full: a clinical atmosphere not unlike an operating theatre: tiled, metallic, gleaming.

With no thought other than suspension in mind, I return to my room, its window overlooking the botanical garden a block away, and, lying down, in no time, am fast asleep.

Clare comes to mind, I recalling this, pleasurably, when I wake.

Someone is in the kitchen.

A woman, slim, middle-aged, dark hair, wearing a white overall, is preparing food at a central table: a pan simmers on one of the two stoves behind her back.

Everything, I conclude, is on the move (the likening of the building to a ship has already come to mind: the accessibility of the sky, the nearby river): the next thing, I reflect, Martha will appear.

'You're Richard,' she tells me: a narrow, ascetic face, dark eyes, olive skin (could well be a nurse): a foreign accent. Slender, practical hands protrude from the sleeves of the overall (or, conceivably, a surgeon). Vegetables, in separate piles, are arranged before her: a knife flicks busily at several. 'I'm Mrs Seagrove's cook,' she adds, irony, facetiousness, even, evident in her voice. She has clearly been bedazzled (enraptured) by Gerry. Maybe – not impossible – something more. 'I'm here to get your dinner. Are you *hungry*? Will you eat a lot?'

Something is cooking in an oven, its smell drifting out to the room.

'I have also something here you could have for lunch. Tonight!' she raises her arms, the knife gleaming in one hand, 'it will be something special! The prodigal's *comeback*, Gerry has told me.' She is smiling, small, even, widely-spaced teeth: everything about her, like the flat, is embracing. 'You sleep.' Injunction or comment.

'Very well.'

'I not wake you.'

'No.'

'I get you lunch in a minute. Unless you get it yourself.'

'I don't know where to start,' I tell her.

'Everything here,' she waves the knife again: an immaculate clinician. 'I know *exactly*. Mrs Seagrove asks me do *everything*. Order the food. Cook. I not let Mrs Marshall in the kitchen. Or Mrs Seagrove when I'm *working*. You an exception. Mrs Marshall clean everything. But not in here.'

'Is Mrs Seagrove at home?' I enquire.

'Mr and Mrs Seagrove are in the West Indies. They have another home. They ask me to go. I say no, my place here. I do not like the sea.'

'Me neither,' I tell her.

Fact is, I get by by liking nothing: a dictum that allies me to everyone – at some point.

'You and I will get on,' she says. 'You are a *mother*'s boy. When you grow up you will have lots of babies. I can tell. I have two children. In Canada, one. In Australia, the other. But they and their children and wives come to visit. Or I go see them. My family, like Mr Seagrove, much travel. My name is Mrs Shapiro.'

'Shapiro,' I repeat.

Lunch is produced on a tray and laid on a low table in the former studio: at the opposite end to the gallery is a marble fireplace: from the books I choose one with reproductions: Victoriana: virtue assailed, moral outrage, final victory: classicana in marble-textured surrounds, water reflecting figures, flowers – a dream-like atmosphere (the room): I wonder if the Whistler plaque is on this façade or the one next door.

My cook-attendant comes in and out, enquiring of the food – its quantity, its quality, its taste ('good?'), removing one plate, presenting another: 'Eat to be big.' She flexes her arm. 'Mr Audlin is strong. A good friend of Mr Seagrove. And Mrs Seagrove. A friend of everyone!' She laughs, her eyes raised upwards, plainly including herself in Gerry's orbit. 'He make me laugh. He make *everybody* laugh. He make Mr Seagrove laugh. He *a very funny man*!'

Something, I have to confess, I've never found: away from home, no doubt (away from me), a different person.

Something new comes up each day.

Rarely of any interest.

Mid-afternoon she leaves: reassurances of a return in the evening (she wouldn't miss Mr Audlin for anything). 'You have a good time. What life for if not a good time?' and she's gone – I, disinclined to follow, remain in the one-time studio (the challenge of what you would do in a place like this), art subsumed by domesticity, as it is – a telephone ringing at intervals in what I discover to be a study at the end of the hall: a panelled desk, an upholstered, swivelled chair, and – again, evidence Gerry has spent time in here – scripts spread on the otherwise uncluttered desk and floor: a filing cabinet, drawers, and, once again, not abstracts but Victorian reproductions (Dante and Beatrice, one).

The hall door has opened: Gerry appears: red-cheeked, breathless, alert: predatory (prepared, at this moment, for anything): I am reminded (prompted, perhaps, by Mrs Shapiro) what a strikingly good-looking phenomenon (no other word for it) he is.

'Okay?' His coat – not unlike the one I've been wearing – he's dropped, as his habit, on the floor behind. A briefcase lies beside it: Eric dispensed with, he must have come in a cab.

'I'm fine.'

We enter the studio-room together: the phone rings once more in the study.

'Meet Mrs Shapiro?'

'She got me lunch.'

'Nice woman.'

'Very.'

He matches my look.

'I asked her to look out for you.'

'She did.'

He looks round for a drink: reminded of its location, he goes to a cabinet beneath the gallery.

'Want one?'

'No, thanks.'

What the fuck are we doing here? I want to ask.

'Like your room?'

'Yes.'

He looks out to the West End view: signals I look also.

'Good?'

'Very.'

'Evidently a painter built the place. Four large studios on top of one another. Maybe a hundred years ago. Whistler painted somewhere round here. Turner, too. Though long before this building.'

'A cultural tour,' I tell him. 'Literature in Hampstead. Art down here. Music in Grosvenor Street, assuming we take it.'

I wait for him to respond.

'Jack and Elise are in the Pacific.' He gestures at the room. 'I've stayed here once before. When you were on vacation.'

'Mrs Shapiro said the West Indies.'

'After the Pacific. They have a house there. Another in Shropshire. We might go there. To either.'

'Wealthy.'

'Very.'

'Films?'

'Inherited. The Seagroves owned hotels. Jack is one of the nephews. We go back a long way. We met in the States. He wanted to be a director. Still does. In an amateur way. Documentaries. That's what he's doing in Thailand. Temples. He also writes. Monographs. Victoriana. Published privately. They're around here.' He gestures at the books in the gallery.

'Idyllic.'

'Idyllic?'

'Life.'

'It is.'

'Enviable.'

Surprised. 'You'd like to live like this?'

'Why not?'

'The past takes care of the past. Forget it.'

Not sure what he means by this, I don't respond.

'A great admirer of Martha,' he adds.

'He is?'

'Elise particularly. Knows all her movies.'

Presumably, at some point, Jack and Elise have been to the house (I wonder if they met Jack and Edith?): amongst the many admirers of Martha (and Gerry) I don't recall their names.

'Why are we staying here?' I finally ask.

'Until we decide about Grosvenor Street.'

'I thought we had.'

'*I* had. You hadn't.'

'I thought the other way around.'

'You've changed your mind?'

I shake my head. 'Are we short of dough?' I ask.

'A bit.'

'What about Martha?'

'Hers we don't touch.'

'Don't,' I ask, 'or can't?'

'It's tied up. I'm a trustee. It all goes to Market Whelling. That takes almost the whole of the interest. She made her dough before the big dough really started. It's partly that which affected her. We make ends meet, but only just.'

He is sitting down, watching me, wondering, no doubt, what he might do: a liability of a brother he can't disown: should he, he must be thinking, shove me back with James and Clare?

'Once this picture's made we'll be afloat.'

'Where?'

'You name it.' He smiles. 'The *work* I've done on this movie. More than on all the others combined.'

'Will you keep the office?'

'Why do you ask?'

'It must cost a lot.'

'Essential.' The drink has softened his mood: it always does: our thin-ice skater speeds away: gracefully, calmly . . .

'You don't have to worry,' he says.

'I like it here,' I tell him.

'You should. On the other hand it's not practical.'

'Why not?'

'The phone, for one thing. The other, it's some way from the office.'

'Not far.'

'Not as near as the place next door.'

'I hoped you might drop it,' I tell him.

'No chance.' He holds his glass in both hands, leaning forward. 'What do you think,' he adds, 'of going back to Jimmy's?'

'Does he want me?'

'I haven't asked.'

'I prefer it down here.'

He regards me for a while in silence: so absorbed is he by his thoughts that he shudders when I cough.

'You slept on a bench last night?'

'More or less.'

'How did you get on with Jimmy?'

'Well.'

'And Clare.'

'I like her.'

'I thought,' he pauses, 'when I was up, you had a thing going for one another.'

'We had.'

'What sort?'

'What you had.'

'Jesus.' He is silent once again, this dismaying him more, conceivably, than the previous hours of waiting. 'Does Jimmy know?'

'He invited me,' I tell him, 'in the end.'

No sound, merely the stare: something profound: what – apart from consternation, horror, or disbelief – estrangement, even – I can't decide.

'You fucked her because he asked you?'

'He gave it *afterwards*,' I tell him, 'his seal of approval. Though not, of course, as simple as that.'

A second profanation. After a moment, he says, 'What about her? Was she willing?'

'From the start.'

He can't take his eyes away, re-visioning everything.

'Was she with you?' I ask.

'The circumstances were different.'

'Was she?'

'I can't remember.'

'Probably was.'

'Probably.' Still his gaze fixed on mine. 'What have I let this kid in for?' he must have been asking; as near to telling him he'd have to shoot the picture all over again (no film in the camera. The labs blew up. The star's developed meningitis).

'It must have been the same with you,' I suggest. 'To that extent.'

'Different.'

'How different?'

'They wanted a kid. Jimmy couldn't have one. Traumatised by the war. What went on in the camp. We had a thing about keeping it in the family. When Clare miscarried it came to an end. A boy. Another boy.' He is thinking again of Ian. 'Somehow, when Martha went down, it all seemed fated. Maybe that's why she made for you. Clare. In which case, you can't go back.'

'Why not?'

'Would you want to?'

'No.'

'It would be a fuck-up if you did.' After a moment, he adds, 'It's a fuck-up if you don't.'

'I don't see why.'

'I can't get onto your wavelength, Rick. I thought Leighcroft Gardens a disaster. It turned you into a recluse. Aged you, I thought, before your time.'

'I don't see that.'

'Too *comfortable*, for fuck's sake. Too easy. You hadn't to do a thing. That's why you came on with all those fucking numbers. Superstition. Boredom. Checking everything. Marking it. In Grosvenor Street, and a crammer – there's one I've dug out in

Notting Hill – a bus-ride away, or even a walk across Hyde Park – it's a job. *Practical.* I made a mistake about community. Community, I've realised, is not for us. We're different. Itinerants. Putting down *roots* delays us.' (Diminishes. Reduces.)

It's a speech, I assume, he's prepared (on the hoof), none the less heartfelt, despite all that. The news about Clare, however, leaves him (leaves us) with a dilemma – determined to persuade me to go up there, even now, should objections to Grosvenor Street persist.

'We'll be here,' he says, 'for five or six weeks. Maybe less if I get things moving. If not,' he waves his hand: about to get up and replenish his drink, he changes his mind. 'How was lunch?'

'Fine.'

'A good cook.'

'She is.'

'Unlike Mrs Hodges.'

'She wasn't bad.'

'She wasn't good. Kept you in line too much, I thought.'

Leighcroft Gardens, whatever I might think, is enclosed in revisionist feeling – communal, historical, domestic . . .

Meanwhile there is the apartment (flat) where he fucks his women: for a moment I'd assumed Grosvenor Street must have been it, until I saw the absence of furniture, its barren spaces.

'What do you feel about Clare?' he asks (curious, mild, full of affection).

'I like her. I miss her.'

'I can't, for your own sake, send you back. Not even for a visit.'

'Why not?'

'It's hardly a situation in which you can flourish.' Having set down his empty glass he waves his hand. 'Any sense of responsibility I might have had has gone clean out of the window.'

'It might be usual but not unprecedented,' I suggest.

Silence, once again.

'Did you *like* it?' he says.

'Yes.'

'She was, when I knew her, one hell of a fuck.'

He is about to add something more to this but, still gazing at me, desists.

'And now she's fucked you.'

'Or the other way around.'

Once more he is about to speak, but doesn't. He even picks up the empty glass.

'You don't have to say anything,' I tell him.

'I suppose I don't,' he says, and then, putting down the glass again, adds, aimlessly, 'What would Martha think?'

'Why Martha?'

He looks up, startled, suddenly grave. 'No need at all,' he says.

'She wouldn't know what we were talking about.'

'She wouldn't.'

His concurrence is swift: coloured – flushed – he looks away.

The telephone ringing causes him to stand: he appears to be on the point of leaving the room.

'I'd better make one or two calls,' he says. 'It's a piss-hot week chasing dough. I'm too old for this racket.'

He's gone.

I hear his voice from the study.

When he comes back he has made up his mind.

'The alternative is a service flat,' he says, 'in Curzon Street.'

'Back to that.'

'While,' he tells me, 'you make up your mind.'

'To do what?'

'Decide where to live. When we leave here, Curzon Street for a month. Maybe three. At the end of which I'll need to get a mortgage. We can't presume on Jack and Elise for longer than a month. They have kids, too, who might want to come.'

A disconsolate figure, my brother rises and stands beside the massive studio window: he views the scene to the east.

'At least,' he adds, 'you like it here.'

'That's right.'

'We could, with a pinch, move in with Gavin. His kids are never there for longer than a day at a time.'

He must have put this to Gavin already.

'No, thanks.'

'He likes you.'

'He hardly knows me.'

'He's known you almost as long as I have.'

A curious remark: I don't pick it up. 'In any case,' I tell him, 'I'm still disturbed.'

'By what?'

'Being nowhere.'

'Nowhere has nowhere been set down as comfortably,' he tells me, 'as here.'

'It helps,' I tell him. 'But also reminds.'

'Of what?'

'I don't belong.'

'Nobody belongs, for fuck's sake,' he says. 'You belong as much as anyone.' Something of his previous concern returns. '*I* can always live out of a suitcase.'

'So I've noticed.'

'In the navy,' he says, 'you had to.'

'I'm not in the navy,' I tell him.

Another thought occurs: 'How about the crammer?' he says.

'Okay.'

'We'll go together. Work out a schedule.' He waits. 'If not Oxford, Harvard. How about Berkeley? You're bound to know someone there.'

'No, thanks.'

'Or London. We'd be available to see one another.'

'No.'

'You'll have to go somewhere.'

'Sure.'

'You'll have to do something.'

Back to that.

'I'll get the qualifications first, and then decide.'

'Get you into a film crew and start from scratch!'

Confirmation as well as suggestion.

'Fuck the cinema.'

Changing his mind about the drink, he gets another: turning to the room, he smiles, salutes with his glass, drinks, and salutes again.

What has the fucker thought of now?

'When you've thought about Grosvenor Street,' he says, 'you'll let me know.'

'Right.'

'Tomorrow.'

'As quick as that?'

'That's how fast we're moving, Rick.'

To me, on one occasion, he announced, 'No one but a fool would live on anything other than credit.'

On another, 'Who'd borrow dough with interest if they didn't have to?'

Inordinate sums, I know, over the years, have moved through his accounts: some I've glimpsed from examining the contents of his desk: for several years he employed a secretary in the house: her filing of his correspondence gave easy access.

Life is in abeyance once again.

BOOK TWO

1

I wake to a sense of apprehension, increasing, once awake, to one of terror: something abstract which appears to originate in the senses, themselves oppressed by the appearance of the wall, the paintwork, the moulding round the ceiling (the lampshade, the light itself): by the sounds, too, however distant, of aircraft, traffic, birds: a vessel's siren on the river – the whole coalescing into a single pang which finally contorts my body: *another thing* – a seizure which, however much I struggle, refuses to let me go.

Two weeks, by this time, at the crammer: anonymous rooms in Notting Hill, twenty-six desks in one, of which twenty-five are occupied most days, the recalcitrant pupil no one but myself. English. History. Geography. Waking shortly after dawn: an other-than-worldly aberration which, instinct tells me, comes from an imbalance in the brain.

Fiercer than anything previously imagined (something formulates, death or something: the fall to the yard, to the footpath below). I get out of bed to a generalised terror . . .

All perceived through a veil of tears: the inconsiderable advantage of not being sane (composed, affected). 'Some place to live, not someone else's,' I tell Gerry, he distracted by other things, incessantly on the phone, even here, the few hours he spends away from the office (he spells the sums out loud: 'Five hundred grand is pissing in the pot. I'm short of fifteen point five million'). Has he been stretched like this before, or are these mountains he's never climbed? Goes off *twice* to see Martha, despite the pressure (is he prizing something out of her?) – hiring a car on each occasion (an unusual occurrence) and driving himself.

On a third of these trips I insist he takes me with him, he curiously at ease driving north and east, getting lost, consulting a map, the turreted, battlemented outline of Whelling Hall finally showing (with a cry of triumph) above the trees: the long run up the drive, Martha walking with an attendant on the lawn, having been forewarned of our arrival – showing no sign, however, of recognition.

'This,' Gerry says, 'is something,' kissing her cheek, stooping – tenderly – to his crazy wife, holding her against him.

She shows no response other than she's tired (brought out, I assume, against her will).

We go indoors, first to a lounge, where we sit, she something of a wraith: a recent loss of weight ('Her appetite hasn't been all it should be,' her attendant has explained. 'If you coax something down her, all to the good'). Then to her room where we sit adjacent to her bed, Gerry on one side, I on the other, she reclining on the covers, supported by pillows, uncertain who we are: *two* of us together: her beatific smile and saintly, sweet-natured incomprehension: the drawn-in cheeks outlining the delicacy of her features: the startled nose, the winsome mouth, the inquisitive brow: the bewilderment, I assume, she is passing on to me.

It is this visit which turns me into something I no longer recognise, Gerry describing, in anodyne terms, his latest project, omitting his principal concern, the money: the director, the writer, the stars: a roller-coaster of a ride, I following his tracks, attached to his tail, inept, graceless . . .

No point issuing further statement.

One of the names she might respond to.

'Martha?' He watches her expression (guilelessness writ large): the vacuous eyes turned in his direction. 'This is Richard. Richard? I'm Gerry. Remember Las Vegas? The boat we sailed at El Guardero? Remember your sister Alice? The snow above Phoenix?'

The eyes examining him from a distance. 'How about *Richard*?' He stresses the name, almost, absurdly, as if I'm not there. '*Rick*?'

The corners of her mouth stir: creased, tightly compressed: a sound, whether of acknowledgement or indigestion, hard to tell.

'Not often, Martha, the three of us together.' He is urging something on, leaning from his chair: her hand, for some time, has been retained in his: in both of them – a tenderness I have rarely seen before.

I re-examine his features: his brow, the broken nose, the caesarian fringe, the line of the jaw, the contour, turned upwards, of his mouth: he looks more youthful than I've ever seen him – searching for a sign of recognition with a concentration which causes him to frown, calling her to him, 'Martha!,' then, strangely, '*Gerry*,' then, 'Geraldine,' then, the ultimate injunction, '*Matty*,' pressing her hand.

Prompted less by his voice than the pressure on her arm, she gazes at him directly.

'I don't like being called Geraldine.' A voice of old, imperious, self-mocking.

'What shall I call you?' he says. He has drawn her hand towards him.

'I don't like being called Geraldine,' she says again.

'Miss O'Neill?' he says, startling her into recognition.

'I don't like being called . . .' the division of identity too much: her eyes flicker, close, widen: we are retracing a familiar path. 'Someone I was telling.' She can't recall. 'My friend.'

'Who?' Gerry enquires.

'I was almost sure.'

Her eyes move to the window.

'Somewhere,' she adds, quite bleakly, 'John.'

The name of her first husband: I see the recognition of failure in Gerry's face.

I am looking at her mouth, the lines like brackets, at each corner – endeavouring to recall an image projected on a screen:

something impersonal yet also 'mine', something intrinsic yet everything but; something in conflict with everything I feel – more relevant, however, than anything I know. I am the abyss into which her memory descends.

'This isn't John,' Gerry says, glancing at me: not so much a brother, or half-brother, as a stranger, looking up to encounter another unknown figure – like he might, I reflect, from a café table – perfunctory, unseeing, weariness, to this degree, virtually unknown: our skater falters and, maybe for the first time, glances back: his skill – his grace, his speed: the fissures, the cracks, are still advancing.

I absorb each detail of the room, determined to recall it yet not knowing why: the pattern of the curtains which, half drawn, let in a filtered light: the lacquer on her fingernails, painted by another hand: the delicacy of her fingers – the enlargement which, mythic, I have witnessed on a screen: the books and magazines beside her bed – untouched, I imagine, since my last visit: the way her legs have retained their shape and lie, discarded, on the bed: similarly, her arms, the hand held by Gerry now released.

He is, in this context, a pitiable figure, his energy expended: at some point he will have to turn and start again: life, with his force removed, would scarcely, if ever, be life at all.

He is looking at me with an air of resignation, as if, in reality, I am a *thing*: transposed, displaced, possibly abandoned (a liability to be disposed of).

His intention in coming has been to unload me – conceivably – onto her: recognition of her name, then of me: failing that, recognition of me, then of her name (jolted back to something): she is, I am, we are (exclusive to ourselves).

He persuades her, finally, off the bed, finds her attendant, and has her accompany us to the hall, she walking between us, oblivious of who we are, and presumably of where we are going. This might be the last we see of her – her dress, summery, fluttering in the breeze, she waving (persuaded by her attendant), Gerry wondering if he could *still* be right, she aware of everything, having decided to withdraw – fleeing to a hilltop, a refuge – at least, a retreat in the English countryside.

The familiar features disappear.

He is silent as he drives – driving, in effect, as he might skate, a 'received' reaction, invoking processes too deep (intrinsic, organic) to fathom – no signal given other than their effect, this metaphorical sweep, sweep, sweep of the arms and legs, the horizon itself constantly reforming: something he knows he will never reach.

'Seems much the same,' I suggest as the first suburbs appear: semi-detached houses interspersed with trees (how often, on the Greenline bus, I have speculated on inhabiting one, lulled to sleep by the monotony of their passing).

'This place?'

He is scarcely aware of where we are, glancing sideways to get his bearings, startled to be brought back from his thoughts.

'Martha.'

'Her?' He isn't, for a moment – amazingly (so far away has he been) – sure who she is, recalling with a backward jolt of the head. 'Maybe I should have seen her on my own. The two of us must have been confusing.'

'Do you still think she's faking?'

'Do you?'

'No,' I tell him, collateral, either way, to the 'world' he represents.

After a while he responds, 'On the other hand . . .' leaving the speculation for me to take up.

I don't.

He concentrates on the thickening traffic.

'She was an actress,' he finally says. '*Actors*,' he stresses, 'are a species to themselves. I say that advisedly. I've known one or two. They're only real when they're not what they are. She *was* – the speculation is, *still is* – no exception. I dream of her, particularly when I'm stressed, like now, and in the dreams she's always as she was, a comedic edge – the quality which, in the first and last analysis, gave her class, as if she were scrutinising her performance the same time as she gave it, *offering* it to the audience as if to say, "This is playing, baby. How about playing with me?" More or less, you could say – though you'd disagree – what she's doing with us.' He glances across. 'She invites you in, or, in this instance, invites you out. The secret of her success.'

'Is that why she cracked?'

'Discounting my own view you'd have to say it's hormonal, chemical, genetic. No two doctors say the same. With one she's schizophrenic, another delusional, with someone else a manic-depressive. One said she suffered from a cellular anomaly, and drew a sketch to take away. Another told me there were missing letters in her DNA. None say it's irreversible, but infer it all the same.'

'What did the sketch look like?'

'A road map with no warning signs, names, or indications of compass bearings.'

He laughs, indicating the congestion ahead.

I am mentally inscribing everything that happens, setting down words like bricks: building structures the design of which I have no idea: edifices, cities: no remedy other than to accede to their erection (the shapes that formulate themselves).

Around the focus – it always feels – of Martha: the linchpin, the core, the heart . . .

'The fact of the matter is . . .'

He doesn't continue, distracted by his driving.

'The fact of the matter is . . .' he says, and, once again, does not continue.

'The fact of the matter is,' I tell him.

'I don't know if there is an answer. After all these years, that's still the bottom line.'

'Maybe we shouldn't look for one,' I tell him.

'Maybe we shouldn't.'

'Maybe it's beyond us.'

'So why the endless *grossing*?' he says. 'It must add up to *something*. If only I could see it. If she's nuts for ever, what's the point in her being alive? What's the point in going to see her?'

The summation of his thoughts: the questions crowd in behind a long-locked door.

'All this *dough* that's going down the drain to keep her in a state of not knowing who or what or where she is, or who anyone else might be, either.'

Maybe he *had* gone with a notion of lifting some of it off her: changing the terms of the trust that paid for this waste.

'But then you think it's faked.'

He reflects a little longer. 'It's the only alternative to thinking she's doing nothing. Assuming she's faking gives me relief. If not, her illness takes over *everything*.'

'Me included?'

'You as well.' He pauses again. 'How do you like what she is?' and when I don't answer, he looks across and adds, '*Not* you as well. *You*, as I've always said, have the whole of your life before you. Isn't that what I've been telling you all these years? That's why I had to get you out of Leighcroft. I had to take action.'

He needed the dough, I assume, as well.

'Precipitate,' I tell him.

'*Somebody* had to do something, Rick,' desperation of a new sort creeping in.

'Where do we go from here?' I ask.

'Home,' he says, 'at least, for the moment. There are *Homes*, of course, in the States, that she could go to.'

A fresh alarm in me.

'She seems happy here,' I tell him.

'Happy?'

'Calm.'

'Sure.'

'*I* prefer to stay. Your work is here. *We* are here.'

'Right.'

'Our past is here.'

'Some of it,' he says. He looks across: a piercing, inquisitive stare.

'Most of it, surely,' I tell him.

'Most of it. That's right,' he says.

The victims and culprits: the suspects and clues: there never will be a bottom line: the criminal (no more red herrings) will never be found.

All this, had I known it, the preliminary stage to cracking up: alone in the flat with Mrs Shapiro, or occasionally the cleaner, Mrs Marshall, an amiable Caribbean woman, or simply alone, journeying to and from the crammer – the hyper-active (foreign) fellow students, the functional interior of the adapted rooms (formerly a house) – add to a record, or so it feels, of displacement: of life going on over there when it should be going on over here.

And Gerry: his preoccupation with his film: the convergence of first shooting with the prospect, if not the certainty, of leaving where we are (occasional letters from Clare: postscripts from James: memoranda, in return, from me), and the fateful waking to a mist, a feeling that the observable world is closing in.

Entombed! a voice like Martha's, in her heyday, informs me.

Enclosure by a sensation that has its source in the walls, the doors, the singular plate glass window overlooking the eastern skyline: incorporated, the whole, as a feature of my mind.

I am taken off by Gerry to see his 'pal': a doctor in Devonshire Street he first visited with Martha (who recommended Market Whelling as a 'refuge' and who, occasionally, at Gerry's prompting, visits her there).

He talks to me (Gerry in the waiting-room) about my feelings of self-enclosure, words refusing to coalesce with feelings, 'appropriate' language no longer the norm, he diagnosing a condition acronymically referred to as GAD: a generalised anxiety disorder

– recommending, in the process, a course of pills, calling Gerry in to discuss it: an avuncular, friendly, broad-shouldered figure, with rounded back and a bowed and balding head (white hair receding decorously at the rear).

'Maybe a home environment would be better for him,' he suggests to Gerry when he calls him in, Gerry responding, '*Home* or home?' I, for a moment, confused, his 'pal' ('Ronnie') replying, 'Domestic, not institutional,' with a laugh. 'The itinerant life, as Richard describes it, is not, at the present, at least, for him.'

'But, then,' Gerry says, 'that's how we live. How we've always lived. Inertia in Hampstead was doing him no good. He – even he – would agree with that.'

'Would you agree?' Ronnie enquires.

'R du Pleiss' is inscribed outside his door.

I shake my head.

'There's Martha, too,' he adds.

He has, perfunctorily, enquired how much, if at all, I like her ('I love her'), how often I see her ('more frequently than Gerry, who hasn't the time').

'The two of them,' Gerry says, 'are very close. He's very attached to her,' identification, his tone suggests, conceivably a problem. 'What's the treatment?' he finally enquires.

'I think it would do him some good to talk.'

'He does talk,' Gerry says.

'To someone,' Ronnie says, 'I can recommend.'

'Sure.' Gerry looks at me. 'Is that okay?'

Implicit in the question is a reckoning of the cost.

'That, together with medication,' Ronnie says (a confidant of stars as well as people behind the scenes, like Gerry).

'Maybe,' I tell him, 'I should give it a try. Nothing lost,' they looking at me as if something in this response is far too prompt.

So I end up at a clinic not a few hundred yards from Dover's and maybe a few hundred of the same from Leighcroft which – three days a week in this impersonal room, in a 'purpose-built' structure not unlike an office block – I walk past occasionally for old time's sake (someone else is living there already).

My interlocutor is someone I have, initially, to resist disliking, a censoriously-featured middle-aged woman with long grey hair which would benefit, in my view, from being cut and which she has trouble controlling: large, heavily-veined hands and slight, flat-heeled shoes like dancing-pumps or slippers: thick-limbed, long-skirted, jerseyed: around her neck hangs, on most days, a string of beads – uniformly-sized, red some days, green or blue on others.

I endeavour to read signals in these changes of colour, but none occurs.

Her eyes are dark, underlined by shadows, her nose pronounced, her mouth thick-lipped (inappropriately coloured), her cheeks jowled: altogether, a sense of unnecessary *weight*.

Gerry makes no attempt to conceal the fact that he is suspicious of me talking to her (Martha has talked to lots not dissimilar in her time), he having seen her on our first visit. Ronnie he 'respects', but, as he often confesses, 'respect' invariably – and not just with Ronnie – leaves him 'blind'. As much as the woman talks me 'in' he endeavours to talk me 'out' – not, at least, to suspend my judgement.

But then, it's my judgement, I tell him, that is allegedly impaired.

Not that I see him often: the one positive element in this latest arrangement is that it keeps me busy: rushing to and from where we are (a comfortable place to go nuts in, which is probably why I've gone) and Notting Hill, and Notting Hill and north London, he's scarcely present at all (my exams postponed until the following year).

We are, too, in no time, on the move: Grosvenor Street, practically next door to the office: 'Not permanent,' he tells me, 'for the duration' (of this film). 'We'll move back to Hampstead, maybe, when I have the dough.'

Disturbance is matched with irregularity, the one a reflection of the other, an air of anxiety (not as acute as mine) characterising

Gerry's features (the shooting at Pinewood underway – the money, allegedly, having come via the Seagroves: all the time we are buying time) to a degree I've seldom seen: a *haggard*, no longer youthful – no longer caesarian (no longer anything you'd care to mention) – look: an aged man staggers out of the top-floor flat at an unearthly hour each morning and an even more aged one crawls back in at night. He has a *fathomed* look, as if his brain has left his body, behind his eyes a cavern from inside of which nothing shows.

'How are you making out with that woman?'

Her name is Pelling: he never uses it (*Marjorie*, I learn).

'Okay.'

'What's the score?' sprawled in a chair: the hotel-suite crap which has been flung around the place by an 'interior' designer: a sparseness which suggests it could be removed any time.

'Evens,' I tell him.

It's Sunday: a brief respite from telephone calls: i.e., only twenty throughout the day.

'What does she ask?'

'What I'm doing at present.'

'Not about the past?'

'Not yet.'

'If you're feeling you're making no progress, let me know. You don't have to go on seeing her.'

'I don't?'

'Not at all.'

'What about Ronnie?'

'He'll understand.'

'Maybe that's why she calls me Ronald.'

'Who?'

'Martha. She's seen him, too.'

'She also calls you Roland, Robert, all the rest. As it is,' he waves his hand, his normally manicured hand, neglected like, I can't help observing, the rest of him, 'it's up to you.'

'Imagine with a surname like du Pleiss being given a personal name like Ronald.'

'We're talking about you.'

'What about the pills?'

'They take time to have effect.'

'I still wake up feeling frightened. Terrified,' I tell him.

He doesn't wish to hear: I am taking the pills, I am seeing Mrs Pelling: 'Doctor M. Pelling' is inscribed on the outside of her door, not, I've been told, a medical appellation.

'Sure.'

'It rarely goes away throughout the day.'

'I feel the same.'

'You're fifty-two. I shouldn't be taking this fucking crap. You're doing something. I'm sitting on my butt.'

'You're working. You're studying. You'll have a career.'

'I'm going mad. I'm going to end up,' I tell him, 'like your wife. Won't that be sufficient?'

That brings him to my side: he sits on the arm of the chair, his arm around my shoulder.

'You're not going the way of Martha.'

'I feel it.'

'She was as bright as a penny at seventeen. Eighteen. So was I.'

I'm not entirely sure what this means: reassurance, or confirmation. 'I'm talking,' I tell him, 'about *me*. I'm full of fear. I'm fucking desperate. I don't belong to anything.'

'You belong to me.' His cheek beside my own: he hasn't shaved all day.

Where all this comes from I've no idea: out of a mist, a forgotten time: places, events, people: Beverly Hills, Beaconsfield, the West End: Hampstead: a passage across a landscape that has no significance other than its passing: everything has 'gone', what's present soon to be gone as well.

I am, I tell Marjorie, not 'founded': I wake up each morning not knowing if I'm there.

'Who experiences the terror?' she asks me.

'No one I know,' I reply.

The pills, meanwhile, are still to take effect.

'There are side-effects, too,' I tell him.

Ronnie made no mention of those.

'Such as?'

'Nausea. Dizziness. Fatigue. You name it. My mouth, most of the time, feels like rubber. I don't know where it is when I speak.'

His cheek compressed against mine: moments later, I realise he is weeping.

'You realise how much I care about you, Rick?' he says.

'We've been through all that,' I tell him, 'before.'

'I'd do anything to keep the two of us – the three of us,' he amends, 'together.'

'I know that.'

'You know what a fucking film is like. Unless I'm *on the spot* the whole thing goes down the shute.'

A disconsolate figure, bereft to a degree I've seldom seen: I'm not sure whether I'm looking at him or me: everything, his manner suggests, is lost. *He* is lost. *I* am lost – except, his manner further suggests, he is thrusting me *out* – the intended sole survivor: two derelicts, cast up on the shore of Martha's dementia: whether to survive, whether to disappear.

Maybe he's not convinced (of what I'm feeling, my capacity to describe it), too much bound up in his own distress: a bum-deal arrangement with someone who's making no 'moves': observant, immobilised. Still.

Bewilderment bordering on contempt: his half-brother Richard must get it from his mother.

The unknown mother.

'The whole strategy, at the moment, is to hang in,' he says. 'Once this picture's finished I'll take a break. We'll go away. We might take Martha. Somewhere where she, and I, and you, have never been. We'll reassess,' his arm relaxing around my shoulder.

He turns, rises, goes to the window.

He – we – might be gazing out of any window onto any street in any city: a representational interlude between something purporting to be one thing while, in reality, it masquerades as another: no local animation, no local name, no variety of custom – the constancy, only, of human nature – such equated with mundanity, relieved by distraction (something conjured up by him).

He wipes his eyes, what he is thinking interpreted by the movement of his hand, the sideways inclination of his head: he runs his knuckles across each cheek: the impropriety of not moving (the precocious arsehole behind his back – suffering while he, Gerry, does for him (by him) all he can).

Suck his thumb: admit nothing but content.

Gerry's back (to me) is his most expressive posture, more vulnerable than when his features might be seen, the face that shows the concentration of the skater, gaze fixed on an objective no one else can see: chasms, voids (going down for ever): velocity, the ice itself: strength, lightness: *speed.*

'All this is to the good,' equilibrium restored. 'Wouldn't you agree we're getting closer?'

'By me,' I tell him, 'going nuts.'

'You're not.'

'Why won't you believe me?' I ask him.

He can't afford to: and hasn't time: already the look in his attractive, revivified eye: 'Look at me! I'm *flying*!'

'Haven't you heard,' he says, 'of adolescence?'

'I'm still going mad.'

'This is backwash,' he says, 'from fucking Clare. Maybe you should go back and finish off. *Grow up*,' he adds, 'and finish off. Finish what you started.'

'All she did,' I tell him, 'was to bring it to the surface. Now that it's happened I don't know what to do.'

'*Everyone*'s taking pills,' he says. He names his star. 'Without pills she'd never get out of bed on a morning. *I*'d never get out of bed. Come down and see what happens. It would *interest* you, even if you did nothing but fucking watch.'

'The cinema is bullshit. The worst distraction yet,' definitive statements, too familiar to be listened to (extracted under pressure): it's disengagement we're involved with, a commonality of experience, purpose – even possessions – moving, however, in opposite directions.

Yet, for an instant, he has wept: something, finally, has reached the eye – emerging from those depths where memories of Ian and Martha in her prime must still exist, I amongst them.

'Get this picture out of the way and we can both,' he tells me, 'reassess.'

'You're not listening to me,' I tell him.

'I'm listening,' everything in motion: his metaphorical arms embrace me – hold me: we will power through this together.

'I don't know how to explain it further.'

'I know precisely how you're feeling. It comes to me when I wake each morning, knowing I've got to go down and *face it*. A hundred, maybe more, waiting for direction. When I open that door and go out on the floor every fucking face is turned towards me. Clare,' he raises his hand, 'thought, no doubt, she was doing you a favour. No need to make an illness out of it. Christ, *I* didn't fuck until I was *nineteen*.'

The dishevelment of his clothes, his hair, together with his unshaven chin, give him an unexpectedly youthful look: back to his favourite subject: so many women must have seen him like this: *glimpsed* him like this: a boy pleading – if not for acceptance – for entertainment.

'If it wasn't her it would have had to be someone else. Someone has to get in first. *She* had a first time. *I* had a first time. You've been lucky. Someone who cares. Someone who *knows*. No incest. No blood link.'

He is talking (with relief) off the top of his head: *everything* happens in the end: we're all in this together: don't think I'm in there on my own.

I am, on the other hand, feeling worse.

'You're bright.' He comes to sit on the arm of a chair (the phone rings in the room he uses as his study: he ignores it). 'The way we've moved around has given you no time with kids. On top of that there's Martha . . .'

He watches me intensely: something, perhaps, he isn't ready to confide (a crack: look out!).

He swerves.

Veers off.

Another tack. 'Those fucking memoranda might have been written by a fucking adult . . .'

Has he gone too far? He is moving fast (something healthy in my distress: *any*body (normal) would feel the same: no need to resort to exclusivity: every *genius* feels like this: look at him (maybe I should see another 'pal'). Did I hear that properly? He has these 'pals' all over the place. I wonder how they refer to *him*? 'Maybe you should talk to someone else.'

'Who?'

'Phil.'

'Phil?'

'O'Connor.'

'He's nuts.'

'Some say. Others not. If he is, you'd have something in common, according to you.'

I've come across O'Connor on several occasions at Gerry's 'cultural' suppers at Leighcroft Gardens: poets, musicians, artists, composers, journalists, hacks, restaurateurs, admirers, politicians, hangers-on (stars): a macabre, limelight-hogging figure: dark (black-pupilled) eyes, pale face, drawn cheeks, a frontally balding head (*shrivelled* features, like those native shrunken 'souvenirs'), black clothes (suit, sweater, socks, shirt): a sinister presence I've never taken to and of whom, if anything, I'm morbidly afraid (a half-hour grilling once, in a corner, on 'how I was'). Notorious as a psychiatrist with authorial leanings, he is frequently to be encountered not only in the broadsheet but the tabloid press – not least for running a 'centre' in the far north-east of London where he treats lunatics without the aid of medication – apart, allegedly, from aspro: often to be seen in his inimitable dress on late-night television advocating the closing of mental institutions and prisons ('much the same thing'). Even occasionally appearing on early evening television news, his Irish accent with its lilting cadence at the end of every word offering comment which, delivered in any other accent, would have the speaker accredited as criminally insane. Gerry is beguiled by him (has put him into one of his films as a disputatious psychiatrist), O'Connor's freakishly bestselling book, *The Nature of Reality: the Reality of Nature: a Phenomenological Error*, lying on his desk (unread) at Leighcroft for the better part of a year.

'I don't understand a word, but,' Gerry has said, 'I respect the authority with which he says it. I've never met a more authoritative man.'

'Or woman.'

'That I'm not so sure of. Martha is very authoritative. *In her way.*'

'Perhaps it's his accent,' I now suggest.

'Maybe it is,' he says, 'but also the *thought.*'

'What thought?'

'Whenever he speaks I always hear something I never heard before.'

'And wouldn't want to again.'

'Always a fucking answer. *That*'s why you ought to see him. If he deals with people who are nuts he definitely is not nuts himself.'

'You want me to go and see him.'

'He is the only person I know, the only *doctor* I know, who has a *belief* informing his judgements.'

'What belief?'

'Read his book. You think you're so fucking clever. An *existential* belief. A definitive, non-doctrinal judgement.'

'What the fuck does that mean?'

He doesn't know himself (maybe Gavin filled him in): he looks to me to explain it, motoring me along, *inertia* the scourge of the age, the disease films are uniquely opposed to: *turpe nescire*: the Socratic rule, disgrace the corollary of ignorance founded in staticity (I'm catching his disease).

'Hasn't he had more suicides amongst his patients than any other shrink on the circuit?'

'Because he sees those who others shy away from.'

'You still want me to see him.'

'I trust him.'

'You *trust* him?'

'Would I ask you to see him if I didn't?'

Showing me the medicine: instantly I'm better.

'These quips you come up with. No thought behind them. Always negative. Always dismissive.'

He is regaining his confidence as well as his temper.

'What about Doctor Pelling?'

'She isn't a doctor.'

'A PhD doctor.'

'She's buttering you along.'

'She could have fooled me.'

'She's *coaxing* you along,' he says.

'She's trying to open me out. I'm beginning to see her method.'

'*Clare* opened you out. How much opening do you want?'

'It's your pal who recommended her.'

'Maybe he was wrong.'

'Maybe he was right.'

Neither of us able, or willing, to concede.

Night is closing in: the moment – the only moment – when I begin to feel relief.

'I don't understand,' he says, 'what goes on inside your fucking head. With most people I wouldn't care. But not with you and Martha.'

He regrets this final observation: he raises his hand to withdraw it.

'I'm relieved about you and Clare. Maybe it would have been better to have been someone different. But she we can trust. Which isn't to diminish the responsibility which, considering her age and position, is hers. And mine.'

A tortuous confession: I wonder how much more he wishes to say, and how, if necessary, I might prompt him.

'I don't regret it,' I tell him.

'You probably miss her.'

'Yes.'

'It couldn't go on.'

'No.'

'I'll give O'Connor a ring.'

'Okay.'

'You'll see him?'

'If you say so.'

'I'm very proud of you,' he says. 'The way we talk. I don't talk to anyone the way I talk to you. It's a measure of the bond between us. Despite all the things you say, that counts,' leaving us looking apprehensively at one another across the almost empty room: two individuals separated by thirty-odd years and something even more in thought and feeling: a father in common, on whom there are strictly divergent views.

'What was my mother like?' I ask.

'I scarcely knew her. Father and I didn't see much of each other at the time of his second marriage.'

He waits: he doesn't like this line of questioning, and never has. At times he even forgets her name: 'Lorna, was it?' he said, the last time I asked him.

'Did you go to the wedding?'

He shakes his head.

'Father cabled me afterwards,' he says.

This, too, he's said before.

'I suppose James didn't go to it, either.'

'As far as I know.' Again he shakes his head. 'I was out of the country. Did James talk about it?' He looks away.

'His attitude,' I tell him, 'was much the same.'

'He didn't like Father, that's for sure.'

'Clare knew nothing of her, either.'

'Father was retired and living on the south coast by the time he re-married.'

'I was born at sea?'

This has been told me several times.

'They were cruising.'

'Wonder you didn't join them.'

'Why?'

'The navy.'

'Behind me, of course, by then.'

'Premature,' I remind him. 'The birth.'

'It's what caused her early death. That and the fucking boat.'

'What fucking boat?'

'It wasn't equipped for childbirth. Not for someone of that age.'

'How old was she?'

'I forget. Certainly in her forties.'

He likes this less and less. 'It's the sort of thing you can talk about with O'Connor.'

'Does he *know* about these things?'

'The relevance of the past,' he says. 'If we count those sort of things.'

'Has O'Connor ever seen Martha?' I ask.

It's the question he's been dreading: at least, I assume so: I watch him stand.

He goes to the window once again: the Sunday evening Grosvenor Street outside, devoid of traffic, devoid of people: an unnatural quiet descends around the place.

'Yes.'

'What did he say?'

'I didn't ask him.'

'Why not?'

He shrugs, his back to me, his shoulders, oddly, remaining raised: a question to which there's no answer, even now.

'*Why not?*'

'I didn't want to know.'

'Didn't he want to tell you?'

'I suppose he did.'

'He must have thought it odd.'

'No odder than a lot of other things.'

'What things?'

'Things he must have come across.'

He turns, dismissing it, his hands in his pockets.

'All I said was would it help or hinder the way I saw her. All he said was, "Neither." "In which case," I said, "don't tell me."'

'Did Martha ever say anything?'

'Apart from saying she thought him strange.'

'Not far from the mark.'

'No.'

'So neither James nor Clare nor you ever liked her?'

'Who?'

'My mother.'

'I wouldn't say that.' He's not sure what he *would* say: the O'Connor decision, with him, is all that counts. 'None of us really knew her,' he adds.

'A hell of a father, too,' I tell him. 'How come they went cruising when he was broke?'

'I sent them money,' he says. 'He'd always wanted a cruise. I was in the States. We intended to meet. Then she fell ill.'

'With me.'

'With you. I paid for the flight back as well, as a matter of fact.' A moment later, avoiding my look, he adds, 'I wouldn't say I knew him too well, either. Particularly as he grew older.'

'Yet an element common to all of us,' I tell him.

There are photographs of James and Gerry, their mother and father: only one of their step-mother and their father: a not unpromising-looking woman gazing flirtatiously into his elderly face some time, evidently, before their marriage (her ideal). I stare at these blurred features as into a mist, recognising nothing: a three-quarters profiled face representing, allegedly, opportunism – calculation, probity: reserve. Somewhere, presumably, I'm buried in all that, the photograph something Gerry, I suspect, regrets preserving (I coming upon it by chance, he unaware he still had it): all other photographs of that period he reportedly 'lost' (perhaps destroyed).

So there I have it: *Mum*!

Life is first awful, then it's worse: the melancholy commentary passes through my head: born to renegades their family have disowned – if latterly with regret.

'Did Martha ever meet her?'

'Who?'

'My mother.'

He shakes his head, the doorbell ringing from the street below. He doesn't respond: bewilderment or denial in his gesture, I can't decide.

The telephone also rings: he doesn't answer that, either.

'I'm never quite sure,' he says, carefully, 'how much you're putting me on.'

Bewilderment, on my part: confusion.

'How much you do know,' he adds, oddly, 'and say you have forgotten.'

'I don't forget anything,' I tell him.

'Nothing?'

'Nothing.'

He smiles, oddly reassured.

'What prompted you to take me to du Pleiss?' I ask.

'I thought it might be something physical.'

'Physical?'

'Mental.'

'Mental?'

'In the fucking head!'

Impatience back again.

'A *physiological* reason,' he adds.

Losing not only patience but his nerve.

'I thought he was a psychiatrist.'

'A neurologist.'

'He didn't take very long. He recommended Doctor Pelling in no time.'

'That I wasn't expecting.'

'What did you expect?'

'Not a shrink.'

'She isn't a shrink. She's a psychotherapist.'

'I wouldn't know the fucking difference.'

Or doesn't want to.

'With O'Connor, at least, we know where we are,' he says.

'A philosopher, just what I've been missing,' I tell him.

'He'll see you as a friend, not a patient.'

'You've spoken to him?' I ask.

'Sure.'

'And didn't tell me.'

'I wanted to know if he'd see you before we went through all this,' he says. 'He'll see you as a friend.'

'I hardly know him.'

'As *my* friend, for fuck's sake.'

The doorbell rings again: Gavin (perhaps) who's phoned and got no answer: who said Sunday wasn't a working day?

Or even one of his women, pissed off waiting.

'I'll call him now,' he says. 'I'll call him now and get it fixed.'

(Why didn't he say 'moving'?)

2

So I end up at Jubilee Hall, a converted community centre built by a local philanthropist ('for the community': good old Gerry has registered that: he's written the address on a piece of paper) before the Second World War – bombed, apparently, and subsequently rebuilt: a pair of battered metal doors leads to a urine-stained, concrete-floored hallway, a telephone hanging from its wire against one wall, a noticeboard pinned with leaflets and handwritten messages facing it. A metal table, with a plastic chair behind, stands adjacent to double wooden doors leading into a hall in which several figures are variously located: some look up but the majority persevere with their principal occupation, which involves observing and commenting on the activities of a woman drawing, or painting, on a large sheet of paper on the floor.

Two other figures are playing table tennis at the far end of the room, one elderly – that's to say, middle-aged – short and stocky, with a balding head, cropped hair, reddened features and protruding eyes, the other a lean, physically uncoordinated youth, possibly younger than myself – who appears not to be focused – is perhaps unfocusable – on what he's attempting to do.

'Nineteen, two!' the older figure calls, serving. 'You're fucking hopeless, Patrick!' adding to me, as the youth misses the ball and trots off to collect it, 'What can we do for you, my friend?'

The surface of the table is decorated with a female face: a series of interlocking circles, with coagulated paint standing up in ridges,

I identify a pair of female breasts and a baby's suckling head.

'I'm looking for Doctor O'Connor,' I tell him, adding '*Phil* O'Connor,' stressing the informality of my visit.

'Out.'

The game recommences, with the same result, the triumphalist figure turning to me again while his opponent once more retrieves the ball.

'What do you want him for?' he adds.

'I have an appoinment.'

'When?'

'Now.'

'What's your name?

'Audlin.'

'Gerry's brother!'

Resting the returned ball in his palm, his bat is raised to hit it.

'Now I see it. "Audlin" written all over you,' he says.

Whether approval or disapproval, hard to tell: I've never thought we are *that* alike.

Distracted by a call from across the room ('Fuckhead is painting her tits again!') he shouts, 'There are penalties for immoderate speech. No supper for you, wanker. I've told you before.' To me, he continues in his previously modulated tone, characterised by a Scottish accent, 'He should be here any minute. You don't play ping-pong, by any chance?'

'No,' I tell him.

'Like to learn?'

'No.'

'You someone who says no to everything?'

'No,' I tell him, and shake my head.

The bulbous nose, the pronounced brow, the mauve cheeks, the protruding eyes, the wide-lipped mouth, the bristled chin: examining me a moment longer, he indicates the youth at the opposite end. 'Patrick learns nothing, despite the lessons I give him. He's not – definitely not – a challenge. You like challenges?' he enquires.

'No.'

'What do you like?' he says.

'Fuck all,' I tell him. 'Certainly not being grilled.'

'I'm Patterson, by the way. Steven, with a "v".' Clipping the ball away, for it to be missed the other end, he puts out his hand. 'How's Gerry?'

'Busy.'

'Always was.'

He grips my hand firmly, flinging it up as if to place it on his shoulder, flinging it down as if to grip his waist, then tossing it away as he releases it.

The youth, having retrieved the ball, the game at an end, has joined the group across the hall.

'Been here before?' Patterson asks, placing the bat on the table.

'No.'

Giving me a swift glance, he says, 'I'll show you round. This is the assembly room. Everything goes on in here when there's nothing better to do. Through there,' he adds, indicating a squared-off arch, 'the dining room. Beyond that,' indicating a further door, through which several other figures are visible, 'the kitchen. We take domestic duties in strict rotation. A bit like swearing, about which no one gives a fuck. Overhead are the sleeping quarters. I'll show you.'

A flight of concrete stairs leads up: the walls are decorated with the same coagulated image which characterises the surface of the table tennis table: concentric rings depicting a female head, breasts, an infant's head, its limbs and torso here intact.

At the top of the stairs an open corridor circles the building: rooms open off on the inner side. Many of the doors to them are ajar, bedding visible inside. In several a figure gazes out, some acknowledging Patterson, without curiosity, the majority not.

'What's your first name?' he asks.

'Richard.'

'Abbreviated?'

'Rick.'

'I get it. I get it. To rhyme with.'

He indicates the interior of one of the rooms, across the floor of which lies a much-stained mattress, the walls decorated with the image familiar from the hall and the stairs.

'This is Ada's room. She's the one downstairs. She used to be a nurse and wants to be an artist. Maybe you'll talk to her, if you get the chance. I got the message you're something of a poet.'

'Poet?'

'One night I was with Phil at your house. Saw you slip across the hall. Said to Gerry, "Who the fuck was that?" So fast. He said, "That's the genius who lives upstairs. Spends all his time writing. Like a *poet*." Or maybe he said, "That's the cunt who lives upstairs." I was high on something at the time. You smoke?'

'No.'

'Not allowed in here.'

Perhaps Gerry imagined I'd meet O'Connor somewhere else: he has a house in a northern suburb and a consulting room, allegedly, in Welbeck Street: have, I wonder, our messages crossed, he, Gerry, too busy to notice?

'We're an outreach of the psychiatry department at the North London Royal,' Patterson is saying, 'financed by them as well as by the charity which owns the building, and the local Council whose area we happen to be in. Fifteen of our chums are long-term patients. Here they live without the usual supervision, other than Phil or me, or some other doctor. I'm *Doctor* Patterson. We have one American and one Canadian medic visiting, with the idea of setting up something not dissimilar over there. In addition we have several volunteers as nurses, our one prescriptive condition is no medication.'

'Does it work?' I ask, as we return towards the stairs.

'Wouldn't you agree everyone is normal? Come downstairs. We'll make some tea.'

A smell of faeces permeates the landing: one room we pass appears to be smeared with it. I don't enquire and Patterson makes no comment, other than – assuming I've noticed the naked figure curled up on the floor – remarking, once we've reached the stairs, 'Eddie's going through retraction.' Adding, as we descend the stairs, 'That's a return to birth and back again,' concluding, 'Quite jolly,' as we reach the hall.

A horror of the place has slowly formed, I wondering if I might leave before O'Connor appears, the thought no sooner established than the man manifests himself in the space before me: small, dark, pale: he hasn't changed his habitual appearance for his interview with me.

He has emerged, in effect, from a room at the foot of the stairs: its door had previously been closed: an interior occupied by a double mattress laid on the floor, covered by coloured rugs, a shelf above it stacked with books. Similarly several piles of books lie around the floor, along (conspicuously) with an alarm clock with two enormous bells above the hours recording ten and two, a fist-shaped hammer between them. There is also a suitcase, its contents strewn across its open lid: files and sheets of paper litter the floor as well as the mattress and its rugs.

'Showing him round?'

'Just,' Patterson tells him.

'Found us,' O'Connor says to me.

No handshake required.

'Yes.'

'First affirmative I've heard,' Patterson says.

O'Connor is tired: his eyes, at any moment, are about to close: black suit, black shirt, black tie: an affectation, if not a uniform.

The (colourless) slit of his thin-lipped mouth – broad, grimacing, expresses pain: thick dark lines, like hooks, link the corners of the same to the blackness of his nostrils: a gargoyle, for a sudden, hallucinatory moment hanging, invisibly suspended, before me.

'Come in the office.' He indicates the room behind, the softness of the voice is Irish, interrogatory, light: 'Steve'll get some tea. Better, make a cup and bring it here. I'll have one as well. First, there's a phone call I have to make.'

He sets off to the entrance, indicating the way to the kitchen.

Several figures, previously glimpsed, are preparing food: mounds of vegetables are arranged on a trestle table, a cauldron steaming on a gas ring. Three of the occupants are women, one young, two elderly – no telling patient (or 'friend') or nurse (or doctor) apart. Two men, both young, are slicing the vegetables, ill-at-ease with their task.

Patterson, for his part, fills a kettle, pushes two mugs across the table, indicates a tin ('tea bags: milk in the fridge. No sugar for Phil') and, setting a flame beneath the kettle, departs.

By the time I've made the tea one of the older women looks up and says, 'You new?'

'Visiting,' I tell her.

'You'll enjoy it here. Everyone does. Isn't that right?' she enquires of the room.

Neither men nor women answer.

'Welcome to Jubilee Hall. Jubilant by name, jubilant by nature. Isn't that right?' she enquires again.

A murmur of assent follows me to the door.

O'Connor's room, if it is his room, is empty, the figures across the hall still preoccupied with the woman painting on the floor.

I set the mugs by the mattress and examine the books on the shelf. Lucretius, Cicero, Plato, Montaigne, Plutarch, Marcus Aurelius (Petrarch, Dante). The remainder are authors I've never heard of: Jaspers, Kierkegaard, Schopenhauer. There's a writing pad, open: I stoop to read it as O'Connor appears in the door.

I hand him one of the mugs.

'How do you like it?'

'The room?'

'The place as a whole.' Taking the mug, he returns it to the floor, kneeling on the mattress; then, turning round, he sits with his back propped against the wall, indicating I do likewise.

Moving several books aside, I take up a similar position on the adjacent wall.

'Fine.'

'Food's monotonous. I'm trying to get them to ginger it up.' He reaches across, retrieving his tea: something companionable about the gesture. 'You live pretty comfortably,' he adds when I fail to respond.

The slit representing his eyes emits an eerie glow: I recall the 'iconic presence' Gerry referred to when I once naively objected to O'Connor coming to the house. 'What's "iconic"?' I asked, evidently a word provided for him by someone else.

'I've known Gerry for quite some while,' O'Connor goes on. 'I can't say I know him well. You not at all. I did see you at that place you had in Hampstead.'

His suit, its neatness; his leanness: the severity of his gaze: the sense of someone reduced to essentials. I observe the smallness of his hands, dark hair emerging from beneath the sleeves of his jacket: a simian presence, not 'iconic'.

'You like your brother?'

'Yes.'

Small teeth are visible inside the thin-lipped mouth: the bloodless lips, the bloodless head: something reptilian, too; smiling, he waits for my reaction.

A figure appears at the door which, since O'Connor's arrival, has remained open.

'Can I smoke?' the youth who has been playing table tennis enquires.

'What's the rule?' O'Connor says.

'You can't.'

'You said it.'

'What if I want to?'

'You have to put up with bad luck, whenever and wherever you find it.'

'If I go outside.'

'You're not allowed outside.'

'If I go with Steve.'

'Steven hasn't the time.'

'If he has.'

'Ask him.'

The youth glances at me.

'Who's this?'

'A guest.'

'Whose guest?'

'Mine. Close the door. I want to talk to him. Ask for Steven.'

Swinging round, the youth closes the door with a backward flick of his heel, as if used to his dismissal.

'Patrick,' O'Connor says. 'He makes not smoking difficult, though I'm sure he's never tried.'

The small-toothed smile reappears.

Only now, with the door closed, is it apparent how confined the interior is.

'Let me,' he leans back, 'talk about you. Or is there something you'd like to ask?'

'No.'

He smiles again: disarmed or disarming, impossible to tell.

'You're seeing Marjorie Pelling?'

'You know her?'

'Well.'

'How come?'

'We're in the same profession. If it is a profession. She's been here once or twice. How do you get on?'

'She's more at ease with men than women.'

'You think so?'

'Could be hard on women,' I tell him.

'Yes?'

'Somewhat softer,' I tell him, 'with men.'

'I see.'

'I could be wrong.'

'You could.' He smiles again. 'I've talked to her. Told her that Gerry asked me to see you.'

'Unusual.'

'With her I'd say not. Talk to her. Next time you see her. Tell her what you think.'

Someone crashes against the door: 'Sorry!' followed by laughter. I recognise Patrick's voice.

'You live here all the time?' I ask.

'Three or four nights a week. I share the shifts with Steve. One doctor has to be present all the time. Terms of our agreement. Fancy staying?'

'No, thanks.'

'Why not?'

'No privacy.'

'You'd soon get used to it.'

'Don't think so.'

His figure realigns itself against the wall.

The more I listen the more relaxed I feel: how significant this is I've no idea.

'How's your sister-in-law?' he says.

'The same.'

'You like her?'

'A lot.'

'She feels the same, I'm told, about you.'

'She shows no sign.'

'I'm sure she does.'

'She's been that way,' I tell him, 'since I've known her.'

'What way?'

He's leaning back, drawn up against the wall.

'Nuts.'

'You give Gerry,' he says, 'a very hard time.'

'The equivalent of what he gives me,' I tell him.

'You like him,' he says: instruction or enquiry.

'I'm dazzled by him.'

'Dazzled?'

'I don't know anyone who moves so fast.'

'Would you like him if he wasn't your brother?'

'Half-brother,' I tell him.

'How about your father?' He opens his hands – much as if he were opening a book.

'How would I feel about that?'

'Sure.'

Affable: I think his eyes have closed: the light, however, a moment later, flickers beneath the lids: his tongue, briefly, wipes his upper lip.

'I'd feel,' I tell him, 'very odd.'

'Assuming you had the choice, who would you choose to be born inside?'

I glance across.

'Man or woman.' He shrugs.

'The only one would be Martha,' I tell him.

'How often do you see her?'

'Not as often as I should.'

'Why "should"?'

'As she *deserves*,' I tell him, and see, for the first time, where he's going – calmly, indifferently, not turning a hair: a sensation like liquid runs up and down my spine.

I'm aware of sounds outside the door: the scuffling of feet on the concrete stairs: an air of indifference dominates the place, casual, elusive.

Someone overhead is crying.

A voice calls out, '*I don't!*'

'Would that,' he says, 'be your only choice?'

'As a surrogate.'

'For real.'

'Biological?'

'Biological.'

Propped there, his presence removed from the room, something other in its place.

'Is this for real?'

He spreads out his hands as if to indicate not only us but the building: he might have said, 'What's real?' Instead he says, 'That's right.'

Sitting, straightened, he clasps his hands about his knees: compact, homely: I'm aware how clean his shoes are, the congruity of his socks (black, like his suit: the whiteness of his calf exposed): he doesn't give a fuck about anything: it leads him into extraordinary places, fearless, untroubled. Aloof and, at the same time, eerily ignited.

'Why did Gerry never tell me?'

'Because of your mother.'

'Martha.'

'Or Geraldine. You have your choice.'

Again the flicker beneath the lids: a reciprocal flicker, below, of his tongue.

'Is she my mother?'

'What do you think?'

The enquiry comes from behind my head: from anywhere other than the thin-lipped mouth.

'All this time.'

'Some problem,' he concedes.

'Afraid I'd go that way myself.'

'That,' he says, 'and her studio contract. Children not allowed. Except to a studio-approved husband.'

Why, I reflect, do I wish to embrace him? The bearer of indifference: news.

'I reassured him that you wouldn't. Go that way yourself. Of course,' he adds, 'I can't be sure. You have every reason not to. He invited me to the house. You may remember. Had me have a look at you. Asked me, if an appropriate moment came, I'd tell you. Couldn't bring himself to do so.'

'He took a lot on trust.'

'Don't we all?'

Statement, not enquiry: moment to reflect.

'He thought I might go nuts like her?'

'More chance if he *didn't* tell you. Or someone did it for him. He thought of Marjorie Pelling, but came back to me. I've visited your mother several times. Like you,' he adds, 'a remarkable person.'

A sound disproportionate to the room erupts around me.

It impels a silence beyond the door.

A similar silence overhead.

His arm, the next moment, is across my back.

'Quite a thing,' he says, his voice beside my ear: an embrace, in that instant, more intimate than Clare's, more bonding, even, than my brother's . . .

BOOK THREE

1

Gerry isn't in: no doubt he's made a point of not being there; perhaps, by now, he's rung O'Connor and been informed that Richard is a rejuvenated (renovated) figure (better keep out of his way until he can be sure: no knowing what he might get, if not already has got, up to).

I consider going round to his office: could ask Gavin for his views on the same; only Gavin (probably like Gerry) will be at Pinewood. On the other hand, I could ring my aunt. Or uncle. Create a precedent: announce – after all these years – my succession. Formulation. Coming out.

On the other hand I might ring Martha (unable to *witness* her expression, however, when finally addressed as 'Mother!'): listen to her breathing (revived, restored, forgiven).

I have, for the first time, come alive.

I am not responsible for what has happened.

Jubilation appropriate to Jubilee Hall (Gerry right to send me).

I hunt round the flat for money, searching his bedroom, going through his clothes: come across several dollars in a wallet and, making my way to the bank in Berkeley Square, change them into pounds, take a bus to Victoria and pick up a Greenline.

I sit at the front (I should have left a note for Dad: 'All is well. Gone to Mother,' but focus on the road ahead).

Martha (Mother), one and a half hours later, is walking on the lawn at the rear of the house, her arm threaded in that of a middle-aged, stout, white-overalled woman who is talking to her (it seems) in a whisper: a conspiratorial exercise: her eyes – my mother's – meet mine: she watches me without slowing.

I'm conscious of how beautiful she looks (radiant) seen through an offspring's eyes – and wonder if my visit has been preceded by a telephone call, if not from O'Connor, Gerry. 'Here's your brother-in-law,' her attendant says. 'Would you like to walk with him?'

I take her arm, the attendant adding, 'Don't walk Mrs Audlin far. She's due indoors to see the doctor. I'll give a call, if you remain in view,' and she's gone, having handed the disengaged arm to me.

I've reflected on the bus how I might introduce the suggestion I am her son (should have checked it out with Gerry: she is, after all, his wife). Walking for a while in silence I wonder if telepathy will do the trick (love, association, empathy): the natural (even, in the circumstance, unnatural) bond between a mother and her child, unique in our particular situation.

I enquire, 'Have you had any children?' expecting no response.

'Yes,' she says, surprising me with the certainty of her answer.

It draws me to a halt.

Her face is fastidiously made up, the blue eyes shaped by liner and mascara: the sensitive presence of her nose: the clarity of her cheek and brow – her hand, delicate, lightly-veined: the perfume reminds me of Clare. Probably the same (the one Gerry gives to all his women: the trail of his progress I'd never otherwise detect – looking for clues, in my fashion).

'How many?' I ask.

'Lots.'

'Boys or girls?'

She has rarely been so communicative.

'Both.'

'In your films, or in life?'

A risky interjection, warned off by Gerry, and doctors, in the past.

'*Films*.' (I can't tell whether enquiry or statement.) She appears relieved, waving her hand, dismissing the speculation.

'In real life you had one.'

'Did I?'

Unusual, too, to speak so promptly, and at such length.

'Do you remember who that was?'

'I don't think I do.' The subject evidently bores her: nothing unusual, however, in that.

'A boy, do you think, or a girl?'

'A boy.'

Illumination of some sort apparent.

'Where is he?' I ask.

'He died.'

'When?'

'Some time ago.'

She glances away: other clues present themselves, somewhere in the distance.

'How long ago?'

'Long ago.'

We have recommenced our walking.

'What if he didn't die?' I ask.

'He did.'

'How do you know?'

'I killed him.'

She turns, her eyes, despite their blueness, darkening.

'It's why they keep me here.' It's the first direct look she's given me for as long as I recall.

'I've been coming to see you all these years. My name is Richard,' I tell her.

'Richard.' Her look turns away.

'There's no reason to pretend that I'm dead. Philip O'Connor has only just told me.'

First I'm an embarrassment, to be denied, secondly the cause of something that has driven her mad – obtusely, obscurely, perversely mad: another performance she's been required to make: I am looking, however, at a stranger, the more intimate, dynamic relationship denied.

'I'm not pretending anything,' she says, the directness and simplicity of her conduct amazing: it's the way she might have spoken to a director (or to Gerry), defending her interpretation of a part, aware of what she is doing, why she's doing it – defending her craft, her skill, her 'art'.

'There's no need to pretend with me,' I tell her again.

She turns towards me, gazing not so much at as into my eyes.

'Do you remember how we used to hunt for clues at Beaconsfield?' I add.

I intend to startle her: one of her 'clues' she might recall. Is this *film*? no doubt she is thinking. Or has it been introduced (without warning) by someone not involved?

Or is it that ubiquitous thing called 'life'?

For a long time I accept her gaze: what's going on behind it I've no idea: for the first time I wonder if I've done the right thing. Will she disappear entirely?

Someone is waving from the terrace: the attendant: a white-clad arm, and her name, or mine, is called.

'Time,' I tell her, 'to see the doctor. I didn't ring up before I came. I'll wait until you've seen him.'

'Her,' she says.

We are walking up the slope to the terrace: once there, we follow the attendant to the hall: I wait outside a door while Martha, my mother, is taken inside. She is there, alarmingly, a considerable time: not a woman's voice, however, but a man's comes from beyond the door. The attendant, who merely closed the door before retiring, reappears and enquires of my seated figure, 'Still there?'

'She is.'

Disbelief gives way, in her, to apprehension.

'How long are you staying?' she enquires.

'As long as it takes,' I tell her.

This, too, she finds disturbing.

'I'm down the corridor,' she says, 'if you need me. It may be I see you before you leave,' and she's gone.

The male voice murmurs on, the sounds interspersed with a female tone which I don't recognise as my mother's. Nor Martha's.

Perhaps O'Connor's got it wrong: another 'plot' intended to mislead: another false trail, another red herring.

The door re-opens, I, by this time, pacing up and down, Martha reappearing, followed by a figure I've never previously seen: stout, wearing glasses, his hair coiled, spring-like, around his head: a benign, if not benevolent expression: dark eyes, a generous mouth, an air, less of disenchantment (a prevailing medical expression) than bemusement, verging on pleasure.

Seeing me, he nods. 'You Richard?'

I indicate I am, standing perplexed before them: Martha – my mother – examines me with a smile: a parent visiting a child at school, full of the reports of his scholarly behaviour.

'Mrs Audlin's well today. Why don't you come in?' he says.

The room is spacious: books line a wall: windows look onto the lawn and the driveway at the front of the house: a desk, laden with telephones and files, suggests an other-than-recreational function. Several upholstered chairs occupy the floor. Indicating one of them he invites me to sit, my mother taking her place in the one, presumably, she's sat in before. The doctor, if it is he, occupies another.

'Martha's feeling well today,' he says again. 'You've spoken to her, I take it?'

I nod.

His benignity remains.

'About anything in particular?'

'Yes.'

'Martha has a clear recollection of what it was.'

He glances at her for confirmation.

She is regarding me with the same unfathomable expression – not unlike that of someone entering a lighted room, accustomed to the dark outside: as if dazzled, assured of her reception.

'I'm Doctor Ryman, by the way.' He reaches across, rising as I shake his hand: something tenuous, almost abandoned, in his hold. 'Martha has been in the care of a colleague who is away today. I have her notes.' He indicates the desk to one side. 'I'd say something unusual has occurred, wouldn't you?'

I nod again, glancing at Martha for confirmation.

Even now, I might have gone too far, O'Connor's revelation suddenly unreal: is this what Gerry has really planned (given his name to, intended)?

I realise how remarkable my mother looks: the slimness of her figure when (pace Mrs Dover) it might so easily have gone to fat: her extraordinary composure (no longer pathological): the way, for instance, she has crossed her legs, her hands clasped, casually, in her lap (the only sign of apprehension the way, after a moment, she bites her lower lip, at one time the prelude to her making an effort to respond to something she suspects is beyond her comprehension).

Her head is in profile against the light from the window: sharp, authoritative, dynamic: a woman in charge of herself.

'She refers to you as her son.'

'That's good,' I tell him. 'I've only just been told myself.'

'I've rung her husband. He's rung me back. A difficult man to get hold of.'

I wait: admonition or approval associated with Doctor Ryman's silence, hard to tell.

'Martha has been able to recall something of your past.'

She, for her part, examines the doctor's face intently: this might be the part she intends (she has been cast) to play – her interpretation of it: a climactic demonstration of her art, summoning up lives – a life – she assumed was past, at the worst had been forgotten.

'That's of interest, isn't it?'

'Yes.'

I'm not inclined to disagree.

'You, for instance, as a child.'

A heated charge around my chest: a sudden burning behind my ears: a constraint, so it feels, on breathing at all.

'In America.'

'Right.'

'A shock.'

'Yes.'

'To you both.'

He looks to her for confirmation: she, more than anyone, looks composed: a body accustomed to playing a role, an intrusion which galvanises others into action.

My love for her, I am aware, has been there all the time, a formality, almost, instinctively presented – requiring no response, no recognition: where she is is where I am: what she is is what I am (all those journeys on Greenline buses).

And maybe, throughout this time, an equally subliminal recognition in her, too: her transposition of the same to an obscure displacement of a clinical need.

'I remember,' she says, gazing vacantly before her, 'a swimming pool. Not long after his mother dies. That was how it all began.'

Tears, a distillation of light, appear around her eyes – moving down her cheek, she raising her hand to arrest them.

I offer her my handkerchief, rising from my chair: she takes it with no sign of recognition, then hands it back. 'Thank you,' she says, but doesn't move her head, her gaze fixed on the doctor as if he is the source of her recollection.

'Swimming with his father,' she adds. 'Confusing, to begin with, not knowing he wasn't to be mine. His mother . . .' she continues, glancing across at me. 'It did him, I believe, a very bad turn. The studio insisted. Gerry said . . . Now I'm here I feel quite well,' this the longest speech I recall her making: mechanically, she extends her hand for me to take: a formal gesture, her fingers warm and hearteningly firm, as if my hand were enclosed by those of a child. 'Like swimming under water for a very long time and coming up in a place where everything has changed,' a radiant, still composed expression.

'Your husband's coming to see you,' the doctor says.

'Here?'

'Here.'

She glances at me.

'Gerry is coming to see you,' she says.

The room takes on an identity other than its own.

'Us,' she amends.

Some while later, holding my hand, we go out to the tea room: a place of tables and basketwork chairs where patients and visitors are seated. Tea is brought on trays from a distant counter, and Ryman, who has suggested this 'break' ('I'll talk to your husband, Mrs Audlin, when he arrives'), having accompanied us to the room, disappears.

'How much did you know?' I ask her.

The question eludes her: she shakes her head.

'My mind is full of drugs,' she says. 'I'm not sure who I am. The same,' she adds, 'must go for you,' a formality still between us (this, too, a part she assumes she must play).

We watch, in silence, the others in the room: it might be a tea room in a tourist hotel.

My identity recedes, in unison with her own: in its place, a space in which nothing of significance occurs, the present too obscure, too tenuous, too fragile to rely on.

Finally, we walk: the corridors, the terrace, the lawn. Gerry arrives as dusk is falling – a studio car, with a chauffeur who, dismissed, goes off in search of a cup of tea – Gerry walking up the steps of the terrace towards us, looking from one face to another, recognising us with something of a startled expression. He embraces us both, she unsure who he is: his arm around each of us, we turn along the terrace.

He doesn't say anything, others observing us from the windows of the house: she is, after all, the 'star' of the place, sheltered, secreted, hidden, in her decline.

A family reunited, a long time, it feels, apart.

'Quite a day,' his voice murmurs above my head: murmurs, too, beside my ear: murmurs, obscurely, something else. The word 'precocious' comes to mind, an allusion to something he fails to understand.

This (evidently) in the midst of filming: 'the greatest crisis of his life'.

'This beats everything I've ever felt,' characteristically looking for superlatives. 'There isn't anything,' evidently, 'to describe it,' drawing back to observe the effect of his announcement, Martha, despite her confusion (it's been a long day), drawing back as if to place herself precisely: is this further role consistent with her previous interpretation?

The doctor summons us from a window, stepping onto the terrace to make the gesture clear. We return to the room where we were before, Gerry retaining my arm as well as Martha's, his look drawn queryingly from face to face. 'You all right?' he asks me as we enter.

'Sure.'

'Was Phil okay?'

'He was.'

A light illuminates the doctor's desk, I realising, suddenly, why there are so many chairs in the room: more than one person, more than two persons, are often involved: two separate pools of light are reflected in the darkening windows: figures still drift along the terrace.

'I've left you – I will leave you – to talk between yourselves,' the doctor says: his wirely-sprung hair glistens in the shaded light – incandescent as he moves his head, his eyes speculative, enquiring.

Gerry looks not merely strained (a day's shooting, then a drive across country, the following week's schedule already on his mind) but vanquished: the thin-ice skater pauses – rocks back on his heels (the cracks catching up on either side – catching up and ever-widening): he has, by some stratagem, to take us with him – or leave us, stranded, on the bank.

'It requires you to readjust yourselves,' the doctor adds, I no longer listening, merely watching: a fractured expression, an assemblage of disparate parts, illuminated eerily by the nearest lamp: he might be all three of us, drawn together.

Gerry, despite his exhaustion, listens intently: he sits, childlike, holding Martha's hand, he the supplicant, she the provider: occasionally he glances across at me, wishing we were closer, I anxious to allow him to witness the miraculous change in her himself. There is much, for instance, he would like to ask: 'Is she cured?' dreading anything other than an affirmative answer.

Yet the doctor is saying she will have to stay. 'Stay on,' he says. 'Though I hope you'll be free to see her,' Gerry's equivocal response to this 'greatest moment in our lives' superseded by another, if of his own invention. 'Until Martha is sure. I'm confident, from what I've seen today, we'll soon be able to tell,' I thinking of the lousy apartment she'll come home to. Events, as usual, have forced themselves upon us. This, I am concluding, is more than we can stand (a suite at the Ritz, or Brown's, in lieu of what she/we pay out here).

I am looking at my parents *in situ*, for the first time seeing them as such together, I suddenly, unmistakably, a *son*.

I travel back with Gerry in the car, an earlier suggestion I stay overnight abandoned when it becomes apparent that the day, for Martha, has been too long: she wilts as we see her to her room, I withdrawing for Gerry to call me in before we leave. Martha sitting there, wearing a nightgown, her tiredness – her absence, even – showing in the light from the bedside lamp: a filmic image (purposely created: 'see us together,' Gerry might have said), he sitting on the bed beside her.

So much for love.

He says little in the car, the driver someone I've only glimpsed before though he drives Gerry to the studio each day (and drives him, occasionally with Gavin, back). He talks, principally, about the day's shooting, implying it's best not to talk about anything else, the conversation upbeat, jolly: a characteristic piece of skating for a spectator he doesn't wish to be well-informed.

Secondly, he talks about Jubilee Hall, though markedly not about my visit. He's been there once to give a talk, and has a standing invitation to give another (lectures something O'Connor is noted for giving, celebrities of every description flooding in to hear him. Several of his performances have, through Gerry's offices, been recorded on film). 'Phil's a celebrity. He has, fortunately, unlike some, a sense of humour,' not caring to expand on this. 'Madness as a social event. How, despite the best intentions, we drive one another crazy.'

The back of the driver's head: the headlights tunnelling in the darkness: we're taking an unfamiliar route.

'I like him,' is Gerry's (confident) summing-up: concordance with the way the day has gone: things are looking up (if the ice is getting thinner, he is still outpacing the cracks). He has taken something out of his pocket: having looked at it, he returns it, inside his jacket. A moment later he switches on a light above his head, extracts what is evidently a sheet of paper – a memo! – unfolds it, gets out a pair of glasses I've never seen before, and reads it. Confirming something (he seems unfazed), he puts it back again, together with the glasses (his effortless gait, one ice-skimming blade alternating with the other) and switches off the light. It's like watching a sprinter's head which, despite the momentum of his body, scarcely appears to move at all.

He looks across, his face illuminated by the reflected glow inside: he touches my arm, the first physical contact since leaving Market Whelling when he'd indicated I get in the car before him. 'We have to make up for a lot of lost time,' his coded message. 'Ever since you went up to Jimmy's things have changed so quickly. Now this.' He nods, indicating, in the presence of the driver, I needn't respond: he is referring to what no doubt he is going to conclude is 'a successful day', the outcome of which, however, he can't be sure. 'Things can never be the same,' signalling with another nod.

'Right,' I tell him.

'We can talk about that later.'

'Sure.'

The driver, unnerved, finally, by the silence behind him (uncharacteristic where transporting Gerry is concerned), remarks about the traffic: 'Easier going in than coming out, Mr Audlin.'

'We had a hell of a job coming out,' Gerry says. 'But for Charlie knowing a back route we'd have been another couple of hours. Normally, going to and from Pinewood, we're against the rush. Coming out to Market Whelling we were caught in the middle.'

The rest of the journey we complete with observations about the route, not Gerry sitting beside me but my father, a father I know as intimately, as confederately, as I would a brother: something we shared has been broken apart, replaced by something the nature of which I will, perhaps, never be able to recognise.

Once in the apartment Gerry makes for the phone, pausing after dialling to pour a drink, the instrument tucked between his chin and shoulder.

Finally, after speaking swiftly, receiving a reply, he speaks once more and replaces the receiver. Turning to me he says, 'Do you want one?' I shaking my head, waiting, as he is, for me to respond. His face is grave: he is sitting across the characterless room: a piece of free-wheeling he can so easily slip into, his figure stretched out along the couch: 'Tell me something!' his eyes voraciously invite.

Maybe we're past the point of saying anything: I am transferring 'authenticity' from one thing to another – in transition, going where, from where, I've no idea. 'Why did you do it?' I (inevitably) ask.

Uncertain how direct an enquiry this is – uncertain, perhaps, what specifically it alludes to, he gets up and crosses to the window (uncurtained: looking out to the vandalised – as offices – houses across the street). Gazing out, he drinks from the glass still in his hand, then crosses to the door and closes it (although there's no one in the place but us).

'To protect you.'

'From what?'

'Do you know what a star's life was *like* in those days? Martha was run by the studios. They didn't approve of her getting married. Let alone to me. The fact that you were on the way made it an unimaginable situation. She refused to abort you. *We* refused to abort you. This was the best way we could think of at the time.'

He has rehearsed this maybe a thousand times: it doesn't come out as he'd intended: bleak, intractable, unforgiving – as if, even, I'm the one to blame.

Having raised his glass to drink, he lowers it: the glass is empty, yet still he holds it.

'I don't know what my father would have thought. Had he been alive. Probably approved, if not applauded. As it was, his widow screwed him for every cent he had. Which wasn't much. She did the best thing by us and died. At the opportune time. We were always worried you'd look up the dates. That's why we said they were both cremated. *Father*'s grave is still up there. Large as life. Jimmy was on tenterhooks you'd ask to see it.'

'I was born at sea,' I remind him.

'Something vague about the sea, don't you think?' (It hasn't ice, for one thing, covering the whole of it.) 'We took off a month before you were due. Before that we bummed around in Mexico, avoiding the press. Puerto Bueno a dump we ended up at. There we borrowed a good friend's yacht. Sailed to the Virgin Islands, hoping you'd pop out on the way. Didn't. Turned round when the press got wind. Sailed in the opposite direction. The midwife we called on board didn't recognise Martha because she lived in a settlement off the St Lawrence Seaway. Gave her a week's cruise during which you belatedly appeared. After that, trusting to luck, we put out the story. I don't think we really cared any more. Not about you. The circumstances. As luck would have it, we didn't have to. Unfortunately, shortly after that, Martha's symptoms first appeared. Post-natal blues evolved into something we could scarcely recognise. It seemed the wisest thing, to stick to what we'd arranged. Luck ran out in an unexpected fashion. Maybe all that time on the boat was not a good idea. It all seemed *fun* to us at the time. Beating the system. As for the studios, they were always good at that sort of thing. Give them a fuck-up and, if it was in their interest, it never occurred.'

He watches me for several seconds, remaining standing.

He is, I can see, in a pre-skating pose: any moment now he will whisk away: perhaps there *is* someone else in the apartment, waiting in his bedroom.

'We were very much in love.'

'So what?'

'The blame for the whole of it lies with me. The fabrication. The *story*. Martha, for her part, loved you very much. She wanted you more than anything. Then grew too ill to do anything about it. It all seemed easier, as time went on, to keep to the arrangement we'd set in place.'

'You didn't want me to think I had a crazy mother.'

'Sure.'

'But I have.'

'You can see my concern, what it's been, all this time.'

'And now?'

'Now we have to sort it out as it is. You're okay. I know it in my gut.'

'You've known a lot of things in your gut,' I tell him.

'Not all of them,' he says, 'have turned out badly.' Not waiting for me to respond, he adds, 'Martha could command any picture she wished to make when you were conceived. Acting was her life.

She loved it. She couldn't *be* married to a limey liaison officer with the American Second Fleet. As for you, the birth *wasn't* difficult, just delayed. The hormonal effect must have changed her. There were times when it seemed she wasn't there. Odd when she'd been able to focus on nothing but you the previous hour. It was as if she took off, *inside*, and left us. *Went*.'

He pauses, not waiting long for my reaction: none forthcoming, he says, 'Jimmy had given her several books. "Murder at the Vicarage" sort of thing. She became preoccupied, first with *England*, then with rural life. Her ancestors, she told me, had come from Devon. She had someone look it up. Beaconsfield, too. We went there. It was near the studios. By the time we got there, however, I was convinced she was nuts. But because she wanted it so much I agreed to it, thinking it might save her. It did for a while. Or seemed to. She made one film over here. Then I discovered she was taking you round the houses, looking in windows, hiding in bushes, looking for *clues*. Some of the locals reported her. If she hadn't have been Geraldine O'Neill she'd have been arrested.'

He is sitting, perched on the edge of the couch, his legs at an angle, I sunk in its depths (receiving this as I might a blow to the head: whether an over-indulgent mark of affection or the prelude to an assault, impossible to tell).

'Maybe what we did was wrong. Hide the fact she'd had a child by a guy who registered less than zero in the picture-making racket. The fact that we pulled it off seemed, at the time, a remarkable feat. As I say, we beat the system.'

He decides to get another drink and, rising, crosses to the cabinet where it's stored.

'Want anything to eat?'

I shake my head.

'I'll get something. I'm starving. Maybe Mrs Summers,' he says, referring to the woman he's hired to look after the place, 'has put something out. I said we'd be late.'

I'm left reflecting on what he's told me: a blind man groping in a room he's never been in before.

For some reason I'm thinking of the girl on the train: I had thought of her rarely while staying with James and Clare (what new identity will I acquire with them?). Why I am thinking of her I have no idea: a peer, a companion, the only one at present 'on a par', and yet unknown and, at this stage, at least, unknowable. A fellow nihilist: a cynic.

Our times have made us both.

No sooner has this thought occurred than Gerry reappears, a sandwich in his hand: he is chewing, intending, perhaps, to invite me to the kitchen – something familiar in the impulse yet, in the current context, dispiriting. He suspects he's 'got away with it', his first triumph capped (compounded) by another. It's no big deal, his manner suggests: he's been doing something not dissimilar all his life: it doesn't change *us*. It binds us, if anything, closer. And Martha: look at the improvement. Ryman has seen nothing like it (even though she isn't his patient). Wait until he tells O'Connor. It's worked out in the end.

Maybe I'm reading too much into it; maybe he's not feeling this at all: he's coasting, allowing his momentum to propel us along – off-hand, exhausted. 'What do you think?'

He doesn't want a direct answer: a euphemism will do: he is looking for a response which will move him, glidingly, away from the bank.

'What about Martha?'

I almost say, 'My mother.'

'Martha?' Concern back in his voice.

'The changes are more than she can cope with. She looked ill, I thought, before we left.'

'You told her about us.'

'Us?'

'You being her son.'

'I tried to.'

'How did she respond?'

'Mixed.'

'Mixed?'

He doesn't like it.

'She thought I'd died.'

'A metaphor,' he says. 'A symbol.' Not sure what he might mean by this, he adds, 'She's had a lot to take in. Or rather,' he goes on, 'to take off. She's removed herself from a *husk*. She's an *actress*. A brilliant one. She's like she would be after a wonderful day's shooting. The following morning – it's all like new.'

The past, until I pronounce it – until *she* pronounces it – has not been appeased: on none of our parts will it go away. Too much is involved.

'Today,' he says, 'has been astonishing. O'Connor's right. It was the *appropriate* thing to do.' He is standing in the door, the sandwich, half-eaten, in his hand. 'There's no longer a need to dissemble. As you say' (have I said it?), 'she plays the leading part. We are, and always were, in the hands of her performance. How did you get on with Phil?'

'Okay.'

He moves from one to the other with familiar speed.

'Like him?'

'Not much.'

'Genius is like that.'

'Is he a genius?'

'Wouldn't you say so?'

'I wouldn't know.'

'He's seen so many people go nuts. His insights, however, are unimpeachable. He sees Martha, of course, as a relavent case.'

'To what?'

'The system.'

'I thought you were the system,' I tell him.

Has always seemed so.

'I was an independent before the word ever got around.'

He is thinking, no doubt, of 'The Studios', a mythology difficult to overrate: nevertheless, I'm sure he does. Overrate. Them and her.

I overrate her, too, if on entirely different grounds.

'You seem to have misgivings,' he says.

'What you did – disguise my birth, ascribe it to another (as it turns out, inappropriate) couple – may have turned her mind. Condemned to live out her life with a surrogate child knowing he wasn't surrogate but her own, turns her *existence* into a surrogate existence – tragic and alarming. A diabolical waste, turning both her public and her private life into a performance. No wonder she became a detective. Convinced there'd been a crime. Someone was responsible. If she looked long enough she might even find a clue. Done, the whole of it, through *love*. Did you ask O'Connor about that?'

He is thinking – a phrase I have overheard him using in reference to his 'brother' – 'he can't get it *all* from me'. Presumably, some, if not a lot of it, comes from *her*: an innate intelligence, implicit in her, explicit in me.

'O'Connor would probably agree that was the *inadvertent* effect,' he says.

'If not the intended one. The subliminally intended one,' I tell him.

The Audlin provenance, going by what he has said about his father (what about his mother?), is not a likeable one.

Father and son, again, in this scenario, in conflict with one another: having consumed the last of the sandwich, another drink in his hand, he sinks on the couch beside me.

'So that's why you think the cinema's crap,' he tells me, summing up.

Side by side, I alert, he similarly so, the glass between his hands.

'Not only that,' I tell him.

'I see what you mean about O'Connor.'

'That's good.'

'The war has a lot to answer for. I see you as a casualty as well.'

'How?'

His remark surprises me: not something he's in the habit of doing.

'The studio system, for instance. The breakup of that a direct result. The system that had made both Martha and me,' a novel experience to be skating, not with Gavin, or his *brother*, but his *son*. 'My mind goes haywire when I'm tired. Maybe we've taken it as far as we can tonight. As you say, it was done in the name of love.'

He is about to add, 'Not in the name but the *reality* of love.' All he does, however, is place his arm around my shoulder and say, 'I love you, kid.'

The poor, suffering, incompetent sonofabitch.

2

I fall asleep on the couch, waking several hours later to find a travelling rug thrown over me and a note laid on the floor between me and the door. 'Go to school. Not to Market Whelling. When we next go we'll go together. Possibly this evening.' And then, incredibly, 'Love. Dad.' Ironically appended, in brackets, 'Your Father'.

We don't go that evening, but in the afternoon: he drops in at the crammer and hauls me out of a class. He has the car with Charlie the chauffeur who drives us to Market Whelling at, in my view, excessive speed (Gerry keen to get back to the set before evening?): a police car, at one point, draws abreast and signals us to ease down.

He hates to be away from the film, yet is keen to press home his advantage: no doubt he's already consulted O'Connor on the best way to proceed (his guru on the psychic front as Gavin, if less so, is on the business).

It's a sunny day, the countryside welcoming, Gerry gesturing at the fields, the hedgerows, the distant hills: 'Fresh. Enlivened. What d'you think?' his confidence increasing. Skating each day on thinning ice, he recognises a safe stretch when he sees one – my credentials as a *son* finally accepted: at one point he begins to sing, the sound scarcely louder than a murmur, the words indecipherable.

A lightening of the heart (even mine) as we enter the drive, a feeling of expectancy (in him), if not of triumph: he lowers the window, breathing deeply, his eyes half-closed: a breeze blows through the car prompting (again, no doubt, in him) a feeling of renewal.

'Take it easy,' he says, as we get out by the pillared porch, 'with our *mother*,' the lightness in his manner persisting – unlike the intensity of his look (one of anticipation): something like this must have characterised him as a youth, or in his first day in the navy, the future an excitingly open book.

She is not in the hall, nor on the terrace, nor visible across the lawns. He has already spoken to her on the phone, though nothing of relevance, he implies, has passed between them.

Most patients, I assume, must be asleep (a post-lunch practice much encouraged): few are evident in the corridors or on the stairs. An unusual air of relaxation characterises the place, associated, presumably, with this time of the day: lassitude, inertia. An odour of food drifts down from the restaurant: a figure passes – young, male: he signals with one finger raised to his brow, a self-mocking salute responded to by Gerry.

Her room door is open, her clothes on the bed. 'Not here,' Gerry says as he approaches her bathroom door.

He remains inside for several minutes: inappropriate, I sense, to follow.

When he comes out his manner has changed. Identifying the phone by the bed, he raises it and, getting no response, replaces it and says, 'We'll find a doctor.'

His face has undergone a remarkable transformation.

'What's the problem?' I ask.

'She's not here.' He speaks in a daze – unusual in someone normally relaxed, the prodigal, prodigious, inveterate 'mover'.

'Did she say anything when you spoke to her this morning?' I ask.

He has turned me to the door, not bothering, oddly, to look in her dressing room, the door of which is also open.

'She sounded okay. Not sure of who I was. To be expected. After all this time.'

He stops a figure in the corridor outside, asking for directions, glancing back for me to follow.

We skate – gracefully, swiftly: the way he holds his head, his neck, his shoulders, particularly, as now, when we move at speed. He knocks on a door, enters, disappears – reappearing to announce, 'Not there.'

'Who are we looking for?' I ask.

'*Anyone*,' he tells me. 'Why have they left her,' he asks me, '*alone*?'

Then we encounter, hurrying towards us, two female attendants I recognise and a suited male figure I have never seen before.

'I heard you'd arrived. We can go in here,' he says, dismissing the two women.

As tall as Gerry – a curious replica of him, if younger – dressed in a grey suit, white shirt, dark tie: I take in the particulars as we enter the room where, the previous day, we've seen Ryman. A figure is standing at the bookshelves, female, skirted, her back to the door. This, too, I take in, assuming, for a moment, it might be her.

'Could you leave us?' the suited figure enquires. He indicates the chairs, still in position from where we have sat the previous evening.

The woman, bowing, has gone to the door, closing it behind her.

'I'm Doctor Stepney. Doctor Ryman is away.' He dismisses this with a wave of his hand, waiting for Gerry to be seated, then myself.

'Has anything happened?' Gerry's gaze – my father's gaze – remains fixed on his younger facsimile's face: a hawk-like presence, rounded eyes set deeply on either side of a prominent nose, the mouth, thin-lipped, broad, used to expelling thought in lieu of feeling.

'I'm afraid I've bad news,' leaning forward to the desk, realities involved of which we cannot, even remotely, be aware – looking to enquire of Gerry if I should stay.

'It's okay.'

The way he would signal a shot on the studio floor: a climactic moment for both of us.

'Mrs Audlin injured herself this lunchtime. She ran the bath in her room, climbed in, and cut her wrists. There's no doubt of her intention.'

Maybe my reaction I'm projecting onto Gerry: a bolt driven, for instance, up the centre of the body: the mind flashes in the message and, just as swiftly, flashes it out.

'Is she dead?' the words placed like objects on the desk, this a scene where the script has several possibilities, not least that she still is alive, the worst of the news already broken.

'I'm very sorry. It was when she failed to come through for lunch . . .'

The words arrive with coldness, precision.

'The wisdom of telling her what she was told yesterday is, of course, in question.'

Of course.

Gerry looks at me as if, at that moment, he is falling off a cliff – or through the ice, this, the look tells me, the end of everything between us.

'Did she speak to anyone?' he asks.

'She spoke to you this morning.'

'Briefly.'

'To no one else we know.'

'I got the impression she was excited at our coming. Very much so. I brought it forward from the evening because of that.'

This is the beginning of lunacy, my inheritance, the legacy she has left me.

'If she's still here I'd like to see her.'

The words could be mine but, more certainly, are his.

My chair is angled to the window: this was where Martha was

sitting the previous evening – someone, in reality, I scarcely knew – and yet know better now than anyone.

Gerry is rising, the figure behind the desk crossing to the door: the route is being described to a hospital. I am, to all intents and purposes, still focused on the chair. What have I done which was incorrect? Has the body she sought turned up at last?

Is everything to be like this for ever?

Charlie's impassive figure before us, we drive in silence, occasionally stopping for instructions – the hospital, a modern edifice, finally appearing across farm fields. The attendant at the reception-counter appears to have been forewarned: we are directed to a corridor leading to the rear of the building: a flight of steps descends to a subterranean passage.

There are chairs around the room to which we are finally shown. Invited to sit we scrutinise the interior – windowless, illuminated by plastic panels let into the ceiling – Gerry unsure, I can see, of what we ought to do, stunned, grave – submitting himself to forces of which he has had no previous experience: none of this accords with how he is: it all goes on without him, without me, I an afterthought (almost an abortion).

I wonder if he will speak: he looks at me, I look at him: his breathing, as in the car, emerges in gasps and groans.

The overalled attendant who has directed us to the room reappears through a further door: he beckons us to enter.

'You don't have to come in,' Gerry says.

'I have to.'

Wordless, he signals me before him.

In the room beyond a figure, unrecognisable as Martha, lies on what I assume to be a bier. There is no light other than from a frosted panel let into the lowered ceiling.

She is lying beneath a sheet, her head considerably smaller than anything I recall, her skin grey, green, obscene: only slowly do I recognise the arching of the nose, the contour of the cheek: the colour of her hair.

How could she choose to end like this? What, I enquire, has she achieved?

The sheet reveals the configuration of her body: her feet, her hips: it ends beneath her chin in a folded, clinical, clear-cut line.

Gerry is feeling for her hand: half his arm disappears beneath the sheet: words, until now unformed, are suddenly clear. 'Oh, my dear,' he says, 'my love.'

I look into her face: her nostrils, her ears, her mouth: it's as if, even now, she's about to speak, her lips, like her eyelids, not fully closed.

Almost mechanically I kiss her brow, her skin colder than anything I have ever known.

'Maybe,' Gerry says, 'I should be alone.'

It's as if he's announcing he, too, has died.

I sit outside for an immeasurable time, Gerry coming into the room so quietly I'm unaware. His eyes are reddened, his face is wet. 'Do you want to see her on your own?' he says.

Placing his hand on my shoulder, he walks me to the door.

The attendant, having entered from a door the other side, is about to remove the body.

I, unable to express precisely what I want, enquire, 'Could I see my mother?'

He goes, his look avoiding mine, adjusting the sheet before departing.

Nothing has changed: I expect her, at any moment, to open her eyes, explain this is a scene which, if rehearsed, has been excised – instead, her silent, impressive, final expression (this, it informs me, the end of the road).

BOOK FOUR

1

I am sitting in the dining car – fuller than on the previous occasion – writing.

She is, at first, I believe, a mirage – taking the seat opposite, putting out her hand, announcing, 'I thought it was you when we first came in,' indicating not one figure but three sitting at a nearby table: her parents, I assume, and the previous companion.

Two other people are sitting at my table. She, concluding from my expression they have nothing to do with me (an elderly man and woman finishing their tea), adds, 'I heard so much about you and your mother.'

The word 'mother' reverberates around the carriage, the macabre story ('the crime') has been prominently in the press (on television, on the radio), wherever the legend of Miss Geraldine O'Neill finds favour.

Only in one report has there been a reference to her 'son': his attendance at the funeral (cremated: the ashes to be taken to – of all places – a so-far unnamed village in Devon). Gerry, meanwhile, the recipient of tributes to his 'stoicism', his 'courage' ('fidelity' to a woman he 'never abandoned': the 'tragedy' of her inglorious decline).

Death doth not leave us but accompanies us in the happiest of guises – runs the rhythm of the wheels as I write my memorandum – glancing up to see her.

'We see a great deal of your *aunt*,' she says.

She gestures to her companions: hazel eyes, reddish hair, a hybrid colouring, pale skin, plainer – significantly plainer, I decide – than on the previous occasion, I realising she wears no make-up.

'And your uncle.'

'How?' I enquire.

'We belong to the same societies. Particularly the Historical. In our town it's very strong.'

I am travelling back to Clare – and James – because, I assume, Gerry can think of nothing else to do with me, the limited time he can give to me increasing his anxiety, which arouses his irritability, his irritability provoking his increasing sense of desolation (our living together impossible).

In addition, of course, I remind him of *her*.

I've seen O'Connor again, at Gerry's (absurd) suggestion – not, this time, at Jubilee Hall but in his flat: he has recently left his wife and children and is living with a ménage of fellow analysts and their admirers above a shop in Marylebone High Street: an unchastened figure, receptive (attentive) to what I have to say (not a lot), he anxious I get my feelings 'into the open'. 'She would have done it in any case. She was only waiting the chance' (his conclusion).

'Did you know that *before* you told me?' I enquire, he regarding me for some time before he shakes his head.

'You were her only chance to do otherwise,' he says.

Tough – and delicate – this current Martha: I wondering why I likened her to someone who was my mother (unlike her in appearance), and realise it is the disregard with which she apprehends everything, not only me (for which I find, surprisingly, I am grateful: a fellow spirit, too, of course).

Gerry is putting me 'in care' ('with someone who loves you. I've talked to her. And James. We've all been very *frank*').

'Odd, the coincidence,' Martha says. 'Meeting like this. I believe in coincidence. Governed by things we otherwise never see.'

Small, even teeth, thin lips, broad and upward-curving: smiling.

'You think so?'

'Yes.'

She looks at me intently: 'You look much *older*,' she adds.

'I am.'

'Even than that.'

She smiles again.

'The Literary Society,' she says, 'is another. An interest which your aunt and particularly your uncle share.'

'I'm not up on literature,' I tell her.

'They tell me that you are.'

'Mistaken.'

'Didn't I see you writing?'

'A reminder.'

'Of what?'

'I forget.'

She laughs, leaning back, at which the couple on the inside table decide to leave, I standing to allow them past: a bow from the man, a smile from the woman.

Another scenario, a different film.

She is – I know the signs – signalling her calling, her hands, her delicate hands – rings on her fingers – additional signs of self-possession.

A dark jacket, a white blouse – presumably a skirt, hair curved, rather than curled, around her ears: her chin, with its hint of stubbornness, reminds me of my mother.

'Another trip to London?' I ask.

'It was.'

'If I'd known we could have met.'

'I thought you'd probably have had enough to deal with,' the fields, the woodland flying past, somewhere in the same latitude as Market Whelling.

I am, seeing my reflection in the glass, marking my removal: Grosvenor Street, the office, Audlin Productions, Pinewood: the cremation, I standing with Gerry at the door (at his insistence) greeting everyone on departure, the 'son and heir' (at last).

Ordained by him, I imagine, this meeting (he, unlike the previous occasion, taking time out to see me off at King's Cross), I, involuntarily, glancing round for the girl, not seeing her, and then, just as absently, forgetting her: another element in the script which he is busily (I imagine) rewriting: 'Don't think this is for ever,' he whispers as he embraces me. 'Just until this film is over,' waving as the train slides out ('We're the only family left,' he tells me. 'But for James and Clare').

He is not cut out for 'family': he is only cut out for speed: anyone passing him in the street would not realise who or what he was. What I am. What *she* is: we speed along together.

'And that other coincidence,' she says.

'Other?' I enquire.

This I've forgotten, her appearance alone my preoccupation.

'I only knew of her as Geraldine O'Neill. Why did she change it to that?'

'Too provincial. Matriarchal. Her surname too *English*.'

This is it, bringing our independent tracks together – wheeling, arrested, rocking back – a dangerous procedure.

'Why don't I introduce you to my parents?'

'Probably not.'

'That's okay.' Amused, she adds, 'Pushing it too far.'

'I very much came up to be on my own.'

'Want me to go?'

'Maybe I should take your number,' copying it down as she dictates, she adding, 'Yours I've got. Mr and Mrs Audlin's,' and, shaking my hand, is gone – taking her seat along the carriage, smiling down the length of it, her parents and her companion glancing back.

It's Clare – more shrunken than before – who recognises me down the platform: our kisses amusingly collide, the intimacy of our previous encounter subsumed in the ambivalence of our embrace:

the moistness of her lips, the smell of her perfume, the fragility of her figure.

In the car her hand comes across to clasp my own (she has come alone to meet me): little, initially, is said, much unspoken. 'You'll see great changes in the garden. Wasn't that Martha Armitage I saw at the station?' she finally enquires. 'Her parents and she we often meet.'

'So she said.'

'You spoke to one another?'

'I took her number.'

I am watching the familiar road unwind as we drive up out of town. 'James is at work,' she explains. 'Though he's looking forward to seeing you. We've missed you,' she concludes, 'so much. Me, need I say, of course, especially.'

The mechanics of the process preoccupy me the most: one in which I have had, previously, by her, to be instructed: the look in her eyes, as if the penetration had reached this far inside, the suffusion flooding the warmth of her face: the final candour of her smile as she draws back to examine mine.

Is this, I reflect, what Gerry (and James) have arranged?

'We must seem,' I tell her, 'a strange household.'

We are back downstairs in the sitting room, awaiting James's return from work (the sun setting on the hill at the back of the house, penetrating the windows at the front).

'Strange to whom?'

I gesture round. 'Your housekeeper. Your friends.'

'You're a celebrity,' she says. 'I can't tell you how high you've risen in their esteem since the tragedy of your mother. I want you to talk about it as freely as you wish. We're able to offer each other so much. The tragedy,' she goes on, 'affects us all. Each one of us has played a part.'

We sit admiring one another – I her humour, her smile (her accessibility) the most constant thing about her: 'We must move forward from this together,' she tells me. 'I spoke to Gavin who says Gerry is more devastated than when Ian died. That man is plagued by tragedy. I don't know why he doesn't leave that business. Surely he's made enough by now? If he hasn't, it's not through want of trying. And Martha. Her estate. It all devolves to you.'

'When I come of age.'

'Held in trust by Gerry.'

I am well endowed, Gerry dependent on me for whatever wealth we have: much, however, has been spent on Homes, though homes, ironically, we've never had.

Or have I finally reached one?

That evening we celebrate my return by going into town: Clare's favourite restaurant: Dougall's: an Edwardian interior of wood-panelled walls, coats-of-arms and discreetly illuminated paintings (landscapes, mainly) – full of women, most of whom she appears to know: the enclosure and, at the same time, the outward-looking, the self-assurance, the generous regard: a 'mother', on the one hand, an idealised 'sport', on the other – one of those agencies put on earth to enthrall, distract (no more untruths or half-truths between us): no more dissemblement, subterfuge, lies: even the waiters call out to her: 'Mrs Audlin! Good to see you!' she taking my arm as we leave.

Life at 'Uplands' – as they have named the house since my previous visit – a plaque on the metal gates – begins: a way of life which takes me, on several occasions, to James's office, a recently converted structure fronting the rejuvenated river, with its walks and gardens, restaurants and flats replacing the quays, warehouses, factories and mills.

His office occupies the second floor of the building, looking across the river to the pleasure craft moored by the opposite bank: a desk stands asymmetrical to the window so that he can simultaneously look out and at whoever comes in the door. From a drawer, on one visit, he produces a file: a ream of closely written-on sheets, the scrawl of ink, at first sight, a hieroglyphic (a sense of writing done with a frantic, ferocious concentration). Similarly, at home, he has shown me his study at the back of the house – looking up to the hill with its crest of pines – producing from his desk seven manuscripts, each creased from being passed from hand to hand, one of which has been recently returned with a suggestion he broadens the confinement of its plot from the world of insurance: 'Not the liveliest subject, but the only one I know.'

'What about your past?' I ask.

'Oh, that,' he says, and waves his hand. 'That,' he adds, 'is a different matter.'

His darkened, habitually frowning, puzzling expression turns from the desk, the manuscript and the publisher's letter to the garden – terraced with rose trees – and the hill beyond. It, the latter, absorbs his attention, something almost artificial in its shape, a tumulus-like construction: it was the hill, he tells me, that sold him on the plot: an aspiration to live on it and, that failing – it belonged to a nearby farmer – to live beside it. 'And we end up below it,' he wryly adds.

'There's also the war,' I tell him.

He glances at me as if to enquire, 'How much do you know of that?'

'The war,' he says, 'I try and forget. Has Gerry spoken much about it?'

'His war?' I say, and shake my head. 'Yours, neither,' I tell him.

'He had a better one than me.'

'How?'

'His charm. Expansiveness. He had something of his mother. Our *real* mother,' he adds, nodding at me. 'I was very enclosed. Always have been.' He might have continued, but merely shrugs. 'It's like some things, too, must be for you. We share something, in that respect, together.' He looks across the desk between us: the desk on which a typewriter stands with a half-typed sheet of paper protruding, a handwritten text beside it: an eighth 'mystery', or his revamping of an old one.

'There's your schoolwork, too, we have to keep up with.'

'Sure.'

'Gerry's arranged all that.'

'By correspondence,' I tell him.

'You can read any of these, by the way,' he says, indicating the manuscripts he's shown me. 'Choose any one.'

The conclusion is I'm obliged to read – at least, to take away – a dog-eared tome which, I assume, has seen many rejections but which he aimlessly recommends with, 'the best of the bunch, in my view, though not in the opinion of others'. A conscientious plod (I discover) through a labyrinth of double-dealing, false accounts, inaccurate statements, duplicitous claims, secret handouts, a body, or a corpse, on almost every page. At the end, if schematically read, I'm unsure who's done what to whom: a tangle of unsubstantiated motives and (invariably) unsurprising explanations.

'I'd recommend the war,' I tell him when I hand it back.

We are sitting in his study before Sunday lunch (the sound of Clare singing in the kitchen below, I having helped her to prepare it earlier).

In front of us is the hill, on this occasion seen through a filter of falling rain: the glistening grass, the absent cattle, the darkened crest of the trees themselves: sombre, strangely menacing: still.

'I don't mind you and Clare,' he says, suddenly, inconsequentially. 'She and I have an understanding. Though we live together, we live apart. I do feel I *am* apart. I see you, in short, as a welcome addition. Far more painful it would be if, for instance, it were someone else. We live very much as brother and sister. At the very least as very good friends.'

'I'd still recommend the war,' I add, hoping to distract him.

'You would?'

'What, after all, have you got to lose?'

His look returns to the hill: he peers at it intensely.

'There was one particular incident I've always felt inclined to write about, but have never known how. We were retreating – though we never made it – towards Dunkirk and came across a group of people pushing a coffin on a cart. An elderly man, two women, and a boy. And a youth who appeared to be partially demented. He ran around the whole time and was never still. They were trying to find a priest. Their own had been killed. They'd been travelling for over a week looking for one to bury the body. The coffin stank. So did they, the body evidently the women's father and the old man's brother. They hadn't eaten for days. We gave them food. Shortly after that we were captured. No ammunition, two wounded. The lowest point of my life. Yet all I could think of were the women, the man, the boy and the youth. Some time later we passed them on the road. The coffin had fallen from the cart. The top of the box was lying open, their bodies strewn around in the road. I began to cry. Shock at everything, I imagine. The hopelessness which came with it. It seemed to me that, even in peacetime, everything is a sham. Species destroying species in an aimless appetite to exist.'

We're silent, Clare passing on the landing, calling, 'Are you boys still talking? Come down for a drink,' the sound of her feet thudding, briskly, from the stairs.

'It haunted me throughout the camp. Nothing that happened there did anything other than confirm it, the terms on which the universe is convened a ghastly error. The arrogance of any religious message, everything there merely to be destroyed, even the supercilious efforts made in attempting to deny it. A malign conception.'

Clare is whistling – an engaging sound – passing to and fro in the hall: we have, as it is, a rota of household chores, over and above those done by Mrs Jenkins: we are, as she and James often say, 'in this together'.

'I don't know why I'm telling you this.'

'A precursor to something you ought to write.'

'Let's go down to lunch,' he says.

The following Sunday morning he knocks on my room door (essays to be posted to my crammer, I writing at my desk).

'I'm not disturbing you?' he says, coming in at my invitation.

Clare is out – strangely, at a church she attends in an outlying village, a social rather than a spiritual occasion, but of that, as of so much in the house, I can't be sure.

'You have a contrary view of life to mine,' he says, picking up on our week-old conversation. 'You believe in life in a way I admire. And envy. You've something of your father in you and, through him, my mother, who despite everything was a lively woman. Not unlike Clare in many respects, I not unlike my father whom I always despised.'

He hands me another manuscript with, 'I wondered if you could see any way I might improve it.'

This confederacy draws us closer: in the evenings we sit, the three of us, reading ('mysteries', Clare and James; something other – text-books – me: this the closest to 'home' I've ever had). When they go out to their various societies I read (and study) alone (occasional calls to and from Gerry: guilt, on his part, reassurance on mine: he never asks me the *nature* of my relationship with Clare). The longer we are together the closer the three of us become – to the point where, one Sunday morning, Clare invites me to accompany her to church.

We drive there: a route beyond the hill at the back of the house, one of lanes and woods and streams and valleys: a Saxon structure, the building, set at the edge of a wood, with zigzag-patterned arches, tiny windows and a narrow, high-roofed nave: a domestic air: scarcely more than a dozen people, all of whom know her and are uninhibitedly curious about me. I am introduced: much interest and avidity to please: invitations to lunch (supper, tea), all of which, 'for the moment', Clare graciously declines.

Everything signals we are a couple, a natural intimacy between us which to the others must be reassuring, not least to the minister who turns to Clare with great – and equally reassuring – animation: he talks of my 'recent bereavement' with compassion, mentioning it in his sermon. I am sitting beside her conscious of experiencing her in a ritualised setting: the austerity and gravity of the place (there are only the simplest decorations, one crucifix and two candle-holders alone on the altar) – allied to this the intimacy evoked by her perfume, the sheen of her stocking, the rising and falling of the hem of her skirt as we kneel and sit and stand.

And her hands – clasped in her lap or held devotedly together: occasionally she reaches for mine, squeezing my fingers before releasing them, a gesture of complicity which intoxicates me to such a degree that, once we have said farewell to the other worshippers and the minister and are in the car, she is obliged to draw up in a secluded lane and announce, 'A walk would do us both some good. It would be so *uncomfortable* returning home feeling as we do at present,' a discomfort which can only finally be appeased in a field beyond the hedge which so conveniently skirts one side of the lane.

Martha rings, inviting the three of us to supper with 'mother and father', an unusually elderly couple for such a young daughter: an evening which goes remarkably well but perhaps not quite fulfilling the hopes of our hostess: 'I so like living in the provinces,' she announces, on our leaving, 'away from all the rivalries of London, *don't you think*?'

However, returning home, James expresses himself 'delighted' with the way things have gone – recognising a more suitable partner, for one thing, for his errant nephew: 'I can see *Martha* has an eye for you. She's a very *serious* girl, I understand, with pronounced views of her own. And their house, too, is lovely,' another out-of-town 'detached dwelling' which, in the darkness, I assume is surrounded by fields. 'Oh, no!' Clare laughs. 'Whetton is *the* suburb to live in, the houses so far apart they're scarcely visible to one another. We'd have gone there, too, only James wished to *pioneer*. He had a fixation on that hill, and also wanted "virgin territory. Starting from scratch".'

'More than we can say of you, dear,' James says, glancing at me to share his laughter.

On the way to the Armitages Clare insists on sitting in the back, our positions reversed, on my insistence, on the way home – largely in order to see my (newfound) aunt and uncle, if in silhouette, as a couple before me, something, I realise, I rarely do: more often, in the car, she and I are alone, not least because of James's recent habit of walking to work on a morning, rising early ('It does me good, and gives me room to think. *New* mysteries, new adventures'). Invariably he takes a taxi home, or Clare drives in to pick him up. Rarely, too, are he and I together, except in the privacy of his study where, increasingly, we have our 'talks' ('I'm sure,' Clare says, 'they do him good'). Occasionally, in the evenings, he taps on my door, enquiring, 'Have you a moment? I don't wish to intrude,' I disinclined to refuse, his excuse, not infrequently, that his writing 'has got into a muddle. I wonder if you'd cast your eye over this?'

'I do these things like crosswords,' he explains on one of these occasions. 'They keep me occupied. In contrast to the work I normally do, which can be extremely tedious at the best of times, I find them entertaining. Like going to the cinema, or the theatre. I don't *ultimately* care if they fail to see the light of day. At least I've done them. They've kept me amused. I've come up with a solution. Solved a mystery. Isn't that what metaphysics is, or are, about? How are you getting on at church, by the way?'

The excursions, particularly the episode which occurs afterwards – eroticism enhanced by the piety and austerity of the place, the endorsement by so many friendly hands and faces – has become an indispensable part of our 'week', it itself characterised not only by the time I spend in James' study but by the amount Clare and I spend in our respective rooms: prior to my arrival she and James have moved to separate bedrooms at the front of the house, on either side of the bifurcated landing, James retaining their original room: one further room, apart from his study, answers as a 'guest' room.

'Maybe I should come with you,' he goes on. 'Though I'm sure Clare wouldn't like it. Church is her provenance, after all, not mine. I can see well enough the pleasure she gets out of going with you. It has for her, I know, an educative function. We are both *educators*, in our differing ways. You coming here has done so much for both of us. I can't tell you how much nicer she is to *me*, and how much more *amiable* she is to everyone else. Before your arrival we were both very rocky, this house our belated attempt to keep things together. We very much *care* for one another, and respect each other's varying needs, but with the limitations placed on our relationship, principally by *my* limitations, it has, at least, until your arrival, been very much touch and go. Social life becomes a hollow alternative when the *heart* is not attended to. With you here the place is full of life. Continuity has been re-established. The Audlin name is carried on. You've so much of Martha in you.'

'Martha?'

'Your mother. Not *Armitage*.' He laughs. 'Though that's a remarkable coincidence, don't you think? Your future may lie there. I don't need to tell you, *coincidence* is what mystery is about. If only to discover it's not coincidence after all!'

The introduction to these 'dialogues', as he's inclined to call them, occasionally takes the form of an invitation to listen to something he's written: considerately, he keeps the readings short. 'Does this make sense?' he'll ask, or, 'How about this at the *beginning* of a chapter?', one such subsequent 'dialogue' drifting off to reflections on the shape of the hill at the back of the house: 'An obvious likeness to a source of nourishment. Something elemental, do you think, in that, but also, don't you think, to a place of ritual? I used to come here as a boy, haunted by its *shape*, and once dug a hole at the top and came across pieces of brick, eighteenth century, or before, and realised there must have been a structure of some sort before the trees. A gazebo. A folly. An observatory, perhaps. The land belonged originally to the local manor. Occasionally I go up there. Often when you and Clare are asleep. I find it a place of solace. Unique, in that respect, less self-conscious, for instance, than a church. Who knows, over the centuries, who may have stood there, gazing out?'

On a subsequent occasion his talk drifts on to the war: 'You're my therapist, Richard,' he announces, laughing, the account inducing a mood of reflectiveness, the intensity of which I haven't previously seen. 'Perhaps I'm regressing,' he concludes.

'Progressing,' I suggest.

'What's the difference, *genius*?' he says, his mood light-hearted. 'In any case, what's the point? It all happened twenty-odd years ago. Much, as we know, has happened since. Everything's moved on.'

'Worth talking about,' I tell him.

'Why?'

'Why not?'

'I suppose you're right.' He pauses, avoiding my expression. 'I couldn't stand the buggery,' he suddenly adds.

The confession is climactic, bleak: and, to him at least, alarming.

'I couldn't fail to notice it going on. A biological perversion which, therefore, you could only assume is a moral one.'

He gazes at me like someone coming in from the dark to a lighted room, his eyelids lowered, his mouth braced: a tortured, vanquished, riven expression.

'It doesn't seem much to me,' I tell him.

'It doesn't?'

'Inevitable,' I add.

'I simply can't get rid of it,' he says. 'If I met any of the men now my immediate reaction would be to assume I didn't know them. I'd cross the street. Alternatively, if I had to face it I'd shoot myself.'

'What with?' I maintain the lightness of my response.

'A pistol. I still have it. A Mauser. I got it, oddly, over here. When we were repatriated at the end of the war. Soldiers waiting to be demobbed. One of them had collected quite an arsenal. In a rucksack. He was selling them off as souvenirs. "I might as well have something to show for all these bloody years," I said, and bought it. I actually borrowed the money from Gerry. Visiting me, the first time we'd seen one another since the beginning of the war, he on his way to Hollywood. And Martha. I occasionally go up the hill and shoot it.' He gestures to the window. 'I got fifty rounds of ammunition. Quite a few soldiers were flogging stuff. I tried to get more. Without the slightest notion of what I intended to do with it. I've only a dozen rounds left. Do you want to see it?'

I shake my head.

'It's why the crimes in my mysteries are often shootings. Invariably with Mausers. Apart from my regulation service revolver it's the only pistol I know. Not *sinister*. Quite practical. Mechanical.' He laughs. 'Know who I shoot?'

Again I shake my head.

'My fellow officers. How's that for a returning hero? A man who sacrificed himself for "future generations". You see at what a price.'

His look turns from me to the hill and back again.

'It affected my relationship with Clare, of course. When she finally did conceive she lost the child. Sex was replaced by social life, for which she has a gift. And, for me, by mysteries in which people I know in real life, though fictionalised, are murdered.'

He's silent for a while, studying my reaction.

'So here we are,' he continues, satisfied with what he's confided. 'The history of our times writ large. I'm sorry to burden you with it. You've had so much to take on. And at such an early age. I always thought Gerry was bringing you up *too fast*. That attempt to "localise" you, as he put it, in London, almost drove him mad. He's never been one for domesticity and used to talk to you as if you were the same age as himself. At six, at seven, at eight, he was addressing you as an *adult*. I used to say, "Talk to Richard as if he were a child." He could never get the hang of it. Perhaps, that, too, was a result of the war. Years in the company of men. I suspect, too, the death of Ian. He never intended to be that vulnerable again.'

'Vulnerable?'

'He loved Martha, it's true, more than I thought he was capable of loving anyone. When she went into decline, so soon after their marriage – almost as if it had precipitated the event – his only recourse was to work. He never changed. Clare used to say *I* was workaholic, and I suppose, after the war, I was. But writing books, thank God, stopped that. Whatever their outcome, they gave me a sense of perspective. My fantasy, when I was working and building up my reputation, was that I'd be moved to the head office in London. Our child dying put a stop to that. Which is when, as I say, the books took over. It's the theme of several of the mysteries, not the camp, but someone taking revenge for what happened in the past. The one element in my fiction, as everyone observes, which invariably weakens the plot. I never make it clear what the *past* was precisely. It's always a euphemism for something I can't admit. Except, of course,' he pauses, 'to you. Apart from Clare, the only one to know.' He pauses again to observe my reaction. 'Your coming has certainly freed us up! I hope we're not imposing on you. You must tell us if we are. We take so much of what has happened for granted. If we can do anything to help we are, as you know, only too anxious to play our part.'

There is an element of mockery in this – self-mockery as well as mockery of Clare and myself, a playfulness he otherwise rarely shows. He doesn't pursue the subject on this occasion, and I refrain from encouraging him.

Gerry, when he rings, keeps his distance: shooting is almost at an end. He is aware I'm being 'intoxicated by those crazy people there'. ('Don't take that as criticism,' he says, 'I'm sure it'll do you good.') He is worried, more, by my lack of schooling, about which Clare – and James – and myself reassure him: he checks up himself on my correspondence with the crammer. 'My chance,' I tell him to be different. Every kid at my age is at school. Let's try an experiment with one who isn't.'

'Okay by me,' he says, 'if you come up with the goods.'

'I'll come up with something,' I reassure him.

'I wait to see it, Rick.' He might have added more, but doesn't. 'Don't take a leaf out of Jimmy's book,' is all he adds. 'Like *creativity* being a part-time job. *Nothing* is a part-time job, least of all for anyone who does it. I've been offered a book,' he goes on. 'Not to film, to write. An autobiography,' he explains.

He is sounding me out if I'm doing the same: an extended memo on the private life of Miss Geraldine O'Neill: what wouldn't they pay for something like that?

'Jesus,' is all I tell him.

'He'll come into it, too.' He laughs. 'It's far too soon, for instance, for *anyone* to write about that.'

'That?'

'Martha.'

The sum offered must have been considerable, I conclude, for him even to have to mention it.

'I'm being offered projects I'd never have got near before. Everybody feels they *owe* me. What they want, of course, is access to her. She once wrote a lot about herself. I must have shown you.'

'No,' I tell him.

'I thought I did.'

'No,' I said. 'I never heard.'

'It must have been Gavin.' He pauses. 'It's too early, Ricky. What d'you think?'

With my agreement, I can see, he'll go ahead: how fast we've moved from my crumby education to his next project, casting, I guess, already underway.

'You're right,' I tell him. 'It's far too soon. If ever,' I add, to torment him.

'You're right.' His voice drops an octave. 'I hope,' he says, 'you're not regressing.'

'What's regressing?'

'Covering up.'

'Repressing.'

'Repressing. Suppressing. Whatever you do when you don't come clean. James, by the way, is a great suppressor.'

'Not any more.'

'Does he say that?'

'You'd better ask him.'

'All he says is you get on well. Exceptionally. I suppose he's suggesting I'm a lousy father and he a better one. I've fucked up with the two of you.'

'Two?'

'You and Ian.'

He adds nothing for a while, I not inclined to help him.

'And Clare. I get the feeling that, too, was not a good idea.'

'I don't like being classified with Ian,' I tell him. 'I am not, as far as I know, scheduled to die.'

'Another mistake. Forget about Clare. Forget the query about Martha.'

He is, I'm aware, moving swiftly on: the hissing of his blades, the ominous creaking on every side: glide! glide! I hear him say: *glide!* his instincts tell him.

'I rely on you a great deal,' he says.

'You do?'

'You have such a different view of things. Sometimes I feel *buried*. Then I see your face and realise why I do these things.'

'Why?'

'Fuck you,' he says, and laughs – or weeps: for a moment I can't tell, the other end. 'Does *Clare* have this impression of you?' he finally adds.

'I've no idea,' I tell him.

'She must say something,' he says.

'We read a great deal.'

'Read? Not Jimmy's fucking novels? Don't tell me they're making you *pay* to stay up there? He sent me one, by the way. I suppose he told you.'

'No.'

'If it's like the one he sent me years ago it must be delirious. I haven't had time to look at it. Who's ever heard of *anyone* but my brother writing for twenty fucking years without publishing a word?'

'Perseverance.'

'Is that what it is.'

He's thinking.

He's thinking like he always thinks, his eyes fixed on a distant and, to everyone else, invisible object.

'Life up there is good?' he asks.

'Okay.'

'You don't want to see a psychiatrist?'

'What about?'

'The way, let's face it, I fucked things up. There's a lot gone on in your short little life. Most of it because of me.'

'I'm off drugs. I don't need to see anyone. I'm feeling fine,' I tell him.

This, more than anything, unnerves him: his mind might be on last week's rushes but his attention is dragged elsewhere.

'I have all the advice I require,' I add.

'I get the message, Rick.' He wheels away, speeding off beneath the stars (with the stars), the sky, reflected in the ice, fractured all around him . . .

2

The church sanctions our arrangement: '*en plein jour*', she refers to the episode which invariably occurs on the journey home (a different field, or wood, every time) – a ritual (almost) with a sacramental edge, raising these occasions to what James, should he have been acquainted with them, would have described as a metaphysical level.

I love to lie beside her and anticipate what might happen next, in much the same way as I might anticipate her next move in the car when we're driving back from a morning or an afternoon in town.

'Even your clothes are blessed,' I tell her, for not infrequently she takes me shopping, selecting garments which she believes will entice me to greater, or more imaginative 'efforts': 'James was never interested. I've had *such* a lot of offers from other men. All of which, I needn't tell you, I declined, you the sole exception.'

'So,' she concludes one Sunday, lying in the grass, 'we are blessed?' Summer is upon us: the sun is shining, clouds scudding, the car parked in the road below the tiny wood: we are in full view of everyone, should they pass, but no longer seem to care. 'The danger of the occasion appears to elude you,' she says (my eagerness precluding us finding a more hidden spot). 'We have to show *some* discretion, if only for James' sake,' she tells me. 'Otherwise,' she goes on, 'there is no problem. He, for his part, spends more time on that hill than he does in his study. He says it's like a hill which overlooked the camp. He spent hours gazing at it, imagining his release. It represented freedom. Everything he'd lost, the sight of it, at that time, his only relief. When he was freed, however, he never had time to visit it. Which is why he goes to stand on this one now.'

I love her in these moods when she's endeavouring to 'place' what we mean to one another: it's why the visits to the church have such appeal, the ecstasy of sitting, kneeling, standing beside her, aware of what, a short while later, will undoubtedly occur.

'You are exceptional,' she says. 'Even Gerry, who's always been reluctant to praise you in case it goes to your head, describes you as "precocious". You're much the same with me. And James. You'll walk the exams next summer.'

'Unless I choose to fail.'

'Will you fail?'

'That's up to you.'

'Why me?'

'I want this to go on for ever.'

'It won't. Even you must realise that,' she says. 'I do, and I am not afraid of it.'

I don't believe her. I don't need to. I make my own conditions. I am ungovernable. Martha, if no one else, has licensed it: why be a genius if it doesn't show?

I play with her hair, her lips (her blouse), with her: how *crude* this is, yet, at the same time, how enthralling. I am, as she frequently tells me, 'biologically' at my peak: 'A pity I can't conceive,' she says. 'We could have had a miraculous baby. I must have absorbed enough for *thousands* by now.'

So we lie, examine the trees, the sky, the grass, reflecting on the sermon, and feel doubly blessed, the secular and the divine mellifluously blended – and hand in hand walk back to the road (unobserved by anyone).

'I've never felt so happy,' she says, as we reach the car. 'Everything about us is both wrong and blessed,' a religiosity, I'm aware, we carry with us into the house, blessing *it*, too, by our presence – James coming down, on this occasion, when we arrive, announcing, 'Let's celebrate. I've turned a corner. At least, with the present piece,' opening a bottle of wine, we more than content to share his triumph with him.

After lunch, the day full of clouds and sunshine, a gentle breeze, he suggests we climb the hill at the back of the house, our agreement as spontaneously forthcoming. A hole he has widened in the hedge at the end of the garden through which he has evidently passed on numerous occasions, a track visible in the grass – strewn with flowers – forming a curiously winding route to the summit, the vegetation thinning where it has been browsed by the cattle. They, we can see, when we reach the trees, are penned in a field below the brow on the other side, a gentler incline giving a view of the route we follow – a hedge-escorted lane – to the church, itself invisible beyond a line of higher hills.

There is something stirring about the asymmetry of the crest: fields descend from it on every side, most steeply of all to where the house nestles in its hollow. Beyond, where the sun descends, the town is visible, stretched across the widening width of the valley where it disburses onto a plain: a festoon of towers and steeples and domes.

The breeze is fresh, Clare panting from the climb – our second (physical) excursion (and exertion) of the day: there's a seductive odour of resin from the trees, mingling with that of her perfume: an intoxicating if not cleansing odour, the sun shifting between the clouds, covering us with shadow one moment, illuminating us brightly the next.

'A glorious day,' James tells us, breathing in the air.

He has brought a camera, an, until now, unremarked-upon endorsement of the significance of the occasion: it hangs around his neck, he moving ahead at one point to take a picture of Clare and I ascending. He now takes several more, of the two of us together, suggesting we stand with our arms around each other, we frowning, at first, then, at his insistence, smiling in the light. He further suggests he takes us singly, first Clare, then I, standing out from the crest of pines. Then I suggest I take one of him, and a second of he and Clare together, he showing me the mechanism with some reluctance before, smilingly, complying: an air of finality, of absolution, hangs about him: an odd, tolerant couple I view through the camera, and wonder how Clare and I, our positions reversed, must have looked to him.

The camera, our visit recorded, is replaced around his neck (another souvenir from Germany, he informs us): the pink bark of the trees luminous in the afternoon sun, he shows us the spot where he dug as a child, the irregular undulations of the ground, soft with needles. He appears transfixed, for that moment, as if removing the trees and imagining the configurations of something which eludes him. 'It must have looked dramatic,' Clare says, intrigued by the view of the house below, of the town beyond, the moors rising on the opposite side of the valley and crossed by the shadows of clouds passing overhead. 'We ought to come up more often. Bring a picnic. I've only been up once before,' she adds to me.

James, meanwhile, is gazing indecisively about him, something other than the view absorbing him, as if endeavouring to locate the source of his preoccupation inside his head.

Moments later, adjusting the camera, he says, 'No need to stay up longer. I'll hang around for a while. I'll see you later. It's often good to be here on my own,' Clare and I setting off, the impress of our ascent still visible in the grass: walking separately, she in front, I admire for a second time her movements against a rural setting: her hips, her thighs, her waist, her legs, her hands, her head, her hair blown back and upwards by the summery breeze: she has changed, for the outing, into flat-heeled shoes, but is still wearing her skirt and blouse and jacket from church: I can see the creases from our earlier outing across her hips and once again preoccupy myself mentally with that region of her body.

Behind us James is visible beneath the trees: he is directing the camera once more towards us, its strap still secured around his neck: lowering it, he waves and, as I wave in return, Clare now descending more swiftly, he waves once more and disappears.

Moments later we hear a shot.

3

Having absorbed so much the mind is inclined to come to a halt: the war played a part (changed the public perception for ever), as it did in my father's life and, by proxy, in my own. On one of his calls Gerry enquires if I'd like to see – or already have seen – a photographic 'memoir' of Martha's life. I decline his offer (I haven't seen it) but come across it, shortly after, in a bookshop in town – a place which, on my own, I wouldn't have entered: we are looking for something for Clare to read and I see her across the shop pausing by the display which I've already spotted, a photograph of Martha in her prime prominently above it: stills, as I see, when I join her – of 'Geraldine O'Neill' – from most of her films: there are additional photographs of her as a child, as a youth, and of Gerry and several of their friends: none of me. The book, I'm aware, came out some time before and has been reissued since her death.

It is like looking at pictures of someone with whom I have no connection: a projection backwards to examine a past for which I can't account: that wonderful face, that wonderful figure: that ironic, canvassing, comedic expression: someone who performs at the edge of reality, allowing you a glimpse of it and fiction at the same time: a revolutionary performer, the screen a foil – one she opposed with so much ease, a self-denominated, self-created 'entertainer'.

It's, curiously, this image of her that comes to mind as I climb back up the hill, wondering if I've imagined the sound – waiting, even, for it to be repeated to clarify my misgivings – glancing behind me to see that Clare has turned as well and is gazing past me, full of apprehension: she has, after all, more knowledge of James than I have.

Reaching the pines I see him some way in, sitting upright, his back to a tree, his head, the only sign of discomposure, slumped to one side: blood, from his temple, has reached his chest; as if alive, the figure moves, a delayed momentum, falling over, his forehead arrested by the ground. In the exposed hand, as if flung from the body, is the gun I refused to allow him to show me.

The scent of pine resin is strong: I am aware of it as a distraction moments before I'm aware of Clare breathless beside me. Maybe she has prepared herself for a scene like this – I involuntarily extending my arm to her shoulders. We stand there as spectators – then I'm stepping forward to see, inexpertly, if there are any signs of life: the angle of the head, the absence of any movement, the camera still about his neck – like the gun, a macabre souvenir, a functional disorder, the omnipotent recorder of contemporary life, its glossy excreta strewn around us.

Clare stands, swaying, as if pinned to the ground: James has moved himself to a distance from where she can no longer touch him, the pink columns of the pines an involuntary chapel, or so it seems – pillars reaching up to the inclines of the foliage, a secular enclosure dedicated to God knows what.

Turning away from the body I offer these phrases (I think) aloud – say something which, afterwards, I can't recall – and see Clare gazing at me in consternation, less a shocked woman than a traumatised child – she surpised, not by the message, the flaccid allusions, but the fact that I've spoken. I am aware of my mother's face again – see it, almost, imposed on the wholly dissimilar features of Clare – think, too, in that instant, of the other Martha, the same metamorphosis in her recalled face, appalled at the cessation of something known and peculiarly cherished – the man who lent me his wife, the wife who abrogated her husband: her first words, 'I'll stay,' followed by, 'I can't leave him here alone,' I taking off my jacket and laying it over his head, adding, 'We'll go down together,' the camera, I notice, as I take her arm, ominously protruding from beneath the coat.

An ambulance arrives, police follow: a line of figures troops up the hill, a cortège, a considerable time later, winding down, a stretchered shape amongst them (the difficulty they have in getting through the hedge, James having widened the hole only to accommodate himself). For a moment, horrifically, I think they're going to bring him through the house, Clare transfixed in the sitting room where, despite my encouragement, she refuses to sit down.

By the evening the summit of the hill is screened off and, after interviews are completed, a solitary policeman is visible, a second at the gate (the 'integrity' of the site preserved).

We don't switch on the light but sit in the dark. At intervals, throughout the night, a police car appears at the end of the drive and the policeman at the gate and the one on the hill are relieved: I finally persuade her to go to bed, going up a short while later to find her, still dressed, lying in the dark. I lie with her for a while, try to contact Gerry (no answer at the flat) and ring Gavin whose home number I have 'for emergencies': Gerry and Gavin are night shooting and can't be reached. I leave a message with a roused wife to ring me in the morning.

In the early hours I hear the phone ring and go downstairs, a police car, at that moment, retreating from the end of the drive: the crunch of the relieving and the relieved officers' steps having preceded it.

'What's happened?' Gerry says. 'We're in Shoreditch. What's the problem?' Patience and exasperation, exhaustion and apprehension: don't inform me of anything I have to *respond* to, his tone suggests.

'Is shooting finished?' A desire to submerge him irrevocably, immovably, in the work he has on hand: nothing will stop him: he sweeps by me on the bank.

'Has something happened to Clare?'

'It's James.'

'Jimmy?' The diminutive at all times.

'There's been an incident.'

Closest to 'accident' without – precisely – being one.

Our thin-ice skater speeds away: a metaphorical figure, a metaphorical distance: is this the 'metaphysics' which James went on about?

'He's shot himself.'

I wonder at the appropriateness of the tense, the improbability and unexpectedness of the announcement sufficient for him to place the telephone – or so it seems – some distance from him: I have a vision of him closing his eyes: he's in a street: there's a murmur of voices and the chugging of a generator engine. The door of a phone booth is suddenly closed.

'Say again.'

'Are you listening?'

'What the fuck do you think I'm doing? Do you mean there's been an accident?'

'I'm sure it was intended.'

'You're not making sense. Where's he got it from? A gun.'

He is about to revoke the whole affair: have it rewritten: he peels away, diverting to another course.

A previously brotherly relationship (fake) is alarmingly in place.

'He had a Mauser. From the war.'

'He never told me.'

'He used to fire it on the hill. The one he was always preoccupied by.'

'What hill?'

Everything I tell him confirms his view that what I'm telling him can't be true: this – a fictionalist himself – is being made up.

'Overlooking the house. It's why he built it here.'

'He never told me.' The affirmation – the condemnation. 'Say again.'

'I thought I'd better tell you before you heard it in some other form.'

'I was talking to him this morning. *Yesterday* morning. Everything, he said, was going well. You were at church. *Church*, for God's sake. He rang me. Everything was fine. Are you okay? I've never heard of a fucking hill. I don't remember.'

'There is one.'

So move it: we'll shoot it somewhere else.

'With trees on top?'

A visual memory – ironically, not his strongest suit.

'We climbed up there this afternoon. He brought his camera. We took pictures of one another. Then he said he wanted to be alone and Clare and I set off back. Halfway down we heard a shot. When I reached him he was sitting down. Against a tree. The gun in his hand. A hole in his head.'

Speaking to a cineaste, I make it exact.

Silence, however, the other end – so prolonged I enquire, 'Are you still there?'

'Of course I'm fucking here.'

Death follows me around (I can hear him thinking). 'The police, I assume, have been involved?'

'They have.'

'It'll be in tomorrow's – *this* morning's – papers.'

'I doubt it.'

'Why not?'

'They won't have made the connection.'

'Don't you doubt it,' he says, in another voice entirely: if the scene can't be re-shot it will have to be re-managed. 'What did they say?'

'They asked questions. Clare's in no state. I gave the answers.'

'Where is she now?'

'Lying down.'

'Is she awake?'

'Probably.'

'I'll speak to her.'

'She's not even speaking to me.'

Everything we touch, he is thinking: everywhere we go.

'I'll come up.'

'When?'

'Now.'

'How?'

'I'll drive.'

Another silence.

'Are you okay?' he adds.

'Sure.'

Am I okay? he's further asking.

'I'm not sure what I feel,' I tell him.

'Better not to think.'

A further pause.

His own philosophy exactly.

'I don't like leaving you on your own,' he says. 'Is there a policeman in the house?'

'At the gate. Another on the hill. The site's screened off.'

'Can you phone someone else in town?'

'The Armitages.'

'Who are they?'

'People I've met up here.'

'Will they come?'

'We'll be all right on our own.'

'I don't like you being on your own. Ask Clare if she'll speak to me.'

'I doubt if she will.'

'Tell her I'm coming.'

The disowning of support he doesn't like.

'I'll be there in three or four hours. The roads are clear this time of night. I'm coming.'

'What about the film?'

'Remember I love you. Don't let Clare be alone. Don't forget to tell her I'm coming.'

I put the phone down and return to Clare's room. I sit in the chair – a comfortable chair – and realise it's covered in her clothes. She's lying under the cover. Her eyes are closed. I'm convinced she's not asleep.

I go back to the chair, fold the clothes and lay them on a chest of drawers. I turn the chair in her direction and remain there, I calculate, for an hour. Another car comes to the end of the drive: there's the crunch of feet followed, after an interval, by the crunch of feet returning: lights from the car sweep across the window: the sound of its engine fades.

I cross to the window and draw the curtains.

'Could you open them?' I hear her say.

'You awake?' I ask.

'Not really.' The voice is confidential. 'I don't know whether I'm asleep or awake. Would you lie here with me?'

Her teeth are chattering, her body trembling. I remove my clothes, pull back the covers, and get in beside her.

Locked together we fall asleep: when a car comes up the drive and I hear Gerry's voice, talking to the driver or to a policeman, or both, I feel I haven't slept at all.

'Gerry's here,' I tell her. 'I'll see him,' the doorbell ringing before I reach the hall.

She, I and Gerry walk – in the countryside beyond the town, she between us, our arms linked, he much on the phone before we leave: a track leads through woods and fields, somewhere I haven't been with her before, I wondering why (until she informs us she and James walked here in their early life), she wishing, I suspect, to place him even further back in time, at least that part of him she wishes to remember.

All the while, meantime, *frissons* of fear – me, and Gerry too, no doubt – as if we are dragging James with us, hauling him along, for Gerry remembers this part of their life as children: we come to a lake behind a low stone wall, enveloped by a wood on one side, a pasture on the other: cattle browse at the edge: here he and James played as boys and, for someone who rejects his past – skates beyond it as quickly as he can – it's not a site to which he wishes to return, pointing out the changes ('It wasn't so polluted. We used to swim'), as if to place it not merely in another time but elsewhere.

It's decided he'll go back the following morning (having prospected leaving that evening: 'I have to get back. The whole thing's almost there'), witnessing the persistence of the police questioning, however, and the calls at the house (a thorough search of James' study and his bedroom); reluctant to 'abandon' me (and Clare) to 'this fucking situation' (blaming 'Jimmy' now 'for so much'), he defers his departure from hour to hour (an hour-long tirade to Gavin on the phone).

Clare is anxious for him to be gone: to be swept away, as if a reminder of where, persistently, she is *not*.

'It's so good no one's *stood back*,' he says. 'The same with Martha. *Everyone* called in. It's moments like this,' he adds, 'when you realise how *good* people are,' taking me aside to announce, Clare on the phone in the hall, we in the kitchen, 'I'm not at all easy leaving you together. Clare's a resourceful woman, and Jimmy, I guess, has been a burden, but she has her limits. Maybe he's threatened her with this before. We all had a war to get rid of. He's behaved like a shit. Taking *you* there to witness it. What sort of a creep is that? After all the effort I've made to get back with him. That *you*'ve made, too,' he adds. 'But there it is. We're not normal. And have never pretended to be.'

Clare's voice comes calmly from the hall: she is, I overhear, talking to the Armitages.

'Let's go to your room,' he says, 'and talk.'

'She'll think we're closing down on her,' I tell him.

So he is looking out at the garden at the back: the terraces and flowerbeds James has had laid out. And the hill.

'That fucking hill.' I'm surprised he hasn't asked to go up it himself, to get a feel of what has happened: no inclination to do so has been expressed at all. In any case, presumably, we wouldn't be allowed beyond the screens.

'Don't you think it odd he should invite you up?' he asks.

He is a 'mystery' man himself and yet not given to enquiry. 'I *demonstrate*,' he has often said. 'Not analyse.'

'He wanted to celebrate,' I tell him.

'What?'

'His writing, he said, had turned a corner.'

'No sign of it on his fucking desk.'

The police have taken away, with Clare's agreement, many of his papers.

'And he took photographs?' he adds.

'We both did.'

'What of?'

'Each other.'

'You hate a fucking camera. Look at the one I bought you. *Unused*.'

'I took them to humour him,' I tell him.

'Why?'

I shake my head. 'I didn't like being taken, at all. I wanted to even it out,' I tell him, not at all sure what I mean.

'He invites you up there. Takes his camera. *And* a gun. Takes shots of you, then you of him. Asks you to leave. Then shoots himself. What the fuck is he trying to say? What the fuck was he trying to *do*?'

'You tell me.'

He shakes his head.

'The complexity of people knows no bounds.'

'Is that from O'Connor?'

'No, arsehole, that's from *you*. Something you said at Leighcroft. Remember?'

'I said a lot of things at Leighcroft.'

'Too fucking right.' He is looking at me intensely. 'Know what I think? You're too precocious for your own fucking good. You'd do everyone a very big favour to think before you fucking speak.'

He is thinking of Martha, and my abortive trip to announce the arrival of her son.

There is silence from the hall: Clare has finished her call. The phone begins to ring again.

She doesn't answer.

Moments later, however, we hear her voice.

'See,' he says, 'how quickly she recovers.'

'She is distracting herself,' I tell him. 'Maybe she, too, is good on ice. She's skating along with the rest of us.'

'What the fuck does that mean?'

'Forget it.'

Disguises fall away on every side: film scenarios – I see the signs – pass through Gerry's head: Martha, him, me, Clare, Jimmy. Who else? The cast increases every second.

'I'll come back up as soon as I can,' he says. 'Definitely for the funeral' (another night's shooting he's about to miss: the conviction the whole thing will fall apart if he isn't there). 'Perhaps you and Clare will change your minds. About coming down. In any case . . .' The scenario drifts on: fiction more real than reality, etc. Nothing beats this for being real. 'Maybe she's talking too much,' he says, her voice chattering on outside. 'Very little gets her down. Not even losing a kid, in the end. She was the first to ring up and talk of Martha when she first cracked up. Not only that, but she talks good sense. Jimmy blamed himself for that, you know. Giving her those fucking murder stories. That's maybe why he went on writing them.'

'Why?'

'To vindicate himself, for fuck's sake.'

He is inviting me to reassure him: that leaving tomorrow will be okay, fleeing the scene of something for which he feels responsible (unloading it where he can on me, and 'Jimmy') – the scenes of his childhood revisited in ways he would have least expected (if anyone should have cracked it should have been me, his hitherto unexpressed prognosis).

Richard, however, is still intact (for all he knows, still writing): on his way into and out of my toilet he must have flicked through the sheets on my table: memoranda – unnumbered. Where, in any case, will he sleep tonight? In the 'guest' room, hitherto unused (not in James's): he's restless, not so much to get Clare off the phone (talking herself into hysteria) but to get on it himself: he has already spoken to Gavin twice, I overhearing the second: 'Not *that* line. The other. Ask him to come up with something better. What's the prickhead paid for? . . . Ask *Richard*? Are you crazy? He *hates* fucking films. He thinks they're fucking up the universe,' catching sight of me passing in the hall and adding, 'Now is not a good time to make arsehole suggestions.'

I leave him to it: go up to my room: not long after I hear his voice, talking to Clare: 'How *is* Richard? That kid has seen too much. He's smarter than the rest of us combined and, worst of all, he knows it.'

Closing my door, disinclined to hear any more, I sit at my desk and stare not at the hill but into the garden: the hill is going from my thoughts. I pick up my pen and write on the sheet before me – aware of a darker scrawl visible below its surface, clearly something Gerry, if he has examined my desk, has missed.

I am confronted, lifting the sheet, by a page of James's familiar scrawl (several of his manuscripts are in ink): a curvilinear, almost lyric line, varying in width and pressure: something inscribed, evidently, with emotion.

If you read this you will know the end of the 'mystery'. Not good to be informed after it has happened, construction – *plotting* – never my strongest suit – always wanting to get to the denouement before the exposition: *motives* were always frustratingly obscure. The device for assuming you won't come across this document immediately (probably not until you sit down to write) is intended to afford me the opportunity to change my mind and retrieve it – if what I intend should happen doesn't. I'm unsure, as always, of my courage. As I am of my determination. However, I've always been a *tenacious* character, not least when I'm doing an inappropriate thing. As true of my *job* as of everything else. Something to do with my upbringing, I'm sure. The decision in question I shan't make until I view you through the camera. You will, if you do read this, recognise the irony of the 'shooting' involved.

What comes to mind, at this point, is the suggestion made by Clare that she 'shoot' James and I together: a photograph, I realise, I have, until now, forgotten – recalling James's initial reluctance, then his peculiarly tortured acquiescence, standing by me, I placing my arm, at Clare's further suggestion, around his shoulder: perhaps it was this contact, brief though it was, that, literally and metaphorically, disarmed him: his insistence on taking Clare and I together had led to a protracted effort to 'frame' us to his satisfaction: perhaps, in reality, he was struggling with thoughts which in his confession he was endeavouring to express: the gun, in the meanwhile, was hidden in an inside pocket – a jacket he had insisted on wearing ('a nice breeze, Clare, but chill') before we went up.

This is my last 'mystery'. I'm convinced I shall not 'commission' another. Perhaps this is what they were all about: *my* participating in events which, until now, I have only imagined. This one is about failure. As a survivor you'll have the privilege of reading it knowing you are safe. I have not the gift of words that you have. Nor have I the gift of Clare to the same degree. Each day I witness how much you bring her. I have never seen her so fulfilled, not even in our youth. Everything about her conveys the fact that she is loved and, in turn, is full of loving, and, to this extent, I see that as my final, perhaps my only genuine achievement: I have brought my beloved back to life – a life, some twenty-odd years ago, I was, inadvertently, almost responsible for destroying. I wasn't made for freedom (look at my brother to see the profligate father we sprang from): freedom for me was first confined, then killed. In the camp I realised I'd been a prisoner all my life, condemned to justify myself to a father I despised. What a trap! One out of which Gerry sprang – our mother's spirit – with no trouble! I've spoken to you of imprisonment but that scarcely conveyed the horror I felt, let alone the terror: the feeling that I was imprisoned for ever.

I am writing to you in a way I have never written before. Writing which, knowing the outcome, I've always resisted. I hated our collusion in Gerry's 'plot' to make you a 'brother' – if only a half one, at that – allegedly to 'save' Martha, on the one hand, and you, on the other. You were bound to find out in the end – by which time, Gerry judged, you'd be 'safe'. Once commissioned, however, he didn't know how to unravel it, 'commissioning' O'Connor to do it for him. With what results! Bowing to the Studios' authority has done for us all. Did he *really* care, as he appears to now? I can only say I took his word for it that it was 'for the best' only to see 'the best' run out of control when he realised he couldn't tell you the truth for fear of condemning you to the stigma of someone who subsequently emerged as a lunatic mother. Clare, in her own way, perhaps is making up for that.

A separate sheet: this is taking longer than I imagined. I've had to refill my pen (not full when I started). These thoughts fly faster than I can write them down. Once released, I find I have too many. Not only that, but I'm beginning to realise the circumstances which must exist if you are to read this. We have talked in the recent past of humanity's aspirations for itself. Maybe that's what took me into insurance: expect the worst and you can't go wrong. After the war I could only recognise humanity in terms of failure, its 'achievements' underlain by a train of horror which even now, after its most potent demonstrations, we are unable to acknowledge: at least, if acknowledge, do little if anything constructive about. We are, in my view, implacably intent on our own destruction, not hubris but hedonism our principal drive, a generic imperative which nothing can overcome: we are condemned, as a species, to invent the means of our own destruction: what sort of saviour do we need for that?

All I should say is measure your life by what I gave, by way of licence, by deferment, standing back: if I can't live with her, I can live for her. She is, to me, my entire world. I envy you, as I envied Gerry: my brother inherited the family grace, the endowment of my cherished mother, who looked to him, I'm afraid, as a reflection of herself. I inherited our father, a man, as I've said, I despised. A mercurial whim of nature. If we'd had a third brother no doubt he would have inherited an equable element of both. Perhaps you are he: a posthumous but equally arbitrary creation.

I am writing this while you are away at church. One look at my beloved's face, on your arrival, will tell me *all* that has happened. And then I will invite you up the hill. With what consequences you will now know. My big decision, as you must have realised, is whether to take you with me: whether shooting with the camera – something, I know, you dislike (and for good reason) – will devolve naturally into shooting you both with a gun.

Your loving uncle,
James.

Rising, I stand back from the desk as, earlier, I had stood back from his body – and find my gaze returning to the window. It's as if he's still up there – that we're still up there – and the event, described in the letter, having been rehearsed, is about to happen.

Gerry's voice murmurs to Clare below: the ringing of the telephone, his louder voice, 'Don't ring again. I'm taking the phone off the hook. I'll ring you.'

I am gliding, wheeling, the ice creaking on every side, 'life' that otherwise burdensome property comprised of 'awareness', nothing else . . .

4

For reasons for which I can't account I don't show James's 'confession' to anyone. The inquest is held, the body released, the ashes scattered, at my suggestion, on the hill. The commentators and photographers who have surrounded the end of the drive (and who have visited the hill, trespassing on an infuriated farmer's land) have disappeared. The house (and the phone calls) return to normal. We go away: to the Lake District, the scene of a childhood holiday for Clare, then to London, meeting Martha (yet again) returning on the train: the group of us, she with her ubiquitous companion, sit at a table in the restaurant car – something like a wake immediately after a funeral: a celebration of what I'm not entirely sure. Clare has aged; at least, sobered – a sobriety she says she acquires from me ('except when you're in the company of Martha Armitage: she brings something other out in you').

We are into new country, hissing along, the ice growing thinner all the while. My 'wealth' is being assessed by lawyers. James has left everything to Clare. We are 'autonomous', as she describes it – Gerry skating effortlessly before us (two other 'projects' underway, one a life of Miss Geraldine O'Neill). The past, whatever its horrors, has been eclipsed: we travel faster than the shadows – or the cracks lengthening on either side.

The photographs, of course, arrive. The police enclose the negatives: a casual, if bureaucratic thought, accompanied not by a letter but a printed slip attributable to the city constabulary and date-stamped by, I presume, a mechanical device.

She and I, arms round one another; she and James, arms linked (the unnoticed bulge visible – for the first time – beneath his jacket); he and I together – the portentous, 'defining' picture; she alone; I alone; she and I walking up the hill, smiling, waving (I'd forgotten our spontaneity) and, curiously, the last one he took of the two of us descending, our backs to the camera, my attention, despite the rear perspective, plainly focused on her.

What held him back? Perhaps her insistence I take a photograph of him, of him being the recipient in or of the picture – something he hadn't anticipated (similarly the two of us together) – or even a remoter aspiration he should, in some form, if only in others' memories, go on living, in her, in me. If not in Gerry.

Or a final gesture of 'insurance', self-enclosure – 'authenticity' adhered to as he watched us walk away, turning from us, sitting down, taking out the gun, placing the muzzle to his head, not others the target but himself.

MEMO

5.9.01, 5:15 a.m.

Thirty (30) years to write this down (31, to be precise: I got up in the early hours to complete it). I've been up most of the night 'improving' the script (crumby writers: I do a better job myself). The studio car is due at six (6). Martha'll get up to see me off, and no doubt Gerry (staying with us, with Clare – though she'll sleep on: the kids, thank God, are all at college). Peculiar household (Leighcroft Gardens), peculiar past. Yesterday Dad doddered in, almost precisely at this hour: he'd set his alarm clock to make sure he caught me before I left (old habit), looking over my shoulder: 'Treat the camera as a friend,' he says. 'If you don't like it, it won't like you'. His staying here, even for a fortnight, while I'm shooting, not a good idea: eighty-two (82) and thinking he'll make another picture. 'Not your fucking masterpiece, I know, but *good* in its way: I the precedent, you the fruition': he gets that from the equally doddery Gavin, a youthful seventy-nine (79), who's also convinced he'll produce another movie: thin-ice skaters never die. They only disappear.

'*Memorandum!*' He comes in in his dressing-gown, picking up the sheet, unable to read it without his glasses. 'Photographs. Of what?' He drops it. 'Another denigration of the greatest art of the past and present century, or, after all this time, has the penny dropped? You fucking crook. Have they *rumbled* you at Pinewood? What goes through your head I can't imagine. After all these fucking years: *Genius*!'

'You or me?' I ask.

I wave to him – and Martha – from the window of the car,

apprehensive of leaving him with her. But then, there's Clare . . . she, too, appearing as the car drives off.

My father has learnt nothing. He doesn't realise what a world we live in, in which dissemblance governs all. He cannot see what is to come – forces which will despatch us as effortlessly, as naturally, as keenly – as guilelessly – as a bird sings in a tree. I, who admire his grace and love his skill: his gyrations, his leaps and whirls, his dancing and his speed are everything . . .

Amen.